FIRST MOON

THE TERNION ORDER

BOOK ONE

DANIEL R. MARVELLO

Published by Magic Fur Press
An imprint of Logical Expressions, Inc.
P.O. Box 383, Ponderay, Idaho 83852, USA

This is a work of fiction. All names, characters, places, and events are either the product of the author's imagination or are used fictitiously. Any resemblance to actual persons, living or dead, business organizations, events, or locales is purely coincidental.

FIRST MOON

ISBN: 978-1-61038-033-1 (paperback)
        978-1-61038-034-8 (EPUB)

Cover art by Victorine E. Leiske
Print layout by Susan C. Daffron
Ebook formatting by Logical Expressions, Inc.

First Moon is dedicated to my lovely and
talented wife.
She is the real magic in my life.

Books by Daniel R. Marvello
<u>The Vaetra Chronicles</u>
Vaetra Unveiled
Vaetra Untrained
Vaetra Unleashed

CHAPTER 1
Dumped

The moment Kyle turned onto his street, he knew something was wrong. Sherry's Subaru was backed into the driveway and the rear door was open. Sherry *never* backed in because she thought she might hit something.

Kyle parked under the spreading maple trees that arched over their avenue, turning it into a long tunnel of green. The two-story house they shared in an older residential section of town was compact and didn't have much of a yard, but it was close to work and shopping.

Grabbing his backpack from the passenger seat, Kyle locked his Explorer and suppressed the urge to hurry his stride. Whatever Sherry might be doing, he had a feeling he wasn't going to like it. As he walked up the driveway alongside her car, Sherry came out of the house with a box and tried to cram it into an available space. The back of her car was already loaded with other boxes as well as her luggage.

Kyle's heart dropped into his stomach. This didn't look like a Goodwill run, and it didn't look like she was packing for an emergency journey, either.

"Taking a trip?" he asked.

Sherry gave the box one last shove and stood to face Kyle with her arms crossed. "I'm leaving."

"You mean, forever? Without even talking to me about it first?"

"We've talked about it a dozen times. You won't listen. I'm not staying here another day."

Kyle had listened; he just didn't agree. Sherry had grown up in Sandpoint, but the things that made this small North Idaho community seem peaceful and charming to most visitors had become boring and stagnant to her.

"Where will you go?"

"Fred and Barbara said I could stay in their spare room until I find a job and get back on my feet."

At least she would be going someplace safe. Sherry practically idolized her old high school buddies because the couple had managed to escape the area and set up a successful life in Portland, Oregon.

His eyes dropped to the engagement ring she wore. "Just like that? What about us?"

Following his gaze, she twisted the ring off her finger and held it out at arm's length. "I'm done with us."

She dropped the ring into his open palm and turned on her heel to scurry back into the house with her head bowed.

Kyle stared at the sparkling diamond ring. The term "solitaire" seemed inappropriate for something that was supposed to be a symbol of togetherness. He closed his fingers over the ring that was still warm from her hand.

He knew she was unhappy, but he had no idea she was miserable enough to throw everything away. They had been working together on some kind of compromise. Just because they hadn't found it yet didn't mean they wouldn't.

He followed her into the house and dropped his pack on the kitchen table next to a small open carton. Peering into the box, he saw some of the kitchen items she had brought into the relationship two years ago. She was also taking a few of the things they had bought together, but it didn't look like she was cleaning him out completely. Not that he cared. Things could be replaced. She couldn't.

Hearing a thump from the upper floor, he went up the stairs to try talking to her again. What could he say to change her mind? Would she accept anything less than his agreement to leave Sandpoint immediately? He'd have to quit his job and leave this land of lakes, forest, and mountains that he'd come to love.

Only yesterday, she had accused him of loving Sandpoint more than he loved her. That wasn't true, of course. It was just that, when they did leave, they needed to plan where they would go next and try to get a job there before making the move. Sherry argued that they had plenty of savings and could afford a little down time while they looked for new work. Her definition of "plenty" didn't come close to his, but that was a different argument.

He couldn't accept that much uncertainty all at once. And apparently Sherry couldn't stand to wait any longer.

Kyle stood in the doorway to their bedroom, watching her pack a few last things that she had laid out on the bed. "Can't we talk about this?"

Although she wiped at the tears that rolled down her cheeks, she didn't look up at him.

She shoved the last few items into the duffel bag and zipped it shut. Picking up the bag, she stopped in front of Kyle. He was still blocking the door.

Her moist, red-rimmed eyes met his. "No. We've talked enough. This is it. Either we leave together or I leave alone. It's your choice."

His choice?

"You aren't giving me a choice! You're giving me an ultimatum," he said, trying not to shout but unable to keep the anger out of his voice.

She took a step back from him and frowned. "Have it your way then. It's an ultimatum. Do you love me enough to go with me?"

How could she be so unreasonable? Of course he loved her. He had asked her to marry him, hadn't he? But he couldn't simply load up his belongings and drive off with her.

"You mean just drive off today?"

"It doesn't have to be today, but I want you to promise me we'll be out of here by the end of August."

The end of August. That gave him less than two months. Kyle would have to wrap up and throw away three years of career-building and new friendships. He'd have to start over wherever he could find a new job. They'd probably have to move to a city where technology jobs were more plentiful, and he'd have to fight traffic every day. When he needed to escape to somewhere peaceful, they'd have to drive for hours. He would be miserable from day one. And how long would she stay happy before she insisted on the next upheaval?

An old saying popped into Kyle's head. *No matter where you go, there you are.* He had a strong suspicion that the changes she demanded wouldn't make her happy. She was running away from something she didn't want, rather than moving toward something she did want. He would be throwing away his life here for nothing because eventually they'd have another conversation exactly like this one. And at some point, he would get sick of capitulating. With a stab of disappointment, he realized that she still had to figure out what she wanted to do with her life, and he didn't want to go along for that ride.

Sherry was staring into his eyes, waiting for his response.

He moved out of the doorway to let her pass. "I can't make that promise. I'm sorry."

She took a deep breath and nodded once, apparently expecting his response. She turned to the side to avoid brushing against him as she went through the doorway. Her feet pounded down the stairs and the contents of the cardboard box on the kitchen table rattled as she picked it up in passing. The thudding slam of her car's rear door was quickly followed by the start of its engine. As she drove off, the weighed-down rear of her car scraped against the surface of the driveway with a loud screech.

The house was utterly silent.

Kyle turned away from the empty bedroom and went back downstairs to close the door that Sherry had left open in her haste.

~

Kyle drove out onto the jetty and found a parking space that was shaded from the late afternoon sun. Sitting with his hands on the wheel, he took a deep breath and let it out. It was time to stop hiding.

In the three weeks since Sherry left, Kyle had become withdrawn. He realized that most of his friends were really *her* friends, and he doubted they would still appreciate his company. He had one buddy from work, but the ashes of his engagement had settled upon him like a shroud and smothered his interest in social interaction. Depending upon the weather, he occupied himself with long stretches of reading, bicycling, and kayaking when he wasn't working.

Tucking his dry bag and deck shoes under his arm, he locked the Explorer and headed down the steps that descended the rocky slope of the jetty to the floating docks below.

Boats bobbed gently in the slips along the docks from the subdued waves that rolled into the protected cove.

The tall masts of the sailboats wobbled to and fro against a cerulean sky, and a cool breeze fluttered the wide leaves of the cottonwoods along the shoreline. It looked like a good afternoon for sailing.

Kyle strode to the last dock of slips, the boards thumping and occasionally squeaking under his feet. His destination lay just ahead: a San Juan 21 with a light blue hull. His friend Greg Hopkins must have arrived early because the sailboat was mostly rigged.

Greg heard Kyle's approach along the dock and looked up from his work on the jib at the bow. Greg waved and shouted, "Just in time. I almost have her ready to go."

Kyle stopped alongside *Sick Day Adventure* and tossed his dry bag into the cockpit. Changing into his deck shoes, he said, "If you'd waited for me, I'd have been glad to help."

"But then we wouldn't be ready to go," Greg said with a wink.

Kyle tightened his laces and called out, "Permission to come aboard?"

Greg braced himself against the anticipated roll of the boat and answered, "Permission granted."

Kyle clambered into the cockpit, lobbed his dry bag and street shoes into the cabin, and looked around to see if he could do anything to help prepare the boat for departure.

Greg stepped off the cabin roof and down into the cockpit. He pushed past Kyle and pivoted the little trolling motor down, submerging the propeller. He looked back at Kyle with a grin.

"Ready to cast off?" he asked.

Kyle answered with a mock salute. "Aye aye, Captain."

Greg got the motor running while Kyle jumped onto the dock and loosened the mooring lines. He stepped back aboard, and by the time he had the lines coiled, Greg had backed the boat out of the slip and they were chugging away from the docks.

Once clear of the cove, Greg manned the rudder to keep them headed into the wind while Kyle hoisted the mainsail. Kyle then turned off the motor and locked it into the raised position.

With the motor off, the only sounds were the waves splashing against the hull of the boat and the sails luffing in the wind. The quiet was what Kyle liked most about sailing. It was so much more peaceful than bouncing across the waves with a massive engine roaring in your ears. A sailboat worked *with* the elements, while a powerboat tried to beat them into submission.

Kyle took hold of the main sheet and sat on the starboard bench. Greg eased the bow to port until the wind started filling the sail. Working with practiced synchrony, Kyle let out the main sheet and Greg adjusted the rudder until the sail was thrumming without a ripple in perfect trim. *Adventure* sliced forward through the waves at a comfortable heel.

Their course took them along the western edge of the bay. They cruised past the graffiti-covered concrete ruins of an old lumber mill that squatted on the shore. Greg was careful to stay far away from the rotting pier supports that jutted above the surface of the water. Tall pines, cottonwood, and quaking aspen crowded the rocky shoreline. The same breeze that powered *Adventure* rushed through the tree leaves, mimicking the sound of a waterfall.

The ruins were a reminder that the lumber industry created most of the towns in the region, although several of the big sawmills had shut down over the past few decades. Now, with the exception of a few technology and manufacturing businesses, most area merchants relied upon tourism for their survival.

"Stand by to come about," Greg ordered.

"Standing by," Kyle confirmed.

"Coming about."

As Greg turned the rudder, Kyle ducked under the boom and shifted to the port-side bench. Kyle trimmed the main sail and *Adventure* leaped forward on a port tack while he adjusted the jib.

Now that they had a long stretch of lake in front of them, both men were able to relax and enjoy the voyage with only minor adjustments to course or sail.

Greg broke the companionable silence first.

"So, how are you doing? I haven't seen much of you lately. Have you heard anything from Sherry?"

When Greg called and invited Kyle to crew on his sailboat, Kyle's initial reaction was to maintain his solitude and refuse. But Greg knew him well enough to insist. Kyle loved sailing and would normally never miss a chance to go out on such a perfect day. The down side was that he'd have to answer questions like the one Greg had just asked.

Kyle nodded and answered his friend. "I called to make sure she got to Portland safely. Haven't heard anything since then."

Greg gave Kyle a sympathetic nod. "Sorry about the breakup, man. That's always tough. How are *you* holding up?"

"I'm fine. I needed some time to sort things out. It's not like I didn't know we had problems, but I thought we mattered enough to each other to work things out. I guess she was right. I love living here more than I loved her."

Greg shook his head and grimaced. "Don't take this all on yourself. Another way to look at it is that she loved the idea of getting away from here more than she loved *you*."

Kyle nodded absently. He'd gone round and round in his own head arguing these points a dozen times over the past few weeks. His conclusion had been that neither one of them loved the other enough to make the necessary sacrifices.

Greg's voice took on a delicate tone. "I've had a few conversations with other people who know her…have you considered the possibility that she was using you?"

Kyle glared at Greg. "You think she would agree to marry me just for a ticket out of town?"

Greg held up one hand in apology. "Sorry. No, I don't think that. But if she got her hopes up, she'd be doubly disappointed when you rained on her parade."

Kyle fell silent, looking up at the sail and thinking through what Greg was suggesting. Yes, it *was* possible that Sherry had originally been attracted to him because he had a decent job and it was likely that he would move on before too long. When he took the job as an Internet developer for a local sporting-goods retailer, he had planned to do exactly that: get a few years of experience and then move somewhere with milder winters.

In the meantime, he and Sherry had fallen in love, or so he thought. She sure seemed giddy enough when he proposed to her. But then he screwed it all up by deciding he wanted to stay here.

Greg interrupted his thoughts. "Sorry I brought it up. Deb thought talking about it might make you feel better. I told her guys don't usually work like that, but she made me promise."

Kyle chuckled and hung his head. Deb was Greg's on-again, off-again girlfriend. Both of them prized their independence, which was why they rarely stayed together for long. But they couldn't seem to stay apart, either.

"Don't worry about it," Kyle said. "She's probably right. I'm sick of thinking about Sherry and what might have been. It's over, and I'm moving on."

Greg grinned. "Glad to hear it. In that case, you should go out to the Pickup Joint tomorrow night with Deb and me. You might find a new filly to break in."

Kyle frowned doubtfully. The Pickup Joint was always loud and crowded. After so much peaceful solitude, it sounded positively nauseating.

"I don't know…"

Greg leaned forward and pressed the invitation. "You said you're moving on, right? I promise that's easier to do with a warm body next to you than it is in a cold bed."

A cold bed was one of the first things that had driven home the fact that Sherry was gone forever. Waking up that first morning to a new life without her had been a bleak moment. It was the one time Kyle had allowed himself to cry over losing her.

"Come on. It will be fun," Greg insisted.

Kyle wasn't particularly interested in meeting someone new to date. He'd had enough relationship drama for a while. But he knew that refusing to socialize could turn into a pattern. Eventually, people stopped inviting you. If he wanted to do something about the solitary mood he was in, he needed to break out of the bubble he was creating for himself.

Kyle looked at his friend and smiled. "Okay, you talked me into it."

Maybe he needed a night on the town. Going with friends would make it easier, and he might meet someone interesting. Where was the harm in that?

Greg gave him a satisfied nod and said, "Good man. You won't regret it."

CHAPTER 2

The Pickup Joint

The next evening, Kyle rode with Greg and Deb to the Pickup Joint. Kyle had dressed in his favorite black cotton pants and a lightweight gray cotton shirt. Sherry had loved the way the outfit looked on him, and he loved how comfortable it was. It was perfect for a summer evening of dancing.

He shook his head and smiled as Greg turned off the highway. The parking lot was bracketed by a series of angled light poles, four on each side. Attached to each pole was an old pickup truck, with the bed toward the ground and the hood toward the sky. They looked like truck rockets, ready for launch. *Only in Idaho*, Kyle mused.

Kyle was willing to bet that the owner got the idea from the Cadillac Ranch in Amarillo, Texas, where ten Cadillacs had been placed nose-first into the ground. But in North Idaho, it had to be pickup trucks.

Greg parked his truck and they all got out. He and Deb were both dressed western-style in jeans, button-up shirts, and boots. Greg looked sharp in a white cowboy hat and Deb wore her dark-brown hair in two braids at the back of her head. She looked a bit like Dorothy from the *Wizard of Oz*, but Kyle knew better than to express that observation out loud.

Greg slapped Kyle on the back and said, "You ready to kick up your heels?"

"As ready as I'll ever be."

"That's the spirit! Nothin' like a few beers, some loud music, and the smile of a pretty lady to chase away the blues."

Deb rolled her eyes. "Don't push him, Greg. We're here to relax and have some fun."

Kyle snorted and shook his head. Greg was normally a pretty straight-up guy, but when he was in party mode, he voice took on a southwestern drawl and you never knew what kind of outrageous thing was going to come out of his mouth—particularly after he'd had a couple of beers.

Lucky for him, Deb had generously volunteered to be the designated driver for the evening. She said she was along for the dancing, not for the buzz. Greg could have as much booze as he wanted, as long as he could keep shuffling his feet around on the dance floor.

Greg put his arm around Kyle's shoulder and pulled him close so he could whisper conspiratorially into his ear, although still loud enough for Deb to overhear. "It's a guy thing. She wouldn't understand."

Kyle laughed and stepped forward to open the door for his friends. Loud country rock blared into the lot while Greg and Deb preceded him inside.

The interior of the bar continued the truck theme. The booths along the left and right walls were made from old pickup beds with bench seats built over the wheel wells. The wall behind each booth was painted with a mural, making it look like you were riding through the countryside in the back of the truck.

A long, horseshoe-shaped bar to his right took up most of the front wall. The back wall had a stage with a DJ booth set up high above the dance floor. About a dozen round tables filled the space between the dance floor and the bar.

It was a typical Saturday night. Several couples were dancing to the music, only a few empty seats remained at the bar, and all but one of the booths were occupied. Most of the tables near the dance floor were still empty, but they always filled up last. Deb made a beeline for the remaining booth and claimed it by tossing her purse into the seat corner and sliding in. Greg sat next to her and Kyle slid in across from them.

Kyle looked around and recognized a couple of people from work. He also spotted one of Sherry's friends across the room, but when their eyes met, she quickly looked away, confirming his suspicion about where he stood with that crowd.

With a sigh, he turned his attention to the mural at the back of their booth. It showed a paved road curving through a forest of deciduous trees displaying their fall colors, with the artist's rendering of the truck cab framing most of the view. An acrylic plaque centered at the bottom of the rear window included a photo of the bed's original pickup and a few statistics. According to the plaque, they were "riding" in the back of a 1979 Ford F-100.

A waitress came by and took their drink orders. She was dressed like Daisy from *Dukes of Hazzard* in cutoff jeans shorts and a plaid shirt that was tied below her breasts. The top buttons had been left undone, revealing a lot of pale flesh and the edge of a white lacy bra.

Kyle watched her walk away, appreciating the sway of her hips and the length of leg revealed between the shorts and her cowboy boots. Greg wiggled his eyebrows at him and grinned.

"I think he's feeling better already," he said to Deb.

She gave him a suspicious look. "So are you, apparently."

Greg put his arm around Deb and squeezed her close while she scrunched up her face. "You're the only woman for me, darlin'."

She reached up and guided his face to hers with the palm of her hand. She gave him a peck on the lips and followed it up with a light slap on his cheek. "Don't you forget it, cowboy."

Greg grinned at her and kissed her palm.

The waitress returned with their drinks and set them down on small square napkins with the Pickup Joint's logo. With Deb keeping an eye on both of them, Greg and Kyle feigned interest in the tabletop and tried to ignore the enhanced view as the waitress bent over their table.

The tables in each booth were made from the tailgate of the corresponding truck bed, so the tabletop was more interesting than one might expect. The tailgate was framed with wood to protect patrons from its metal corners, and a sheet of glass covered the top, giving it a flat surface. Photos of smiling people posing with their trucks were strewn across the tailgate under the glass. Patrons who owned the year and model matching the booth's truck bed were encouraged to donate a photo to the funky montage.

Greg pointed at one of the photos and said, "Nice restoration job. You suppose those headlights are original?"

The waitress narrowed her eyes at him suspiciously before moving on to the next table.

"Thanks," Kyle called to her back.

Deb punched Greg in the arm, and he made a mock show of pain. "Don't be a jerk," she said. "You're going to have to give her a big tip to make up for that."

"Hell, I'd give her a big tip anyway," he said with a snicker.

Deb shook her head and pushed Greg toward the end of the booth. "That's it. You owe me a dance."

"But my drink just got here," he complained.

"Well, bottoms up, Buttercup. We need to put some of that feisty energy to good use."

Greg grabbed the pilsner glass and tilted it up as fast as he could swallow the contents. In about three seconds, it was gone. He made a face and pounded his chest with his fist. Covering his mouth, he let out the inevitable belch as quietly as possible while Deb leaned away from him. Eyes watering, he turned to her and said, "Ready."

She gave him another shove toward the end of the booth and muttered, "You're disgusting."

Kyle took a few swallows of his beer and looked around the room for likely partners. He'd need a bit more liquid courage before he'd be ready to hit the dance floor, but it wouldn't hurt to scope out the possibilities in advance.

Three well-dressed women sat together at one of the round tables. One of them looked familiar; possibly someone he'd seen at work. His company was one of the largest employers in town, and he knew only a small fraction of the three-hundred people who worked there. He'd keep an eye on the trio as a possibility.

He scanned the people who were standing and sitting at the bar. It was mostly single guys, but there were a few women. One woman in particular caught his attention. She had her back to the bar and was leaning her arms on it behind her while she watched the people on the dance floor. She wore a dark-green sleeveless dress with a low-cut front and medium-length skirt. Her clothing and posture revealed a well-toned body and an appealing figure. She turned her head his direction, almost as if she sensed that he was checking her out. Kyle quickly broke his stare and moved his eyes on to other parts of the room.

The waitress eventually came by and asked him if he was ready for another beer. He told her that he was and ordered one for Greg as well.

The new drinks arrived at the same time Deb and Greg returned from the dance floor. Both of his friends' faces were flushed and sweat beaded on their foreheads. Deb used the damp, cool napkin from her drink to mop her brow. Greg took off his hat and wiped a bandanna across his forehead.

"Whew! They need to kick up the AC a bit," he exclaimed. "Thanks for gettin' me another beer."

"No problem. Cheers," Kyle said, clinking his glass against Greg's and taking a deep swig.

"So, when are you gonna get out there?" Greg asked him.

Kyle held up his glass. "In about six ounces."

"Well, you better git on it, or all the good ones will be taken." He tilted his head toward the table of three women Kyle had noticed earlier. Sure enough, a couple of guys were chatting them up. One of the women rose from her seat and accompanied the lucky fellow to the dance floor. The other man sat in the vacated chair and talked with the remaining two women, who smiled politely at his animated attempt to win them over.

Kyle drained his glass and thumped it down on the table. "All righty then. Wish me luck."

The beer was doing its job, so Kyle was more at ease than when he'd arrived. He was ready to ask someone to dance and face the possibility of being shot down in flames. Not that being rejected was a common occurrence. At twenty-seven, Kyle was in his prime and had learned that most women saw him as tall, dark, and handsome. They were willing to give him the benefit of the doubt ... at first. It wasn't until they discovered what a nerd he was that they made excuses and backed away.

Kyle slid across the bench seat and stepped out of the booth. He decided to cruise past the tables and take a seat at the bar for a closer look at his options. He could get another drink while he was at it.

Kyle found an empty stool between an older man who was talking with the bartender and a young woman with a

Rubenesque figure who looked to be barely legal drinking age. As he sat down, the girl glanced over to check him out, and the older man nodded to him in greeting. The bartender took Kyle's order for a highball. *What the hell, I'm not driving tonight.*

After the drink arrived, Kyle turned his glass on the napkin, evaluating the other patrons. The bar's horseshoe configuration and the mirrors behind the wall of booze made it easy to scope out the pickings.

The girl next to him was cute, but a little too young. Also, it seemed like she might be with the guy who was sitting next to her, although they weren't talking.

He spotted two other possibilities. A woman who was about his age met his eyes and smiled before turning away. She had a pleasant face and was dressed to the nines in a maroon dress with a French manicure, perfectly coiffed blonde hair, and expertly applied makeup. She might be fun to dance with, but her appearance screamed High Maintenance.

The second woman was the one he'd spotted earlier from the booth. Now that he was closer, he could see that she was much older than he'd originally estimated—probably in her mid-forties. She had her profile to him and was fascinating to watch. Every movement was smooth and sensual. Some women wore their femininity with confidence and pride, and this lady appeared to be one of them.

Kyle had difficulty looking away from her taut, smooth arms and the suggestive curves at the front of her dress. Her shoulder-length, dark-brown, wavy hair obscured part of her face, so he didn't see it coming when she turned her head his way and locked eyes with him. His heart stopped. *Busted.*

Normally, Kyle would have looked away in embarrassment, but not this time. Her unusual green eyes seemed to get closer the longer he stared into them. A slow smile curved the corners of her sensuous lips, and she winked at him before breaking eye contact and taking a sip of her drink.

Kyle blinked a few times and then looked down at his own drink, eyes unfocused. Remembering to breathe again, his neck flushed warm and his heart started to pound from a brief rush of adrenaline. He couldn't decide if he was excited, embarrassed, or afraid. There was something … *dangerous* … about her.

Kyle looked over his shoulder to where Greg and Deb were dancing. Greg had apparently witnessed the brief exchange and he gave Kyle a grin and a thumbs-up. Kyle glanced over at the green-eyed woman, hoping she hadn't seen his gesture. She was looking down at her drink, but she wore a bemused smile as if she knew exactly what was going on.

Kyle mentally scratched her off his dance card. That woman was *way* out of his league.

Kyle took a long slug of his drink to calm his nerves and went back to observing the room, carefully avoiding looking in the direction of the woman in the dark-green dress.

The alcohol was working its magic and Kyle found himself tapping his foot in time to the music. The DJ played a mixture of country and rock, appealing to the tastes of a mixed crowd in a small town. Every once in a while he'd slow it down for the lovers and hopefuls.

Over the music, Kyle heard the girl next to him complain to the guy on her other side. "If we aren't going to dance, take me home. I don't want to just sit here and get drunk."

Her date shrugged. "I don't feel like dancing tonight, and I ain't done with my beer." He took a small sip to illustrate his point. His glass was only about a quarter full and he could have easily downed the last of it in one gulp.

Her voice went frosty. "Fine. I'll be in the car. If you aren't there in two minutes, I'm leaving without you." She got up and stomped out of the bar, her wide hips swaying her skirt back and forth with each step.

"Shit," swore the young fellow. He downed his beer and left a few bills on the bar before hurrying out after her.

Kyle shook his head. *Yep. The things we do for love.*

"I think he's in for a disappointing evening," said a sultry voice next to him. Kyle looked up to find the green-eyed woman standing only a couple of feet away.

"May I?" she asked, indicating the newly-vacated stool next to him.

She was close enough that Kyle could smell the subtle perfume she wore. It made his pulse pound in his neck. "P-Please do," he stuttered, straightening his back and rotating his seat toward her.

She sat down and called the bartender over.

"I'll have what he's having," she said. The bartender was quick to comply.

She turned those amazing eyes back to Kyle and held out her hand. Kyle could feel her body heat as he reached out to accept the handshake. Her fingers were long and strong and surprisingly warm as they curved around his.

"I'm Clarissa," she said, moving his hand slowly up and then down.

"Kyle … I'm Kyle. Nice to meet you." He was acting like a dork. *Get it under control, dumbass.*

She smiled. "It's a *pleasure* to meet you too, Kyle."

The way she'd said "pleasure" made Kyle's bones melt. He wanted to ask her to say it again just so he could watch her full lips form the word. His initial assessment had been right. She *was* out of his league, and he was in over his head.

The bartender delivered her drink and she leaned sideways to take a sip, leaving her knee touching Kyle's.

Say something, idiot.

But his mind was a blank. All he could do was absorb the presence of this sleek panther of a woman. The soft cloth of her dress draped flatteringly over her body, showing the curve of her breasts and dropping enticingly into the valley between her toned legs. Kyle gulped and squirmed to reposition his natural response to her potent sexuality.

She leaned an elbow on the bar with languid ease and bumped her knee against his again. "So tell me about yourself, Kyle. Do you live in the area or are you visiting?"

Kyle had trouble concentrating on her words when she looked at him like that. He couldn't have looked away if he wanted to, and he didn't want to. His delay in answering stretched long enough that she tilted her head toward him as if to say, "Well? …"

Kyle shook his head slightly and broke eye contact. "Here … yes … I live here in Sandpoint. How about you?"

That was better. If he looked anywhere other than into those eyes, he might be able to keep it together. He rotated his seat back toward the bar and toyed with his drink.

She turned toward the bar as well, but that put her body even closer to his. He looked up into the mirrors behind the bar and met her eyes again through the reflection. Okay. That wasn't as bad. He could still think.

She stirred her drink slowly with the little red plastic straw. "I live here too, north of town. What do you do for a living?"

Here came hurdle number one. When Kyle told people what he did for a living, they usually changed the subject quickly. When he told *women* what he did for a living— women who had seemed interested in him up to that point— they usually remembered that they needed to be somewhere else.

This time, Kyle wasn't afraid to reveal his job. This woman made him uncomfortable; he'd never felt so much like prey. If his work scared her off, he'd breathe a sigh of relief.

In a matter-of-fact tone, he replied, "I'm a software developer for Northern Peaks Sports Equipment."

"Good for you," she said with a dip of her head. "That's a great job, particularly for this area. I have an ex who did programming." She moved her forearm so it was alongside his, the warmth of her bare skin soaking right through his sleeve. "You must be intelligent and have good concentration skills."

Kyle glanced at her to see if she was teasing him, but her expression was friendly and open. So much for chasing her off that way.

Kyle raised an eyebrow. "My concentration skills were fine until about five minutes ago."

Clarissa responded with a throaty and intensely personal laugh that made Kyle's breath catch. Once again, he had the sensation that he was in the crosshairs. What he didn't understand was how this woman could possibly be interested in *him*.

Kyle tipped up his glass and finished his drink. He decided it was time to cut this short. He was about to say that he needed to return to his friends when her hand closed around his forearm. He automatically turned his head and met her eyes again. *Damn.*

"Would you like to dance with me, Kyle?"

Well, he had come to dance, and he could do worse for a partner. At least he'd have someone nice to look at on the dance floor. "Okay," he answered, but his doubts came through in his voice.

She arched one thin eyebrow. "Are you sure? Is something wrong?"

"It's your eyes. They're beautiful … but so distracting."

She smiled at the compliment and leaned toward him, placing her face less than a foot from his. "I have a confession," she whispered. "This is not my natural eye color."

Up close, Kyle could see the contact lenses floating over her irises. "Colored lenses?"

Clarissa nodded and took his hand in hers. She led him around the tables and onto the dance floor, passing Greg and Deb's booth on the way. Kyle looked over at his friends as he went by and gave them a thin-lipped smile and a shrug. Greg was grinning broadly, but Deb was frowning at Clarissa.

What's her problem? Kyle wondered.

Kyle wasn't a great dancer, but he had a decent sense of rhythm and could adapt his moves to complement his partner's. Sherry had been a country-music fan and had taught him a couple of western dance steps, but Kyle's preference was classic rock.

The song was "Mister Blue Sky" by the Electric Light Orchestra, a bouncy tune that celebrated sunny days, something that anyone who lived in the Northwest for any length of time could appreciate.

But Clarissa's fluid movement and brief touches turned even that song into something inviting and sexy. Kyle wasn't sure what to do with his feet and hands, but managed to keep moving somehow. Her eyes left his only when she raised her arms and swayed in a full circle, showing him every inch of her lean form. She sidled up to him frequently, pressing the length of her body against his. She fit well against his six-foot frame. Her strappy sandals had a modest heel that brought her height up to about five eight.

By the time the song ended, Kyle was blushing and ready to head back to the booth. He smiled at her and was about to excuse himself when the DJ started a slow song. Clarissa stepped in close and put her arms on his shoulders, tilting her face up to his.

Their lips were only inches apart. He could feel her warm breath on his chin, and her breasts pushed softly against his chest. When she started swaying to the music, he automatically put his arms around her waist and matched her motion, staring down at her. *Those amazing eyes.*

Kyle lost track of time while they swayed around the dance floor, never once breaking eye contact. Clarissa looked good, smelled good, and felt good. Kyle's doubts melted away as his desire for her grew.

Near the end of the song, she rested her head on his shoulder and pressed herself even closer, moving her leg between his. Kyle's breath caught and his heart rate jumped in response to the intimacy of their embrace.

Kyle glanced over her shoulder at his friends, who had returned to their booth. Deb looked positively agitated, and even Greg had a puzzled expression. True, things were moving pretty fast, but wasn't *this* why Greg had invited him to the bar tonight?

Clarissa seemed to sense his wandering attention. She raised her head and asked, "Are you enjoying yourself, Kyle?"

Kyle answered with a low chuckle. "Can't you tell?"

She smiled and rolled the front of her hip slowly against his groin. "Oh my. This *is* a good sign."

When the song ended, they both stopped moving and stood together. She backed up a half step, creating a narrow gap between them. Kyle took shallow breaths, trying to force himself to settle down, resisting the urge to crush her against him and feel her soft warmth again. *Maybe later.*

A tap on his shoulder jolted Kyle from his thoughts. He turned to find Greg and Deb standing together. The DJ started a new song, and the four of them moved to the edge of the dance floor. They had to speak up to be heard over the music.

Greg checked out Clarissa and looked distinctly uncomfortable about interrupting. Deb nudged him with her elbow, prompting him to speak. "We're thinking of heading out. Do you want a ride home?"

Kyle gave his friend a puzzled look. "Already? I thought you guys wanted to dance."

Greg looked at Deb before answering. "Uh, yeah, we did. And we have."

Kyle shook his head in confusion and looked at Deb, who was watching Clarissa and frowning. "Is something wrong, Deb?"

Deb's eyes darted to Kyle. "No. We were thinking about getting something to eat. I'm buying."

Deb was acting strangely, as if she didn't approve of his dance partner. Why would she care?

Kyle looked over at Clarissa. She wore an enigmatic smile and simply arched an eyebrow at him. Her warm hand was still in his, and he didn't want to let go of her yet. "I think I'll stay a while longer and take a cab home."

Deb's eyes grew wider, and she opened her mouth as if she were about to object, but then she closed her lips into a compressed frown.

Clarissa gave Kyle's hand a squeeze and said, "I'll make sure he gets home okay."

Deb narrowed her eyes. "Whose home?" Greg looked down at her with a puzzled expression, as surprised as Kyle at her rudeness.

Clarissa kept a polite smile on her face as she glanced at Kyle.

Kyle met Deb's eyes and used his most reasonable tone. "I'm fine, Deb. We're just dancing. You and Greg go get something to eat and I'll call you tomorrow."

Deb blinked at him a couple of times and her concerned look faded. She put her hand on his arm. Her eyes seemed to want to stray toward Clarissa, but she kept bringing them back to his face. "Sorry, Kyle. It's none of my business. Enjoy your evening." Deb turned on her heel and strode toward the exit.

Greg shrugged and raised his hands in exasperation. "Sorry about that. It was nice to meet you … Miss …"

"Clarissa," Kyle supplied. "And this is my friend Greg," he said to her.

By then Deb had reached the door and was holding it open, glaring over her shoulder at Greg.

"Well, I'd better get going," Greg said. He waved farewell as he stepped away and then hurried to follow Deb outside.

Clarissa still wore the enigmatic half-smile when Kyle turned to face her. "I'm so sorry. I hope she didn't upset you."

Clarissa gave a short laugh and rolled her eyes. "Believe me, I'm used to it. Other women often feel threatened when I'm around. I have very few female friends."

Kyle eyed her up and down appreciatively. "I think I understand why."

She chuckled low in her throat and let go of his hand so she could put her arms around his waist. She brought her face so close to his that their noses were practically touching. Kyle accepted the invitation and moved his head forward those last few tantalizing inches, touching his lips to hers.

The kiss was tender at first, a soft brushing and pressing of tingling lips. But as Kyle inhaled her scent and pulled her close, the kiss became an urgent exchange of tongue and an exploration of fresh intimacy.

After a moment, Kyle became aware that they were still standing at the edge of the dance floor in full view of everyone, and he reluctantly pulled back. A quick glance around the room told him that several people had witnessed the kiss, and their reactions ranged from bemused to surprised to disapproving. Kyle's face grew hot, but he couldn't suppress his smile.

"Nice," Clarissa said with a wicked smile of her own.

They still held each other close, and the excitement from their kiss burned in Kyle's chest. He took a deep breath to calm himself and let it out slowly through his nose.

When the buzzing in his head had subsided, Kyle asked, "Uh, do you want another drink?"

Clarissa rubbed her hand slowly across Kyle's back, letting the tips of her fingers drift low into the curve near the bottom of his spine.

With an innocent expression but a suggestive tone, she asked, "What do *you* want, Kyle?"

Kyle blushed again at the cascade of images that entered his mind in answer to her question. Most women would have slapped him if he'd given voice to any of them, but he had a feeling she would take his fantasies as a compliment.

The wicked smile returned to her face and she nodded knowingly. "That's what I thought," she said before giving him a light pat on the butt.

She took his hand and led him to the exit. As they walked out of the Pickup Joint, Kyle looked over to where Greg had parked, but his friend's truck was gone, thank goodness. Night had fallen, and the parking-lot lights had come on, shining down on the posed pickups as if they were paintings in a gallery.

Feeling like a dog on a leash, Kyle let Clarissa guide him across the parking lot. She stopped at the passenger side of a low-slung black convertible Jaguar and opened the door for him. The musky smell of soft leather wafted out, inviting him into the rich interior. He hesitated, confused by the high sill and placement of the seat, then chose to put one foot into the car and lower himself onto the seat before swinging in his other leg. He eyed the rocker switches that were lined up side-by-side across the center of the dashboard and the five round gauges filling the space above them. She closed his door as soon as he was settled.

She slid into the driver's seat, sitting first and then swinging in both long legs. She dug into her purse and extracted her keys.

"This is one fine automobile," he said with reverence.

She grinned and arched an eyebrow at him. "Just wait until she's on the move."

Clarissa turned the key in the ignition and the motor started on the first turn, settling immediately into a low purr. She buckled her seat belt and Kyle followed her example. Kyle caught her watching him with a secret smile while he soaked up every detail of the Jag's interior. She backed out of the parking spot and rolled through the lot toward the exit. As she swung the long front end onto the highway, Kyle sat back and enjoyed the powerful and smooth acceleration. The car reached for more road with every shift of her practiced hand, and in no time they were cruising at sixty miles an hour.

Kyle glanced at Clarissa and shook his head. *I was right. She is SO very out of my league.*

CHAPTER 3

One-Night Stand

By the time they reached her turn, Kyle had added owning a Jaguar Type E to his wish list. According to Clarissa, her baby was a 1969 Series 2. She said the automobile had a top speed of 150 miles per hour, but she'd never gone faster than 120.

Awesome.

The tires crunched on gravel as they turned off the highway onto a dirt road. None of the roads out here in the county had street lights, but the full moon was bright enough to turn the trees into silhouettes and to paint shadows onto the road. Clarissa slowed the car down to walking speed and was careful to dodge every rock and pothole.

"Must be a pain to live on a dirt road when your car has such low ground clearance," Kyle observed.

Clarissa nodded, but didn't take her eyes from the patch of road directly in front of the car. "That's why she only comes out to play in summer."

During the drive, Kyle's head cleared of the intoxication from the alcohol as well as her touch. The anticipation of a sexual interlude with such an amazing woman both excited and alarmed him. Did Clarissa see him as a one-night stand, or would she expect more from him?

He decided he was over-thinking the situation, as he often did. She was the one who had seduced him on the dance floor and practically dragged him to her car. If she wanted to use him and then discard him, he could go along with that.

Even if he didn't know anything about her.

"What are you thinking over there, Kyle?"

He hoped she couldn't see how her question made him blush. "Me? Nothing. Just enjoying the ride."

She glanced at him with a sly smile. "Don't worry. I don't bite. At least, not unless you want me to. Hang tight for another minute. We're almost there."

"There" turned out to be a cute, single-level, ranch-style home nestled back in the trees with no view of neighboring houses. It had fake log siding with a covered screened-in porch next to the main entry.

As she turned onto the driveway, Clarissa reached in front of Kyle and took a remote out of the glove compartment. She opened the door to a detached garage and parked the Jaguar inside. Kyle was strangely disappointed when she turned off the engine and silence descended.

Kyle opened the long passenger door, careful not to let it bump the wall, and levered himself out of the seat. He joined Clarissa outside the garage and she closed the garage door. It rolled down, concealing the Jaguar like the curtain at the end of a show.

"Thank you," Kyle said. "I've never ridden in one of those before. It was quite an experience."

She took his hand and started walking toward the house. "Don't thank me yet. The best is yet to come."

She'd had the foresight to leave the entryway light on, so she had no trouble finding the door key and letting them in. When she turned on the interior lights, they revealed a tidy, cozy little home. She had a taste for rustic log furniture—the type that was popular in northwest resorts. It was handmade and expensive. She kicked her shoes off onto a mat at the entryway, and Kyle followed her lead.

"Have a seat on the couch, and I'll make us a couple of drinks," she said over her shoulder as she padded around a corner.

Kyle did as instructed, sitting on the edge of the cushion while he looked around the room. The fireplace was a masterpiece of natural stone with a thick finished-timber mantle. An exquisitely carved wooden owl perched at one end of the mantle, staring balefully at Kyle. On the opposite end was an equally detailed carving of a wolf on the prowl. Red crystals glowed in the wolf's eyes, giving it a demonic stare. The wolf's eyes were so eerie that Kyle shifted his position on the couch until the light no longer reflected the glow toward him.

Clarissa entered with a drink in each hand and caught the direction of his uncomfortable stare.

She handed Kyle his drink. "Don't mind the wolf. People seem to either love him or hate him."

"He's beautiful. The eyes got to me."

She smiled and held up her glass in a toast. As his eyes met hers, she said, "They always do."

They clinked their glasses together and Kyle took a sip. She had poured him another highball, and it was pretty strong.

Clarissa crossed her legs and let her dangling bare foot rest against Kyle's calf while she considered him over her glass. Kyle took a gulp of his drink to hide his discomfort and tried to think of something to say.

But she didn't give him time. She set her glass on the coffee table decisively and then took his glass from him and set it next to hers. She sidled up to him on the couch and draped one leg across his lap. Cupping the back of his head in her hand, she drew him to her and kissed him deeply.

Kyle responded by putting his hand on her leg, caressing the length of her thigh. When her dress slid up and his hand met bare flesh, she broke their kiss with a short gasp. He let his hand wander farther up her thigh to rest on her hip.

She let out a needy growl and moved up onto his lap with a leg on either side. She kissed him again, harder this time, and with an urgency that sent tingles down his spine. Kyle put his hands on her firm rear and pulled her closer. She moaned when he brought his hands around to cup her breasts, which were disappointingly cushioned by her bra.

She eased away from him with a lustful smile, grinding her hips against his. "Let's move this somewhere more comfortable."

Kyle didn't want to let go of her as she slowly wriggled off his lap and stood up. She reached a hand toward him, and he let her lead him down the hall to the bedroom. The heady glow from their passionate moment on the couch made him feel like he was moving in some kind of dream. He still couldn't quite believe it was happening.

Her bedroom was furnished in the same style as the living room, with a log four-poster bed and rustic nightstands. She stopped next to the bed and turned her back to him, asking him to unzip her dress. He slid the zipper down, wondering how she'd managed to zip it up in the first place. It was one of many female mysteries.

She let the dress slide to the floor and pool around her feet, giving him a nice view of her bare back and long legs that met at a petite butt. Black lace panties covered but didn't do much to obscure her smooth, muscular rear. She stepped out of the dress, picked it up, and laid it on a chair in the corner of the room. Then she came back to stand in front of him wearing nothing but a black strapless bra and panties.

Smiling at the hunger in Kyle's eyes, she reached behind her back and unhooked her bra. She caught it as it popped forward and fell away from her breasts. With a flip of her wrist, she tossed it toward the corner where it landed on top of her dress.

Wow. Kyle decided that Clarissa was either younger than he originally thought, or she took remarkably good care of herself. She leaned over to the nightstand and turned a knob that extinguished the table lamps and sent power to a series of tiny white lights that went all the way around the room where the ceiling met the wall. It was like being outside at night with a sky full of stars. The diminished light made her look even more alluring, subtly erasing her few flaws.

Kyle had no doubt that Clarissa wanted to control the action, and he was fine with that. He let her fold down the bed covers, undress him, and then guide him onto the bed. She reached into the top drawer of the nightstand and withdrew a condom, which she deftly applied. In a tangle of lips and limbs, Kyle followed her lead and gave himself over to the most delicious sexual encounter of his life.

At last, Clarissa straddled him with her fingers digging into his chest. They moved together, her hair swinging down around her face. As Kyle neared the limit of his ability to restrain himself, she stiffened and gasped almost as if she were in pain. Kyle smiled to himself when she moaned and started moving again, thinking he no longer had a reason to hold back.

With his hands resting on her hips, he closed his eyes and relaxed into the sensations of their lovemaking. Her movements became more frantic and her fingers arched until her fingernails were like claws digging into his chest. Her moan had turned into a series of low growls that was both sexy and scary at the same time. Kyle didn't want to do anything to interrupt the moment, but her fingernails were digging in hard enough to be painful.

He moved his hands up to her wrists and opened his eyes.

Clarissa leaned forward and pressed harder on his chest. But she also sped up her rocking motion and Kyle forgot all about the pain. He tightened his grip on her wrists and matched her tempo until he couldn't take it anymore. With a grunting sigh, he let go and rode a satisfying wave of release.

At the moment of Kyle's grand finale, Clarissa drove her hips down onto him and held him in place. She arched her back and let out a throaty scream that was nearly a howl. Kyle instinctively froze in response to her chilling cry and goose bumps rose in the aftermath of a tremor that passed through him from head to toe. When she quieted and collapsed on top of him with a sigh, he was glad that they weren't in a hotel room or apartment. They'd have had neighbors banging on the walls or door for sure.

Clarissa rolled off him, trailing her hand across his chest. A cooling wet sensation made him look down, and he was alarmed to see that her fingers had left thin blood trails that streaked across his chest from tiny crescent-shaped fingernail wounds.

As the scent of blood reached his nostrils and mingled with the musky fragrance of their intercourse, a strong wave of dizziness washed over Kyle, robbing him of consciousness.

～

Kyle awoke with a mild headache from the prior evening's indulgences. At some point during the night, he had pulled a cover over himself, but otherwise he was still naked and unwashed.

Opening his eyes, he was briefly disoriented by his surroundings and the unfamiliar feel of the sheets and bed. *Where am I? What happened?*

As memories from the prior evening resolved in his mind, he turned his head to the side. Clarissa lay there, her face relaxed in peaceful sleep.

A lock of hair draped across her cheek. He reached over to move it aside, but moving his arm caused a crusty tightness and stinging on his chest. He looked down and found dried blood trails crossing his chest. The puncture marks from her fingernails reminded him of the surreal experience of the night before. He snorted to himself. *A little pain was worth it.*

Kyle's fingers grazed her face as he shifted the lock of hair. He jerked his hand back when his fingers touched skin that was cool and slightly stiff—not the warm, soft flesh he had enjoyed the previous night. He scrambled away from her and jumped out of the bed, staring agape at her unmoving form. She wasn't breathing and her body didn't move with the shifting of the bed as it should have.

Clarissa was dead.

Kyle's heart pounded so hard that he could feel the blood pulsing in his neck. He shook from the adrenaline coursing through his veins and he had a strong desire to run. He looked for his clothes and pulled on his underwear and pants, nearly tripping in the rush to dress. Finding his shirt, he stopped and looked down at her.

What should I do? Why is she dead? Did I kill her?

Forcing himself to take a few deep breaths, Kyle tried to think. The last thing he remembered was passing out after she rolled off him. Judging by the unchanged position of her body, she was already dead by that time or she'd died as soon as she came to rest next to him. The fingernails of the hand that lay on the place he'd vacated were still tipped in his blood, which was dried now and nearly matched the dark-red polish she wore.

Dread crawled through Kyle, tightening his chest and making his stomach twist. He put his hand over his mouth and swallowed an urge to gag. He was in big trouble. A vibrant and healthy woman was dead, with his blood and possibly his skin under her fingernails.

Running wasn't a realistic option. He couldn't involve anyone who knew him. He'd have to call a cab or steal her car. But the police would surely find the cab driver during their investigation, and her car drew far too much attention.

Besides, he'd done nothing wrong. The cops would figure that out, right? They would undoubtedly see him as a suspect at first, but an autopsy would have to reveal what really happened. *I hope.*

Kyle finished dressing while he considered his next move. The only thing to do was to call the police and get this over with. He looked at the clock. Five thirty in the morning. It was starting to get light outside, which was probably what had awakened him.

Clarissa certainly didn't wake him. She slept like the dead. Kyle giggled in distress at the inappropriate humor. This wasn't his fault! What would the cops charge him with? Screwing her to death? Kyle's hysterical giggling turned into tears and he covered his face with his hands. He tried to get his hiccupping sobs under control and wiped the moisture from his eyes.

A phone was on the night stand next to Clarissa's side of the bed.

Kyle walked around the bed, staring down at Clarissa's nude body. The lithe form that had seemed so sexy last night was now an object of horror. He was relieved to see no obvious marks or bruises that would point a finger at him, and the only blood on the sheets or on Clarissa was his. He was tempted to draw the sheet over her to cover her nakedness, but he'd seen enough cop shows on television to know that he shouldn't touch or change anything. This was now a possible crime scene.

Picking up the phone, Kyle dialed 911.

Two sheriff's deputies and an ambulance arrived within fifteen minutes of his call to secure the scene and take his statement. The deputies were professional and calm, and they seemed to accept Kyle's narrative of what happened.

The female deputy, who had introduced herself as Deputy Arpin, noticed the blood on Clarissa's fingernails and asked Kyle about it. Kyle opened his shirt and blushed when he showed her the fingernail marks on his chest. She instructed Kyle to have the medics treat the wounds after the detective had a chance to photograph them.

The detective arrived about ten minutes after the deputies and took control of the scene. He had his own questions for Kyle, many of which were uncomfortable. No, Kyle had never met Clarissa before last night. No, in spite of the fact that it appeared Clarissa liked to play rough, they didn't engage in asphyxiation games or other dangerous activities. They had used no drugs other than alcohol.

Shortly after the detective arrived, the medical examiner and the CSI team showed up. Kyle didn't see what happened in the bedroom, but after a few minutes, the medics rolled a gurney through the living room where the detective was still questioning Kyle. As Clarissa's body rolled by, Kyle closed his eyes and hung his head.

What a nightmare.

The medical examiner found no evidence that Kyle had been directly responsible for Clarissa's death, so the detective did not place him under arrest. He warned Kyle that he was still a person of interest in the investigation and that he would need to remain available for additional questions. The deputies offered Kyle a ride home, which he gratefully accepted.

When the officers dropped Kyle off at his house, Deputy Arpin opened the door of the cruiser for him. As he climbed out of the backseat, she handed him a business card and then closed the car door.

Keeping her voice low, she said, "Give Dr. Rutlinger a call if you need help dealing with any unusual side effects from your ordeal."

Kyle looked down at the card. All that was printed on it was "Dr. Adolphus Rutlinger" with an address and phone number. Kyle couldn't tell from the card what kind of doctor Rutlinger was. Kyle absently touched the bandaged wounds on his chest. "You mean like for an infection? Or counseling?"

The deputy smiled. She said, "Whatever you need," and got back into the patrol car. The officers drove away, leaving Kyle confused and standing on the sidewalk with the card in his hand.

Chapter 4
Symptomatic

Kyle walked into McWort's, his favorite local brewpub, and took a seat at a small table near the entrance. His seat overlooked the small brewing area where the owners brewed their tap beers. The microbrewery fermented some pretty mild fare—mostly "session ales," in brewing terms—but it went well with food and was suited to palates accustomed to the barley pop produced by the large American breweries.

What brought Kyle back time after time wasn't their beer, it was their veggie burger. They served a patty made from their own recipe that was the best Kyle had ever tasted. Kyle's mouth watered just thinking about pepper jack melted across the patty with alfalfa sprouts on a whole-grain, poppy-seed kaiser roll. His stomach grumbled in anticipation.

Kyle looked around for a familiar face, scratching absently at the front of his shirt. It had been a little over a week since the terrifying incident at Clarissa's home, but his chest still ached and itched where her fingernails had dug in. He caught himself scratching and stopped. It never seemed to make the discomfort go away, and anyone observing him would think he had fleas or something. The itch was probably all in his mind anyway, since the wounds had healed and practically vanished by the next day. Maybe this was one of the things Deputy Arpin was talking about when she'd mentioned "unusual side effects." Perhaps trauma victims routinely picked up odd quirks.

Thankfully, the sheriff's department had contacted him only once since the incident. They basically called to say he was off the hook. Clarissa had a known heart problem and had been taking medication for it for years. She didn't let it slow her down though. Associates testified that she habitually pushed herself harder than she should have, refusing to let her illness take control of her life. The coroner confirmed that she had died from natural causes due to her medical condition, not from any criminal action on Kyle's part. Kyle was relieved, but he wished Clarissa had picked someone else to be her final partner.

Kyle had arrived at McWort's early, before prime lunch time, so the brewpub was sparsely populated with patrons. He saw no familiar faces, which was fine. Earlier in the week, the newspaper had run a short article on Clarissa's death. It included a quote from Kyle, and some rather embarrassing details of the events leading up to the tragedy. Thank goodness the only picture they'd run was one of Clarissa.

The waitress came by not long after he sat down, and Kyle ordered the veggie burger with fries as well as the house porter. He glanced at his watch. He had given himself plenty of time to get some food and then meet Greg and Deb at the marina for an afternoon sail.

When the food arrived, Kyle started eating with enthusiasm. After a few bites though, he put the burger down. It didn't taste right, but he couldn't tell exactly why. He waited until the waitress came by again and waved her over.

She was carrying a platter with several plates on it. "Can I get you something?" she asked pleasantly.

An aroma from the top plate on her stack caught Kyle's attention. The plate had a mostly eaten hamburger on it, and the bit of meat patty that remained was red and juicy. Kyle had given up red meat the prior year and had never missed it, but the leftover burger made him lick his lips.

Kyle tore his eyes away from the food and focused on the waitress, who was waiting for his reply. "Uh, yeah, I have a question about the veggie burger. Did you guys change the recipe or something?"

She shook her head. "No … not that I know of. Is there something wrong with it?"

Kyle looked down at his plate. "I'm not sure. I get this all the time, but it tastes funny today."

The waitress leaned down and took his plate. "I'm sorry. Let me take that. Would you like me to get you another one, or do you want something else?"

Kyle glanced at the burger again. "You know, I think I'll have a regular burger today. Cooked like that one," he said, angling his head toward her platter.

The waitress smiled. "No problem. Medium rare then? Coming right up."

After she left, Kyle shook his head in dismay. The *thought* of eating a regular hamburger didn't appeal at all, but his body seemed to be craving real meat. Maybe it was some kind of vitamin deficiency related to the stress of the past week. He hoped eating meat after all this time wouldn't make him sick.

With the first juicy bite, Kyle's doubts about his decision evaporated. Suddenly famished, he consumed half the burger in four bites and then set it down to catch his breath and take a sip of his porter.

"That was impressive. I'm guessing you haven't eaten for a few days?"

Kyle looked up, not recognizing the woman who had spoken. She stood next to his table with her purse slung over her shoulder. She had apparently just entered the brewpub and been treated to his swinish display. Her full lips were curved into a friendly smile that carried up into her hazel eyes. Straight, dark-brown hair flowed down her back and curved over the swell of her breasts in front.

"Sorry you had to witness that," Kyle said. "It's been a rough week."

The woman hung her purse strap over the back of the chair opposite Kyle. "Mind if I join you?" she asked as she slid into the seat.

Kyle glanced around the brewpub. The lunch crowd had starting filtering in, but plenty of tables were still open. Why she would want to sit with him was unclear, but he could do worse for an eating companion. Still, she was being a bit presumptuous.

"Please, have a seat," Kyle said sardonically, holding out his right hand toward the chair she now occupied.

She didn't miss a beat. She took his hand in hers and shook it. "Thank you. I'm Amanda."

Her hand was small and cool. When they shook, a charge went up his arm, and he nearly jerked his hand back.

"Sorry," she said, releasing his hand. "I'm a little static-y today. I think it's the shoes."

"I'm Kyle. Pleased to meet you, Amanda."

The waitress came to the table and asked Amanda if she'd like to order anything. Amanda asked for a half sandwich and salad.

Kyle had stopped eating the moment Amanda arrived. After the waitress left, Amanda insisted he go ahead and finish his meal while it was still warm.

She nodded toward his plate. "You like your burgers with some pink in them."

Kyle picked up the half-eaten burger and stared at it. "You know, normally I'd have a veggie burger. This is the first red meat I've eaten in over a year." Kyle took a bite and savored the warm, juicy texture and the slight tang of the rare center.

Amanda's food arrived and she started on her salad. "You mentioned you had a rough week," she said between bites. "Do you want to talk about it?"

With a stranger?

Her question seemed oddly personal, considering they'd just met. Kyle grew suspicious of how easily she had placed herself at his table.

"Are you a reporter or something?" he asked.

She smiled and tossed her hair over her shoulder. "No. Just nosy, I guess." She took a bite of her sandwich, watching him while she chewed.

Kyle wiped his hands on his napkin and rested his forearms on the table. "I think I'd better go now." He looked around for the waitress.

"Kyle, wait," she said, drawing his attention back to her. "Don't go." She reached across the table toward him, but her hand grazed the top of her water glass and the stemmed goblet tilted toward Kyle.

Kyle reacted without thinking. Everything seemed to happen in slow motion. Her light bump pushed the glass past the tipping point and the water inside sloshed toward the rim, speeding its descent. Kyle's hand reached the half-full glass an instant before the water rolled over the rim, and in one smooth motion, he righted it and pulled it toward him exactly enough to compensate for the motion of the water. The next thing he knew, he was holding up her glass and the water inside it was perfectly still.

Amanda blinked at the goblet a couple of times. "Nice reflexes," she said, barely above a whisper.

Kyle set her glass back down where it had been, suspecting she might have tipped it over on purpose. "What do you want, Amanda?"

"Just some friendly conversation." She kept eating her sandwich as if nothing had happened.

Kyle picked up a fry and chewed on it, considering the pretty girl across from him. He guessed she was about his age, maybe a little younger. She seemed relaxed and confident, but there was an edge of excitement in her voice and a sparkle in her eyes. Like she knew something he didn't and was dying to tell him about it. The only odd thing about her was the earring that she'd revealed when she'd pulled her hair back. It was a silver pentagram.

"You know who I am, don't you?" he said. "Coming in here and sitting at my table was no coincidence."

Amanda put her sandwich down. All that remained was a corner of crust. She used her napkin and shrugged. "Okay, yes. I know who you are and what happened last week."

Kyle started to get up from his seat. He'd find the waitress, settle his bill, and get the hell out of there.

"Kyle, please hear me out," Amanda said, putting her hand on his arm. The tingle that her touch gave him this time could not be explained away by static electricity. "Sorry, I have to quit doing that."

Kyle lowered himself slowly back into his seat. There was something earnest about her expression that made him want to give her a chance to explain, and she didn't carry herself with the smug entitlement of a reporter. He drank the remaining third of his beer in a couple of gulps, hoping it would help him relax. "I'm listening."

"I'm here because I think I can help you." Her hazel eyes held his, and she appeared to be genuinely concerned.

Kyle narrowed his eyes at her. "Help me do what?"

She struggled to say whatever it was she wanted to say. "Well … get better, I guess."

Kyle sat back and shook his head. "What do you mean, *get better*? I'm fine. Still a little freaked-out by what happened, but anybody would be."

Amanda poked at her salad with her fork. "So, you haven't noticed anything different in the past week? Other than maybe a change in appetite and improved reflexes?"

Kyle snorted. "I don't think there's anything unusual about craving a burger. As for your water glass, I got lucky."

Amanda stopped playing with her salad and watched Kyle closely as she asked her next question. "What about the wounds on your chest?"

Kyle closed his eyes and sighed. That was one of the embarrassing details included in the article. The reporter had thought it highly amusing that the throes of passion had ended in a literal death grip. Greg had assured him that everyone thought the article was in extremely poor taste, but Kyle had overheard enough snickering over the past week to make him wish he'd taken some time off and stayed home.

"Look, I don't know why you are interested in this, but someone died last week and I was there. It isn't something I really feel like talking about."

He stared Amanda down, but her gaze remained steady and serious. "Just tell me this. Did she draw blood with her teeth or nails?"

Oh, man. What kind of freak show am I dealing with here?

"Listen to yourself, Amanda. Do you have any idea how creepy that question is?"

Amanda looked over Kyle's shoulder and her eyes lost their focus. Then she chuckled and shook her head. "I guess I see what you mean. Let me try again. If she did hurt you, did the wounds heal faster than normal?"

The hair on Kyle's neck stood up and a shiver ran down his spine. Her question was only marginally less creepy, and it put a sinister light on something he'd thought was a blessing. He decided he needed to understand where she was going with all this.

"What are you getting at?"

Amanda took a deep breath, put her fork down, and set her hands in her lap. "Clarissa Laughton may have passed something to you during your … interaction."

"Passed something? Like a disease?" he asked quietly but forcefully. He'd been wearing a condom that night, but condoms don't protect you from *everything*.

Amanda nodded slowly. "In a manner of speaking, yes."

"Did you know Clarissa? How would *you* know about any disease she might have had?"

It wouldn't have surprised Kyle in the slightest to learn that Clarissa had recreated with both genders. Maybe Amanda knew Clarissa intimately.

Amanda seemed to recognize the direction his thoughts had taken. She blushed and looked down at her plate. "I didn't know Clarissa *personally*, but I knew *of* her. She belonged to a group of others who share her … condition."

"And you're part of that group?"

Amanda shuddered. "No, thank the Light. But I keep an eye on them."

Her shudder disturbed Kyle. This *condition* she was dancing around was apparently pretty bad. And he was tired of the dance.

"Look, just lay it on the line for me. What is this condition you're talking about, and why do you think I may have it?"

The waitress came by right then and dropped their checks on the table. Amanda picked up her fork and pushed her salad around until the waitress had left. She finally looked up and met Kyle's eyes.

"Before I alarm you any more than I already have, let me ask you about the symptoms first. It's only been a week, but some may have started to manifest. In any case, you'll know what to watch for."

Kyle leaned forward, putting his arms on the table. "Okay. What are the symptoms?"

Amanda pushed her plate aside and leaned forward as well. "First, there's unusually fast healing."

Kyle nodded, but said nothing. The wounds on his chest had healed quickly, but they may have been superficial. The blood Clarissa had drawn suggested otherwise, but he was no expert on puncture wounds.

"Next, your physical strength and dexterity improve to unusually high levels."

Kyle gave her a wry smile. She *had* tipped the glass over on purpose—to test him. So far, these so-called symptoms sounded pretty good.

"Your eyes will start to change color." Her hazel eyes searched his brown ones, but she didn't seem to find what she was looking for.

"What color?" Kyle interrupted.

"It varies a little, but golden amber is most common."

Kyle nodded and Amanda went on.

"In the first month, you'll have strange dreams. You'll feel compelled to find others who have your condition."

Kyle was taken aback. "That's odd. It has a psychological aspect? What kind of disease is this?"

Amanda took a breath to answer and then released it through her nose. Finally, she shook her head and said with regret, "Lycanthropy."

Kyle was sure he heard wrong. "Lycanthropy? As in werewolves?"

Amanda gave him an apologetic look. "Sorry. That's what Clarissa was. Last Saturday was the full moon. If she shifted even part way and scratched or bit you, you could become one too."

Kyle watched Amanda, waiting for the punch line. Greg must have set this up as some kind of practical joke. But the look she leveled at him was deadly serious.

Kyle sat back and laughed. Shaking his head, he grabbed his check from the table and stood up. "It was nice to meet you, Amanda. I'm not sure who put you up to this, but tell them it was a good one. You had me going there for a while."

"Before you go, Kyle, know this. I believe I can help you, but we only have until the next full moon. If you want to contact me, leave a message at Butterflies and Rainbows."

Kyle frowned down at her. Butterflies and Rainbows was a small local store that specialized in spiritual books and curios that catered to the crystal-hugging crowd. The venue, coupled with her pentagram earring and her *thank the Light* comment, told him she was probably some kind of religious or superstitious nut-job who was fascinated by his bizarre experience last week.

She wouldn't be the first. At work, a woman from a different department had propositioned him, convinced he had a thing for older women. Another woman had made hints in the lunch line that she thought men who "liked it rough" were exciting. That stupid newspaper article had shattered his privacy and was attracting the crazies to him. He wondered briefly if he had grounds for a lawsuit.

Still frowning, he said, "Goodbye, Amanda," and went to pay his bill.

While waiting for his credit card to clear, he glanced back at the table. Her check was tucked under her plate along with some cash, but the woman herself was gone.

Good riddance.

Chapter 5

Dr. Adolphus Rutlinger

Kyle parked his blue Ford Explorer in a shady spot and went around the side of the brick professional building. The sign by the road had listed several businesses, including doctors' offices, accountants, and lawyers. Dr. Adolphus Rutlinger was in Suite 102, as it said on the business card the deputy had given him. The good doctor's name was followed by the letters "DVM," which meant nothing to Kyle. He'd expected to see MD or PhD, but he wasn't familiar with the various medical designations.

Kyle stopped when he reached the door to the office. "Rutlinger Pet Clinic," the sign above the door declared. The DVM on the sign must have meant "Doctor of *Veterinary* Medicine." Kyle looked down in confusion at the card in his hand. The deputy had recommended a vet? Was this some kind of joke?

As Amanda had predicted, Kyle had been waking up in a sweat from the strangest nightmares every night since he'd met her. The dreams usually involved chasing something or being chased, and it always ended bloody. He couldn't decide if she might know something after all, or if her crazy claims had messed with his head and *caused* his nightmares.

Amanda had gotten to him so thoroughly that he even caught himself checking his eyes in the mirror each morning to see if they were changing color. Had his eyes always had that thin ridge of amber circling the brown iris? Probably.

He'd just never had a reason to obsessively check his eyes for every nuance before then.

That morning, Kyle had woken up exhausted and on edge after another night with little sleep. He decided that he needed help, but not whatever kind of help Amanda thought she could give. He'd give Dr. Rutlinger a try.

Now he was reconsidering that decision.

Shrugging, Kyle pushed through the door and entered the waiting room. He'd probably be able to figure out pretty quickly if the cop had been messing with him as well.

A woman with a toddler sat waiting in one of the chairs along the wall. A husky puppy sat on the floor, wiggling its over-sized ears while it chewed on its leash and stared up at Kyle with pale blue eyes.

"Can I help you?" asked the woman at the reception counter.

Kyle stepped up to the counter and spoke quietly. "I'm looking for a Dr. Rutlinger, but I think there may have been some kind of mistake. A sheriff's deputy gave me this card and suggested I contact him." Kyle laid the card on the counter so the receptionist could read it.

She looked at the card and then quickly back at Kyle. "May I have your name?"

"Kyle Nelson."

"Please wait here, Kyle. I'll be right back."

She bustled out of the room and into the back offices with some haste. Her reaction was so unexpected that Kyle snatched the card off the counter and seriously considered getting out of there. Was everyone around him acting strangely, or was he imagining things?

Kyle was about to bolt when the door to the waiting room opened and a man stepped out. He was taller than Kyle's six feet and had dark hair going gray at the temples. Not a hair was out of place. His white lab coat hung open to reveal a dark tailored suit.

With a welcoming smile, the man stepped over to Kyle and held out his hand. "Hello Kyle. I'm Adolphus Rutlinger. I understand Deputy Arpin sent you to me."

The doctor spoke with a slight European accent of some kind. Kyle guessed it might be German or Austrian.

"Yes, sir. She suggested I contact you if I ran into any … difficulties." Kyle glanced toward the woman who was waiting. She thumbed idly through a magazine, appearing to be uninterested in their conversation.

The doctor nodded. "I understand. Come with me, and we'll talk in private."

Kyle followed Dr. Rutlinger through the door and down a short hallway to an examination room. The doctor closed the exam-room door and asked Kyle to have a seat next to the exam table in one of the room's two chairs.

The doctor sat opposite him and folded his hands in his lap. He gave Kyle an assessing look. "I'm glad you came by today, Kyle. I was wondering when I would see you."

Kyle tensed. "You knew I was coming? How?"

He smiled and answered with a reassuring tone. "Don't be alarmed. The good deputy told me that she gave you my card. In my experience, you were bound to come looking for answers eventually."

Kyle shook his head. "I'm confused. No offense, but why would a veterinarian have the answers? Shouldn't I be seeing a people-doctor or a psychiatrist?"

"An MD would find nothing wrong with you, and a psychiatrist would not be able to help you either, although you'd pay dearly to discover that. I operate a foundation that exists for the sole purpose of helping people in our situation."

Our situation? "What exactly *is* our situation?"

Dr. Rutlinger held up a hand. "Before I explain more, we should be sure you have reason for concern. It would be a shame for you to worry over nothing, yes?"

Kyle nodded, wondering what the doctor had in mind.

The doctor scooted his chair closer until his knees were practically touching Kyle's.

"I want you to look into my eyes and tell me exactly what happened the night you met Clarissa."

Kyle did as the doctor asked. Up close, it was easy to spot the brown-tinted contact lenses that floated over the man's irises. He wondered what color they hid.

Kyle started relating the story of his evening with Clarissa. When he grew uncomfortable or started to hold back, the doctor prompted him with soft-voiced questions like, "How did that make you feel?" His soothing interest in Kyle's experience made it easier for him to keep talking. Eventually, Kyle got to the part where Clarissa and he were sitting on the couch. He started to hesitate, but the doctor reassured him again.

"Please continue, Kyle. I'm well aware of Clarissa's sexually aggressive nature. You will not shock me."

In spite of the reassurances, Kyle felt reluctant to share the intimate experience, but he supposed the doctor was trying to help. As he continued, Dr. Rutlinger's eyes conveyed no judgment or amusement—just intense interest.

At the end of the story, the doctor slowed Kyle down and asked about Clarissa's final moments. "You say she clawed you and screamed right before she died?"

Having already spilled most of the story, Kyle felt more comfortable talking about it. "Yeah, but it was more like a howl than a scream. Honestly, it kinda freaked me out."

"May I see where she scratched you?" the doctor asked.

Kyle lifted his t-shirt and pointed to the locations on his pectoral muscles where the fingernail cuts had been. "The marks were here and here, but you can hardly tell where they were now."

"So the wounds were superficial? Scrapes, perhaps?"

"No, I was bleeding pretty well at the time. But within a couple of days, the wounds were completely healed."

"I see."

Kyle lowered his shirt while the doctor stared at him in silence. After a moment of that, Kyle started feeling uncomfortable. "What are you thinking?" he finally asked.

Dr. Rutlinger sat back in his chair with what appeared to be a satisfied smile. "Well, Kyle, I have good news and I have bad news. The bad news is that Clarissa probably *has* passed her condition to you. The good news is that you qualify for assistance from the foundation."

Kyle sat in stunned silence. The nightmare apparently wasn't over yet. Clarissa had infected him with something that modern science couldn't treat—that modern science couldn't even detect.

Wait a minute. This was all starting to smell like some kind of scam. First the cop gives him a card, then some girl comes out of the blue and fills his head with horror stories, and now a veterinarian wants to offer him the assistance of his foundation. What was *that* going to cost him?

Kyle stood up and began to pace the room. The doctor folded his arms and waited patiently.

The more he thought about it, the more convinced Kyle became. "Amanda's part of this whole setup, isn't she? She spooks me and you reel me in."

The doctor cocked his head to the side and narrowed his eyes. "Amanda? The young witch? You spoke with her?"

Young witch? Well, that explains the pentagrams. And the insanity.

Kyle rounded on the doctor. "She interrupted my lunch the other day, as if you didn't know. She tried to tell me that I'll turn into a werewolf without her help."

Dr. Rutlinger nodded his head slowly and then stood. With a sigh he said, "The witch cannot help you. She can only put you in danger. Only I can help you deal with your condition. The foundation has served our kind for generations."

Kyle frowned at the doctor. "You still haven't explained what this *condition* entails. I hope your story is better than that I'm turning into a werewolf."

The doctor took a step closer to Kyle, entering his personal space. "I understand that this is upsetting. When you are ready to calm down and listen, we will talk again."

Kyle eased back until the overpowering *presence* of the man faded. He nodded his understanding, although he had no intention of visiting Rutlinger Pet Clinic ever again.

The doctor took a note pad and pen from his lab-coat pocket and bent over the exam table. He wrote down what looked like a date and an address, and he handed the piece of paper to Kyle. "The foundation is having a party this weekend. Come see for yourself what we are about, and I will answer all of your questions. Now I have patients I must attend to. Have a good day."

The doctor opened the door to the examination room and walked out, leaving Kyle standing alone in the room holding the piece of paper. Kyle was tempted to drop it in the trash can next to the door, but he couldn't bring himself to do it. Unlike Amanda, the doctor at least seemed sane. So far, anyway.

Kyle stuffed the piece of paper into his pocket and headed back to the waiting room. The first thing he needed to do was get out of that clinic. Then he was going to make an appointment with a *real* doctor and get a second opinion.

One nice thing about living in a small town was that it was usually easy to get a doctor's appointment on short notice. Kyle was able to see Dr. Basile, his regular physician, the morning after his visit to the pet clinic.

Dr. Basile gave Kyle a regular checkup and prescribed some medication to help him sleep, but found nothing obvious wrong with him physically. The doctor ran a full blood panel and said the results would be back in a day or two. That might tell them more, but the doctor warned Kyle that they were testing only for specific things that might or might not relate to his sleeping difficulties.

In reality, Kyle had learned nothing, but he felt better about things anyway. It was comforting to be back in the rational world of normal medical science. He'd had enough of doomsayer witches and creepy veterinarians.

Back at work, Kyle happily engrossed himself in his current project. His desk was in a partitioned section of a large, rectangular cubicle dedicated to his team. He pounded away on his keyboard, writing a database script while Vivaldi played through his headphones.

An e-mail notification popped up in the lower right corner of his monitor, and he stopped to check the sender and subject of the message before it faded away. It was his boss. She wanted to see him as soon as possible.

Her office was at the end of the hall, and he had waved to her when he'd arrived earlier, so she knew he was here. Kyle sighed, saved his work, and locked his computer session. It wasn't that he didn't trust his teammates; it was company policy. He personally never understood what could be so secret about programming a web site for a sports-equipment retailer, but he knew better than to quibble.

She was on the phone when he walked into her office. She waved him to close the door and he did so. He sat in one of the visitor chairs and waited for her to finish her call.

Vanya Raine was generally a good supervisor. You always knew where you stood with her, and she understood the unpredictable nature of software development. She was firm but forgiving. Her main failing was that she was too easily influenced by the shifting priorities of other departments, who were essentially the IT team's internal customers. Her eagerness to please had inspired Kyle's team to come up with their own saying about priorities, which they used when she was out of earshot: "When every task is Number One, not a single thing gets done."

The fire of the moment was the project Kyle was working on.

She held up her index finger to let Kyle know she was almost finished with her call. "Sure, thanks, Jennifer. I've got one of the developers in my office right now, so I'll have an update for you later today. Okay. 'Bye."

She hung up the phone and wrote a quick note before looking up at Kyle. "Thanks for coming so fast. I wasn't sure if you were in the middle of something."

Kyle shrugged. "No problem. I'm always in the middle of something, so now is as good a time as any."

She nodded. "That's one of the things I like about you Kyle. You get stuff done. Speaking of which, how are things going with the data warehouse project?"

Kyle thought for a moment about where he was with the project and how much more he had to do. "I should have the new tables and scripts done by the end of this week. I think we can schedule a test run with the data warehouse group early next week."

"Great. That makes us only a few days late. Do you think you'll need more time off?"

Kyle didn't miss the not-so-subtle hint that the project was already running late because he had been out for all of the prior day and part of that morning.

She held her hand up before he could say anything and continued. "It's okay if you do. I don't want you to come in if you aren't feeling well. But I need to know if I need to assign someone else to fill in for you."

Having someone else take over Kyle's tasks wasn't a practical idea, and he was sure she knew that. Only one other person on the team had the necessary skills and that person was up to his eyebrows in a different high-priority project. It would take as long to bring someone else up to speed as it would to just finish the damned project.

Kyle grimaced and tried not to let his annoyance into his voice. "That won't be necessary. My doctor says I'm fine and that I just need more rest. He gave me something to help with that."

Vanya seemed to realize she'd pushed a little too hard. "Sorry, Kyle. I know you had an awful experience last week, but I've got VPs breathing down my neck on some of these projects."

Kyle took a deep breath and straightened his back, pushing aside a wave of exhaustion. Putting confidence into his voice that he didn't truly feel, he said, "I understand, and I won't let you down."

She smiled at him and sat back in her chair. "I know you won't. Well, I guess I'd better let you get back to it. Keep me posted on how things are going, and warn me if it starts to look like the coding will slip into next week."

Kyle nodded and stood up. "Will do."

Kyle suspected that one of the hallmarks of a good supervisor was to be a pain in the ass. There was a saying that work expands to fit the time available, but a good boss also knew that work *contracts* to fit the time available—within limits. Vanya's job was to make sure that all available time was filled with as much work as possible, and she was good at it.

Kyle walked back toward his desk, passing his friend Greg along the way. Greg looked up as he went by and pantomimed cracking a whip. Kyle snorted and rolled his eyes.

Kyle stopped when two men came his way pushing a cart with a wide steel cabinet. He started to back up, but one of the men said he was fine where he was. They would be turning at the next hallway before they got to him.

One man pulled on the handle of the wheeled cart while the other pushed from behind. As they turned the corner, they miscalculated the swing of the cart and jammed it against the wall. The momentum of the cart along with the angled force of the man who was pushing caused the cabinet to tip toward Kyle.

"Grab it!" yelled the man pulling the cart, but the other man was already fully extended and had no leverage.

In two swift steps, Kyle came forward and caught the top edge of the cabinet inches before it slammed to the floor. He pushed it back into position on the cart and dusted his hands.

The two workmen looked at him like he'd grown a second head.

"Holy crap!" The lead man said. "Somebody's been working out. It took both of us to get that mother onto the cart."

The other guy shook his head. "I told you we should have taken all that stuff out of it. It's too top-heavy."

The lead man shrugged and held out his hand. "Anyway, thanks for the catch. Those cabinets ain't cheap, and I'm glad I don't have to explain how it got busted."

Kyle smiled and shook the man's hand. "No problem. Glad I could help."

The two workmen successfully renegotiated the corner and wheeled the cabinet toward its destination. Kyle continued down the hall to his cubicle with a dark foreboding descending upon him. Yes, he was in good shape, but not *that* good.

Kyle sat at his desk and put his headphones on. He unlocked his computer and stared blankly at the script he had been working on. What was happening to him? Being strong was cool, but what was the cost? Would he really turn into some kind of furry beast at the next full moon?

A crumpled slip of paper still sat on his dresser at home. Maybe he *should* go to Rutlinger's gathering. The doctor said that others with his "condition" would be there. Maybe he could get a straight answer from one of *them*.

CHAPTER 6
The Foundation

Kyle's palms began to sweat as he turned off the highway. He slowed down about a half mile up the dirt road and his knuckles went white on the steering wheel. There was the driveway to Clarissa's house. Shuddering, he stepped on the accelerator and resumed his journey.

The road wound up into the hills, curving past isolated homes and patches of meadow fenced for gardens or livestock. The housing varied from gorgeous new log or timber homes to run-down trailers with cardboard duct-taped over the windows. This strange mixture of home quality was typical of nearly every area Kyle had visited in North Idaho, where neighborhood covenants and deed restrictions were rare.

The farther Kyle drove into the mountains, the harder his Explorer had to work. Long stretches of relatively flat road degenerated into nasty washboards, and patchy shade obscured suspension-challenging potholes. Kyle slowed down substantially after going around a corner and slamming into a rock that stuck above the road surface. The last thing he needed was a flat tire out in the middle of nowhere. He owned a cell phone for emergency calling, but he seriously doubted he'd get a signal with forested hills rising on both sides of the road.

Right about the time he was starting to think he might have missed a turn, Kyle came upon a driveway that curved up and disappeared over the ridge to his right. A rock retaining wall with a concrete sign built into it supported the driveway's incline along the hillside. The sign said, "Rutlinger

Foundation." To the right of the driveway, a different sign said, "Private Drive, Invited Guests Only."

Kyle turned and drove up the smooth gravel driveway. At the top of the ridge, the road continued for about fifty yards before it widened into a large circle in front of a black wrought-iron gate supported by a tall block wall. Each gate panel had been decorated in the center with a stylized snarling wolf's head. Concrete wolf sculptures sat on the top of each gate post, calmly staring ahead.

So, the doctor had a thing for wolves. The witch-girl Amanda probably knew that and let her over-active imagination run wild with it.

After Kyle slowed to a stop in front of the gate, movement caught his eye. He spotted a camera adjusting its position under a protective overhang. Unsure of what he should do, he started lowering his side window in case he needed to announce himself, but then the gate began to swing open for him.

Past the gate, the driveway curved around a small copse of pines. When he drove past the trees and reached the other side of the ridge, the scene before him made his jaw drop.

The Rutlinger Foundation building was a European-style manor with a gray rough-hewn block exterior. An angled pair of two-story wings extended from each side of the three-story main building. The dark-green metal roof was pitched steeply to deal with winter snow.

Kyle pulled into a parking space opposite the six-car garage, marveling at the money it would cost to build and maintain such a place. Just the block wall that encircled the grounds would have cost a fortune. The Rutlinger Foundation was apparently doing well.

Kyle grabbed a wine bottle from behind the passenger seat and started walking toward the building. He wasn't sure if the party was a random get-together or if it was someone's birthday, so he brought the wine as a generic gift, just in case.

He strode off the gravel of the parking lot onto a cobbled stone walkway that passed through a well-tended garden filled with flowers and low shrubs. His steps faltered uncertainly until he came to a stop.

Ahead of him, an enormous wolf had stepped out from behind a shrub and onto the path, staring at him with intense amber eyes. It paused and sniffed the air a few times before continuing across the walkway into the garden on the other side.

Kyle swallowed hard and gave the creature a moment to go on its way. He assumed that it belonged to the Foundation and must be tame. Surely it would be too dangerous to let a wild wolf stalk the grounds with visitors arriving. Taking a deep breath, Kyle slowly resumed his trek toward the building, shooting nervous glances in the direction the wolf had gone.

Mounting the front steps, Kyle searched for a doorbell or knocker. The front doors were made of narrow wood planks set into a tall arch, each door filling half the archway. Before Kyle could reach for the doorbell button, a face flashed in one of the narrow windows alongside the doors and the latch clicked.

The door swung open and Dr. Rutlinger extended his hand toward Kyle.

"Kyle! I'm glad you could make it. Please, come inside."

Kyle followed the doctor through the door and found himself in an open foyer. He held up the bottle of wine, thinking maybe he should have chosen a more expensive brand. "I wasn't sure what the occasion is, so I brought this."

The doctor took the bottle from him and rotated it to inspect the label. "Ah, the local huckleberry wine. Excellent."

He smiled and raised an eyebrow at Kyle. "Did someone tell you this is one of my favorites?"

"No sir, although I'm glad to hear you like it. I gambled on it because it's a popular wine, and I figured I'd drink it even if no one else did."

The doctor chuckled. "Very practical, but you will not drink alone today." He turned and motioned Kyle to follow. "Come. Meet the others."

The foyer stepped down into a wide living space with an open-front stone fireplace that had to be four feet wide. A pair of long black leather couches faced each other across a glass table made in the same rustic log style Kyle had seen at Clarissa's. Classical music played softly in the background from speakers set high in the four corners of the space. As Kyle followed the doctor into the living room, two people rose from the couches.

Kyle almost didn't recognize Deputy Arpin out of uniform. She wore a summer dress with a light blue print. The soft fabric followed curves that hinted at a nice figure, and the thigh-length skirt showed off her trim legs. Her long blonde hair cascaded around her shoulders, framing a face that looked much more relaxed than the last time he'd seen her.

"I believe you have already met Skyler Arpin," the doctor said.

Kyle nodded. "Yes, nice to see you again, Deputy."

She smiled and nodded back. "I'm glad you could make it. And you can call me Skyler when I'm not on duty."

The doctor held out a hand toward the other occupant of the room. "And this is Fenris Kellen, our legal counsel."

A lawyer. Well, that explained the clean shave, neatly trimmed hair, dress slacks, and button-up shirt. The man's only concession to relaxing for the weekend seemed to be the lack of a tie.

"Hello, Kyle," he said without warmth or welcome in his voice.

Kyle stopped himself from extending his hand, sensing that Fenris had no intention of doing the same. The man simply stood there, staring at Kyle as if he were waiting for Kyle to go away.

The doctor frowned at the lawyer. Turning back to Kyle, he said, "Please have a seat. I'll pour us some wine." He took the bottle toward a buffet that was set against one wall.

Uncertain of the protocol, Kyle sat in the middle of the couch. Skyler chose the same couch, but sat at one end, half-turned toward Kyle with her back against the corner cushions. She crossed her legs and discreetly arranged the skirt of her dress. The lawyer sat on the edge of the opposite couch, leaning forward with his arms braced on his legs.

Kyle looked around and realized it was only the four of them—not many people for a party. "Am I early?"

Fenris snorted. "You mean, where is everybody?" He shook his head in mock sadness and said to Skyler, "I guess we aren't enough."

Skyler narrowed her eyes at him and responded in a level tone, "Be nice to our guest, Fenris."

Fenris looked at the floor and let out a frustrated sigh. "Sorry, Kyle. I'm in a bad mood today."

The doctor returned with four glasses of wine and handed one to each of them. "Perhaps this will cheer you up," he said as he gave Fenris his wine. Everyone took a sip.

Fenris pursed his lips and nodded in appreciation. "I'm not much for sweet girlie wines, but this isn't bad."

The doctor rolled his eyes and shrugged apologetically to Kyle. "In answer to your question, other guests may stop by, but for now it's just the four of us. I thought you might feel more comfortable discussing the Foundation in a smaller group."

Kyle sipped his wine. "Thank you, I appreciate that. I'm sure you're right."

The doctor waved his glass around the room. "So, what do you think so far?"

"You have a beautiful facility," Kyle answered. "The gardens out front are impressive. Although I was surprised to see a wolf cross the path in front of me."

The doctor wasn't surprised and waved away Kyle's concern. "That's Reggie. He likes to wander the grounds when the weather is good. He has a taste for pocket gophers and ground squirrels." Skyler giggled into her glass and struggled to swallow the sip of wine she'd just taken.

"So he *is* tame," Kyle muttered with relief.

Kyle wondered if he'd said something wrong when everyone stopped and stared at him for a moment.

Finally, the doctor tilted his head back and forth in a *yes-and-no* motion. "Most of the time," he said.

This elicited another giggle from Skyler. It seemed out of character for a sheriff's deputy to giggle over a glass of wine and look so good in a summer dress, but Kyle was starting to like her.

The doctor cleared his throat and set his glass down on the table. "Since you came today, I assume you have thought about our conversation at the clinic."

Kyle nodded and set his glass down as well. "I have. I visited my doctor, and as you predicted, he wasn't able to find anything wrong. I was hoping you would tell me more about this condition I seem to have."

The doctor nodded and relaxed into the couch, draping an arm over the back. "Absolutely. I would have explained sooner, but you were not ready to hear."

Kyle sighed. "You're right. I wasn't. Sorry if I was rude."

The doctor shrugged. "You are entitled to your feelings, but you should know that you are not alone. All of us have been through what you are experiencing now. That is why we are here."

Kyle had wondered about that. If the Foundation were dedicated to patients or victims or whatever you called people with this condition, would all of the people at the gathering be among the afflicted? Apparently, yes.

"I guess my biggest question is what will happen to me? What are the symptoms?"

Dr. Rutlinger answered, "You probably know of the symptoms already. You will grow in strength and speed, and you will heal from cuts and abrasions more quickly than normal."

So far, this was sounding pretty good. Kyle figured everyone would want to get infected.

The doctor continued. "You may also have disturbing dreams and difficulty sleeping. The dreams will get worse during the first month, but go away after that."

Kyle nodded, thankful for the drugs his doctor had given him to help him sleep. It sounded like he was going to need them.

"So after a few weeks of bad dreams, I'm stronger, faster, and able to heal quickly? That doesn't sound too bad."

His companions exchanged glances with each other, alerting Kyle that there was probably more to be told.

"So what's the down side?"

After a momentary hesitation, the doctor answered. "Most people undergo a significant change in personality because of their new abilities. They sever contact with former friends and family, who often become uncomfortable around them. That is why the Foundation was established—to help others like us who feel out of place among the rest of society. Here we have safety and fellowship."

Kyle couldn't imagine telling Greg that he never wanted to go sailing with him again. Would his personality change so much that he wouldn't like sailing at all? And what about cutting ties with his entire family? Most of his family still lived in Southern California. They had never been particularly *close*, but still ....

He had a feeling there was more. This obsession with wolves had to mean something. What was that all about? There was only one way to find out, but he wasn't sure he wanted the answer.

Gathering his courage, he lifted his chin and asked, "How do wolves tie into this?"

The doctor smiled and looked down at his hands, which were folded over the knee of his crossed leg. Fenris exhaled and sat back against the cushion, folding his arms. Skyler drained the last of her wine and set the glass down on the table before relaxing against the couch with her hands in her lap.

"Let me answer that," demanded a deep male voice from the foyer. A tall man with an incredible physique stepped into the living room. He wore blue jeans and a plain white t-shirt that fit him like a second skin and contrasted with his tanned arms and neck. He moved silently on bare feet that were also deeply tanned.

He went to the buffet and poured the last of the huckleberry wine into a waiting glass, grumbling something about "pussy wine." He downed it in one gulp and clunked the glass down on the buffet.

Walking over to the couches, he reached past Skyler, forcing her to huddle deeper into her corner, and held his hand out to Kyle.

"You must be Kyle. I'm Reginald Clark."

Kyle shook the man's large, warm hand, cringing from a grip that was almost painful. "Nice to meet you, Mr. Clark."

"Reggie is fine. No need for formality here."

Reggie. Like the wandering wolf outside. It was either an amusing coincidence or a not-so-amusing joke at Kyle's expense.

Reggie remained standing with his hands on his hips. He rolled his head around to stretch his neck and then addressed Kyle. "I'd like to ask you something, and I want you to give the question serious thought before you answer."

"Uh, sure. Go ahead."

"If you had the ability to transform yourself into a wolf and then back into a human, would you do it?"

The question was everything Kyle had feared. His pulse started pounding in his head. He seriously considered running out to his vehicle, driving away, and never looking back. When he looked into Reggie's eyes to see if the man was serious or making a joke, his heart nearly stopped. He beheld the same intense amber gaze that had considered him on the front path.

Oddly, staring into Reggie's eyes calmed him. He sensed no danger or malice from the man, just extreme confidence and genuine curiosity.

Reggie's question echoed in his head. *If you could turn into a wolf, would you do it?* Kyle loved to hike the area trails and get out into nature as often as possible. How amazing would it be to travel the wilderness as a wolf? He could go *anywhere*. He'd smell and hear things that no human had ever known.

Kyle found he was slowly nodding. "Yeah. I think I would. As long as I could transform back."

Reggie grinned and threw his hands up. "Well, there you go. You have nothing to worry about."

Kyle still couldn't quite accept what he was hearing. "So Amanda was right," he said under his breath while he tried to work out how it could be possible.

Fenris tensed and leaned forward, putting his hands on his knees. Glaring at Kyle, he said, "Amanda? The meddling witch?" He turned the glare to Dr. Rutlinger. "Something needs to be done about her."

The doctor waved his hand, dismissing Fenris's concern. "She is harmless. Kyle's reaction to her proves it."

It was true that Kyle hadn't believed Amanda before, but now he was learning that he probably should have. He wasn't sure what Fenris might *do about her*, but he hoped he hadn't just gotten her into some kind of trouble. She seemed like a nice girl, other than being a loon. And now it seemed she wasn't so crazy after all.

Everyone was staring at Kyle, and it occurred to him that he had been the center of attention since his arrival. "I'm getting the impression that you didn't really have a party planned for today," he said to Dr. Rutlinger.

"On the contrary," he responded. He tilted his wine glass toward Kyle. "I simply neglected to mention that you are the guest of honor."

The doctor's presumption caused a flash of annoyance. "You must have been pretty sure I'd come."

"The odds were in my favor. Your condition compels you to seek answers, and you know I have those answers."

The doctor was good at deflecting concern, and Kyle couldn't argue with the man's reasoning. He *had* come for answers, after all.

Kyle finished the bit of wine left in his glass and stood up. "Thank you for inviting me. You've given me a lot to think about."

Everyone in the room tensed and Reggie shifted his position subtly, putting his intimidating figure in the path between Kyle and the exit. Kyle narrowed his eyes at the doctor.

The doctor spoke as if nothing unusual were happening. "Leaving so soon? But I haven't told you the best part."

Kyle froze. *Dum-de-dum-dum*—the dramatic music played in the back of his mind. *This* was where the doctor would reveal what he really wanted. Kyle slowly sat back down.

Once Kyle was seated, the doctor went on. "I invited you here today so you could meet some of us and see our facility. Your next couple of weeks will be difficult. If you wish, you may stay here. We know how to keep you comfortable until the worst is past."

Relief eased the tension in Kyle's chest. "Thank you for the offer. But what about my job?"

Skyler shifted herself closer to Kyle and answered. "If you can't get time off from work, the commute from here to town isn't bad. About a half hour. Maybe a little more."

Taking more time off work was definitely out of the question. He'd miss his usual ten-minute commute, but half an hour was doable. He could verify that estimate on his drive back to town.

But was staying here a reasonable option? They knew almost nothing about him. Why would they be willing to put him up for two weeks? He couldn't help but cynically wonder what they would be getting out of it.

He decided to play dumb. "I'm not exactly loaded. What would it cost me to stay here for two weeks?"

The doctor chuckled. "There is no charge. The Foundation was created to help people like us."

Kyle shook his head. The facility itself was worth a fortune, and several people seemed to call it home. "Where does all the money come from?" he wondered aloud. He glanced up, hoping the doctor wouldn't think he was being rude.

The doctor took the question in stride. "The Foundation is funded by its members. We pool our resources, and in return we want for nothing."

Like a commune. That kind of an arrangement didn't appeal to Kyle at all. He liked his privacy too much and wanted the flexibility to go wherever and whenever he wanted.

"May I take some time to think about it?" Kyle asked.

The doctor waved his glass magnanimously and smiled. "Of course. Take as long as you like. The offer does not expire."

Kyle got tentatively to his feet again. "Well, I do appreciate the offer and promise to give it serious consideration. I'm sure it would be interesting to stay here with you, but that's a big decision."

The doctor set down his wine and rose to his feet. Fenris and Skyler followed his example. Everyone shook Kyle's hand and escorted him to the foyer, exchanging farewell pleasantries.

When Kyle left the building and walked back to his SUV, the outside world seemed extra bright and harsh, like an overexposed photograph. He started the Explorer and sat staring out the front window. His life had taken such a surreal turn that he had trouble imagining what his future might look like.

Putting the vehicle into gear, he backed out and then drove toward the main gate. Although the doctor had answered his questions, Kyle was sure he still wasn't getting the whole story. Maybe Amanda could give him a different perspective.

Chapter 7

Butterflies and Rainbows

On the drive back, Kyle thought about Fenris's remarks regarding Amanda. His guilt over calling attention to her grew until a sense of urgency made him decide to warn her as soon as possible. Looking at his watch, he figured the shops would still be open, so he headed into Sandpoint.

He parked his rig in the central lot downtown. Locking the door to the Explorer, he chuckled to himself, remembering how quickly he'd adopted the local term "rig" to describe any SUV or truck. Walking the side streets to the main drag, he dodged tourists, dogs, strollers, and skateboarders to reach the front door of Butterflies and Rainbows. He glanced up and down the street, hoping that no one who knew him would see him entering the shop.

Tiny bells hanging above the doorway chimed as he went inside. Strong incense immediately assaulted his nose, and he blinked a few times to clear the itch from his eyes. He stood near the entrance waiting for his vision to adjust to the interior gloom.

A tall portly woman with long white hair and a no-nonsense expression pushed aside a rainbow-patterned wall hanging that covered a door at the back of the shop. When her eyes locked on him, he nearly turned and fled. He felt like an intruder who had been caught trespassing. After a quick assessment of her new customer, the woman's eyes widened and she rushed forward, the wide sleeves of her long white cotton dress flapping as if she were taking flight.

Startled, Kyle took a step backward as she approached, but her hand reached out and gently took his arm, arresting his escape. She craned her neck looking him over as if he were a horse she was inspecting for purchase.

"Hello, young man. I see you are having difficulties. Come with me and we'll see what we can do about your aura."

Kyle held his ground as she tugged on his arm. "I'm afraid there's been a misunderstanding. I'm not here because of ... my aura. I was hoping to leave a message for Amanda. Sorry, but I don't remember her last name."

The woman released his arm and patted it. "That's fine, dear. I know who Amanda is."

Kyle's eyes had adjusted and he glanced around. The shop was decorated with hanging dream catchers and wind chimes. Book shelves bowed under the weight of books on every occult and arcane subject imaginable. A glass display case featured crystals in many shapes and colors, and a barrister bookshelf behind the counter held dozens of tarot decks and several other kinds of cards.

Butterflies and Rainbows really was crystal-hugger central.

He turned his attention back to the woman. "I stopped by to warn Amanda about something. Do you have a piece of paper so I could leave her a note?"

The woman nodded sagely. "Ah, a warning. Very ominous. You should not trust such an important message to a hastily scribbled note. Share the warning with me so I can report it to her with the proper urgency."

Was she serious or was she was mocking him? He opened his mouth to speak, but then closed it again, unable to decide if he should confide in her.

She shook her head impatiently and took his arm again. "Well, come on then. You don't have time to waste standing around looking confused." She reached around Kyle and flipped over a sign that read, "Back in 15 minutes," and locked the deadbolt on the door. Of course, no one would know when the fifteen minutes had started, but he imagined the sign was typical of the woman who had him in her grip.

Kyle reluctantly let her pull him through the central aisle of the store to the back left corner, where a short counter was draped with black velvet cloth. She released Kyle and waved him toward a bar stool on the near side of the counter while she went behind it and reached underneath.

By the time he had settled on the stool, the woman had a deck of tarot cards in her hands and had started shuffling them. "Tell me your name, dear."

"Kyle."

"Thank you, Kyle. I'm Lucille, and Amanda is a good friend of mine. Now tell me what you wanted to warn her about."

Kyle relaxed as he watched the woman smoothly work the cards with practiced hands. Even if he did leave a note, Lucille would probably read it. Besides, Amanda wouldn't have suggested he leave the message here if she didn't trust the proprietor, right?

Kyle sighed. "Okay." He wasn't sure where to begin. "It's hard to explain. Amanda tried to warn *me* about something last week, but I didn't listen to her. It turns out she was right. And when her name came up in conversation, a certain lawyer was unhappy with her meddling, as he put it. I think he might be planning to make trouble for her."

Lucille shook her head and pursed her lips, still shuffling the cards. "Amanda does like to meddle. And lawyers do like to make trouble." She gathered the cards into a neat stack and placed them in front of Kyle. "Cut those once, please, while I make a quick call." She leaned over, picked up a phone receiver, and punched in a phone number.

Kyle cut the deck while the line rang. A click followed by an answering voice came through the receiver.

"Come down to the shop, Amanda. Your friend Kyle is here and you should hear what he has to say in person."

Kyle started to wave at Lucille and tell her not to interrupt whatever Amanda was doing, but she had already hung up.

Kyle let out an exasperated sigh. "You didn't need to do that. It's not a big deal. I probably shouldn't have said anything."

Lucille picked up the deck and split it into four piles. "Don't fight the Universe. Your conscience guided you here and you must learn to trust those feelings. Now, let's see what this is all about."

Kyle frowned at the cards with trepidation. All of this hocus-pocus spiritual stuff gave him the willies. Even if the world *was* full of unseen forces and spirits, it was probably better to leave them alone.

Ignoring his discomfort, Lucille pulled the top card off each pile. She placed the second, third, and fourth cards in a row, centered under the first one. Kyle couldn't help being fascinated by the detailed drawings on each card. At least the artwork was nice to look at, even if tarot was a bunch of nonsense.

Lucille's hand trembled over the last card she'd placed. "Oh my," she mumbled. She looked up at Kyle and cleared her throat.

"The three cards in the bottom row represent the major influences on your life." She pointed to them from left to right. "Past, present, and future. They reinforce the top card, which shows you what's immediately at hand."

The cards meant nothing to Kyle, so he had no idea what surprised her when she laid them out. In spite of his skepticism, his curiosity prompted him to ask, "What do they say?"

"They say quite a bit," she said in a musing tone. "Every card is from the Major Arcana, which is rare and tells me significant things are afoot with you."

"How much did Amanda tell you about me?" he asked, suspicion tinging his voice.

Lucille narrowed her eyes at him and tapped her index finger rapidly on the counter. "She told me a little about what happened to you and said you refused to listen to her." She waved her hand over the cards. "But I'm not making this up. If you doubt me, feel free to research the card meanings yourself."

Kyle sighed and slumped in his seat. "No, that's fine. Go ahead." None of this mattered anyway. He'd let her do the reading, for what it was worth.

Lucille seemed to recognize that he was humoring her and gave him a disapproving frown. She pointed to the top center card and her next words seemed almost vindictive.

"The Tower is the card of destruction. It represents the tearing down of illusions and plans that must be abandoned. Many people fear the Death card, but I'll take Death over The Tower any day."

Next, she pointed to the first card in the bottom row. "The Wheel of Fortune as a past influence says you have taken risks and must now face the consequences. It's reversed, which indicates negative consequences and suggests you should seek help from others to deal with them."

Kyle did take a risk by going home with Clarissa, and he was certainly facing the consequences of *that* decision. As for getting outside help, he had no shortage of volunteers between Dr. Rutlinger and Amanda.

Lucille moved on to the center card on the bottom row. "This card shows present influences. When it's upright like this, The Moon refers to strong dreams and emotional upheaval. Your intuition is at its peak, which is why you were moved to come here today, but your emotions make you vulnerable to deception. Coupled with The Tower, I would say that you are faced with serious and unpleasant life events, and that you lack the emotional stability to deal with them. You will have to rely on others for help, but you won't know whom to trust."

As she spoke, the hairs on the back of Kyle's neck stood up. Her assessment was eerie and frightening. As much as he didn't believe that cards could control his life, she had interpreted his current dilemma in the way he feared most.

The trick was figuring out who was trying to deceive him and who wasn't. He was indeed irritable and jumpy from the stress after his night with Clarissa and the nightmares that had been ruining his sleep. Whatever intuition he might have didn't seem to be working properly. Kyle started to wonder how much of this reading was being customized for his particular circumstances. She could say the cards meant anything and he wouldn't know any better.

"What do I do?"

He meant it as a rhetorical question, but she answered him in a sympathetic voice. "I can't answer that for you, but the cards suggest that you choose someone to trust and rely on that person to guide you."

Kyle nodded thoughtfully but said nothing.

Returning her gaze to the spread, Lucille said, "We do have one more card to interpret." She pointed to the last card in the lower row. "This final position is about the future.

When reversed, The Hanged Man suggests that you must open your mind to alternative courses of action, but be decisive. Don't let your worries distract you, or you will lose the opportunity to choose for yourself."

That card didn't make any sense. As far as Kyle knew, his fate had been sealed the night Clarissa infected him. What alternative courses of action did he have? Was she talking about the option of staying at the Rutlinger Foundation?

Kyle silently berated himself for taking this drivel seriously, even if only for a moment. It was time to get out of here. He had enough to think about without all this psychic mumbo-jumbo distracting him.

He slid off the bar stool and got out his wallet. "Thanks for the reading, but I need to be going. How much do I owe you?"

Lucille huffed and shook her head while she picked up the cards and put them away. "That was on the house. You may not have asked for it, but I know a troubled soul when I see one."

Kyle put his wallet away. "Sorry if I offended you. Psychics and magic aren't my thing."

The older woman laughed. "If you say so, dear."

Kyle edged back toward the door to make his escape, but right then the lock turned and Amanda stepped in. She closed and locked the door, and then paused when she spotted Kyle.

Amanda came down the aisle toward him and stopped a couple of paces away. Her dark-brown hair was windblown, and she had tucked the forward strands behind her ears. He'd forgotten how pretty she was until her hazel eyes met his and he found he couldn't speak.

"Hi, Kyle. I'm glad you came by." She didn't smile, but she sounded sincere.

"Hi, Amanda. I think I owe you an apology."

"For what?"

Kyle looked down at the floor. "For a couple of things, actually. I'm sorry I was rude when you sat with me at lunch. I guess you were only trying to help."

She waved a hand in dismissal. "Don't worry about that. I'm used to it."

He brought his eyes back to her face. Along the way, he noticed that she was wearing white tennis shoes, blue jeans, and a long-sleeved white shirt with lacy frills at the edges of the sleeves and collar. Over the shirt, she wore a purple velvet vest. The odd ensemble came together nicely over her feminine curves.

She noticed his lingering gaze and smirked, raising an eyebrow. "And the other thing?"

"What? Oh, yeah. I think I may have gotten you in some trouble today … accidentally."

The look she gave him was curious, but not concerned. With a teasing tone, she said, "Now Kyle, what have you done?"

"I was talking with some people at a place called the Rutlinger Foundation and your name came up."

Amanda's eyes grew wide and she went still.

Kyle continued. "Anyway, the lawyer—some guy named Fenris—seemed to get pretty steamed when he found out that you talked to me about … you know."

Amanda's brows drew together and she took a step forward. Kyle felt like a jerk for scaring her like this when it was probably nothing.

"What did he say, Kyle? His exact words."

Kyle shrugged. "I'm not sure I can remember his *exact* words, but it was something like they needed to do something about that meddling witch. It's probably nothing to worry about. He can't sue you for talking to me."

She moved forward until she was only a couple of feet away. She smelled like warm vanilla. "But it worried you. That's why you're here."

Kyle nodded. "Some of the things they told me confirmed what you said at McWort's. Your name slipped out while I was thinking about that."

"That's okay. I can take care of myself." She glanced at Lucille. "Plus, I have friends who are looking out for me."

Kyle sighed. "Must be nice. I can't talk to my friends about this. They'd think I've lost my mind. *I'm* starting to think I've lost my mind."

"Don't worry about it. You're doing fine … for now. What did they tell you at the Foundation?"

"Mostly the same stuff you told me."

Amanda looked surprised. "They told you about the shape-shifting?"

"Yes. I asked about it, and they said it was something I could control. As for the rest, they said the symptoms will get bad over the next couple of weeks, and they offered to let me stay with them until I get past the worst of it."

Amanda folded her arms and nodded. "Mmm-hmm. And did they tell you *why* everything gets better after the next couple of weeks?"

Kyle had assumed that the initial symptoms just settled down after a while. "Not really. I guess the worst of it just goes away."

Amanda snorted and leaned toward him. "No. It gets better because *you* just go away."

A chill ran down Kyle's spine. "What do you mean?"

Amanda tilted her head at him and narrowed her eyes. "They stuck to the story that this is some kind of disease, right?"

Kyle shrugged. "Isn't it? Clarissa infected me and there's no cure."

Amanda slowly shook her head and gave him a pitying look. "*Infected* isn't the correct word for what Clarissa did to you. She passed something to you all right, but it wasn't a disease."

"I thought that's what lycanthropy was—a disease that gets passed on when someone is bitten or scratched by a werewolf."

"That's what the legends say, but it's not entirely accurate. Lycanthropy is caused by a *lupusdaemon*. It's not a disease, it's a form of demon possession."

Kyle swallowed hard and wobbled on his feet. Amanda and Lucille each took an arm and guided him back to the bar stool. He barely noticed the tingle when Amanda gripped his arm. He sat down and put his face into his hands.

A demon? Inside him? A sick feeling twisted in his stomach and his throat closed up. He tried to take a deep breath, but that only made him feel worse. He groaned and took fast shallow breaths, panicked and on the verge of tears. Amanda rubbed his back until the dizziness passed.

When Kyle finally raised his head, both Amanda and Lucille looked at him with sympathy. He remembered something Amanda had said at McWort's. He grabbed both of her arms above the elbows and pulled her toward him, speaking with a demanding tone. "You said you could help. Can you get it out of me? Can you exorcise this thing or something?"

Amanda grimaced and looked down at his hands. Kyle released her and clenched his hands in his lap. "I'm sorry. I didn't mean to …"

Amanda's tone was forgiving. "I understand. You're upset, and for good reason. Not everyone has to deal with their inner demons so literally."

Kyle let out a nervous laugh and then groaned. "So now I'm going to have to live with a demon in my head for the rest of my life?"

Amanda put her hand on his shoulder and waited until he met her eyes. "No. Only until *Erst Mond.*"

Kyle blinked several times. The term sounded European and he was sure he'd never heard it before. "I don't understand. What does that mean?"

"It means First Moon. The demon shifted from Clarissa to you during *Vollmondritus*—the Full Moon Ritual. The demon establishes itself during the subsequent month and takes over at the next full moon—First Moon."

"Takes over? I won't be in control of my own body?" Kyle couldn't imagine the horror of having to watch helplessly while a demon used his body for its own purposes. Did transforming into a wolf put the demon in charge?

"Kyle, you won't even *be* in your body. You'll be gone."

Gone. That sounded like a euphemism. "You mean dead."

"Yes."

Kyle suddenly felt light-headed and thought he might faint. Amanda's hand on his shoulder was no longer reassuring. According to her, he had about two weeks left to live.

"I thought you said you could help me," Kyle said in a defeated tone.

Amanda started nodding but then changed her head motion into a side-to-side "maybe" movement.

"I'm a hunter with an organization called the Ternion Order. We watch for paranormal activity and monitor known paranormals operating in our region. We've known about the Selkirk Pack for decades, and we have a sort of truce with them. They don't make trouble for normals, and we don't make trouble for them."

Kyle got up from the bar stool and waved his arms in agitation. "How does possessing me with a demon *not* count as making trouble?"

Amanda shrugged. "It's a gray area, but it gives us some latitude."

Kyle shot her an incredulous look. "Gray area? I'm going to die!"

Amanda spoke soothingly. "We have until First Moon to stop it. But after that, there's nothing we can do."

If she was still talking about stopping this, there had to be hope. Kyle gave her a sidelong glance. "So there is a cure."

Her voice became cautionary. "There's a *record* of a cure, but no details on how it works. I've been researching it off and on for a couple of years, but to be honest, it hasn't been a high priority because your situation is actually quite rare."

Kyle snorted. "Low priority. That's great."

"Well, if it makes you feel any better, it's a high priority now. For me, anyway."

This was crazy. His life depended upon a witch finding a rumored cure for lycanthropy. Meanwhile, a werewolf pack was trying to convince him to hang out with them at their cozy little mansion in the mountains. His life was out of control in the most surreal way.

He shook his head, unable to see a way out. "What can I do to help?"

"First of all, don't let the Pack get wind of the fact that I'm working on a cure. I'm sure they would try to stop me, and they'd probably succeed."

Kyle didn't want to think about how they might stop her. It was starting to sound like she was putting her life at risk for him. If she succeeded in saving him, he was going to owe her in a big way.

"No problem. I have no intention of visiting the Rutlinger Foundation ever again."

"That might be more difficult than you think," she said. "They protect their own. If you don't go to them, they'll come to you. You've already shown an interest by visiting their facility. If you suddenly cut off all contact, they'll wonder why."

Kyle knew himself well enough to know that he wasn't that great at lying or acting. "I can't hang out with them and pretend to go along with their plan to kill me."

"I understand. Tell them you want to try working through the next couple of weeks on your own, but stay cordial. If they get suspicious, reluctantly tell them that you know about their little demonic secret. It will piss them off, but they believe that nothing short of killing you will prevent full possession at First Moon. All they have to do is wait. They win by default."

The best way to avoid giving away their plan would be to minimize contact with both the Pack and Amanda. But he couldn't sit around and wait to see if she succeeded in discovering the secrets relating to this supposed cure. He had to be useful somehow, and the idea of spending more time with Amanda had its appeal as well.

"Can I help you with your research?"

Amanda considered his question for a moment, and then shared a long look with Lucille. Lucille shook her head slowly from side to side.

Amanda frowned and finally answered. "That wouldn't be a good idea. The less you know about my progress the better. To be honest, telling you about the potential for a cure was risky."

Kyle's brow furrowed. How could giving him hope be risky? There was no way he would voluntarily share her secret with the demons.

With a shock, Kyle understood her concerns. *He* wouldn't share her secrets, but the demon inside him would. He sat down on the bar stool again as the feelings of nausea and dizziness returned.

In a shaky voice, Kyle said, "It's hearing all of this, isn't it?"

Lucille answered for Amanda. "It knows what you know. In another two weeks, it will be able to impersonate you well enough to take your place."

Kyle wanted to run, but there was no place to go. He wanted to deny this ridiculous story Amanda was spinning for him, but he didn't want to miss what might be his last opportunity to survive this nightmare. He was in a battle for his own body with no way to fight back. Somehow, he had to get this thing out of him.

His desperate mind went back to an earlier idea. "What about exorcism? Can't a priest remove the demon and send it back to Hell or something?"

Amanda shook her head. "It's been tried. An exorcism somehow isn't enough. The theory is that *lupusdaemons* have been among us for more than a thousand years, and now they are bound to the earth. As far as we can tell, the only way to force them back to Hell is by destroying their host body."

Kyle straightened, his eyes wide with alarm. "That's the cure? Destroy the host body?"

"No. That's how you get rid of them after First Moon. It's too late for any kind of exorcism at that point."

"But these demons have been successfully removed before First Moon, right?"

"Once, supposedly, about a hundred and fifty years ago."

Kyle closed his eyes. His fate rested on the rumor of a technique that had been lost since the years of the American Civil War. For the first time, he seriously considered ending the nightmare on his own terms. He would rather take his own life than surrender his body to some demon.

Amanda seemed to know the direction his thoughts had taken. "Hang in there, Kyle. I know the stakes are high, but we still have some time. Don't give up on yourself. And don't give up on me."

Kyle opened his eyes. "If you think of any way I can help you, please let me know."

"I will," she promised. "For now, you need to go on as if nothing has changed. Distract yourself with work and the things you'd normally do for fun in the summer."

In a wry tone, Kyle said, "Sure. I might as well live it up for my last two weeks on Earth."

Amanda nodded. "And pray Dr. Rutlinger believes it."

CHAPTER 8

Boomerang

Kyle groaned and rolled over, throwing the too-warm covers off his sweating body. Another crappy nightmare. The sleeping pills had helped at first, but lately they were wearing off about halfway through the night. He'd have to ask his doctor to give him something stronger.

He got up and turned off the alarm. It would have gone off at any moment anyway, so he figured he might as well get up. He had a standing appointment with Greg to go sailing on Sunday mornings, and he needed to get ready.

After his conversation with Amanda the previous day, he had gone home and moved around the house like a zombie, trying to assimilate what he'd learned. How was he supposed to act like everything was normal? He was so scared that he could hardly think. He wanted to call Amanda and make sure she was working on his problem, but he knew pestering her would only piss her off and slow her down. She knew how serious this was. He had no choice but to trust her claim that he was her top priority. He had never felt so completely helpless.

Kyle padded to the bathroom to use the facilities, get a drink of water, and wash his face. The drugs always left him feeling a little hungover the next morning, but that was better than how he'd feel after a totally sleepless night.

He shook his head at his reflection in the mirror; it looked like a mug shot. He had dark circles under his eyes, his short brown hair was tousled from tossing and turning, and worry lines creased his brow.

He leaned forward to closely inspect his eyes and then quickly backed away from the mirror. The amber ring around his irises had definitely widened. Soon people would start to notice. He could wear sunglasses on the boat today, but tomorrow he'd look pretty stupid wearing them while he worked at his computer.

Staring at his reflection, he wondered how else the demon was changing him. He suspected that the nightmares were more than simply dreams—the demon was trying to take over his mind. Eventually, it would succeed and Kyle Nelson would cease to exist. Kyle closed his eyes and turned away from his waking nightmare.

After a quick shower and shave, Kyle dressed for a day on the boat. To minimize the area he'd have to cover with sunscreen, he wore a long-sleeved t-shirt and cargo shorts. He was gathering his things and throwing them into his dry bag when he heard a car pull into the driveway. He peered through the kitchen window and saw Deputy Skyler Arpin stepping out of her cruiser.

Spotting him through the window, she smiled and waved.

She was one of the last people he wanted to talk with right now. But she knew he was here, so he couldn't hide and pretend he wasn't.

Heart pounding with anxiety, Kyle went to the front door. He had to play this cool. Not wanting to invite her into his house, Kyle grabbed his stuff and went out onto the front porch as she was coming up the steps.

"Good morning, Deputy Arpin. I was just heading out. Is there something I can do for you?"

She smiled sweetly, and he saw past the uniform to the sexy woman he'd encountered at the Foundation the day before. Under other circumstances, he might have been attracted to her, but something about there being a demon behind her pretty face cooled his ardor.

"I won't keep you long," she said. "Dr. Rutlinger asked me to come by and find out if you've decided to stay with us at the Foundation."

"Already? It hasn't even been twenty-four hours."

"True, but it's not that tough of a decision. You can always come back here, once you are feeling better."

Liar, Kyle accused silently. He kept his face impassive, not trusting himself to say anything yet.

She glanced up and down the street before stepping closer and lowering her voice. "We really can make the next couple of weeks more comfortable for you." She raised one eyebrow suggestively.

You mean my last *couple of weeks.*

Kyle took a deep breath and slowly moved back to put more distance between them. "I guess you're right. I don't need more time to think."

She grinned and moved forward again, taking his hand in hers. "I'm so glad to hear that. I can be at the Foundation by about four o'clock today. I'd love to give you a tour of the place and help you get settled in."

From the way she said it, Kyle had little doubt about what she meant by offering to help him "get settled in." *Good grief. Are all werewolves as promiscuous as Clarissa and Skyler?*

Kyle slipped his hand from hers and tried to step back farther, but he bumped into the door.

"Um, I think you misunderstood. I've decided I *don't* want to stay at the Foundation."

Her eyebrows went up in surprise and then she gave him an exaggerated pout. "Why not? Is it me? I can make myself scarce if you don't want to hang out."

"No, no, it's not you. I want to stay in my own place and be with my friends. Staying at the Foundation seems … complicated."

Deputy Arpin narrowed her eyes at him and chewed her lower lip for a moment. "I see. Dr. Rutlinger will be disappointed."

Kyle half turned and locked the front door, hoping she'd take the hint that he wanted to leave. "He asked me to make a choice, and I made it. Sorry, Deputy."

She pursed her lips and shrugged. With disappointment in her voice, she said, "I hope you know what you're doing. The next couple of weeks can be tough. I don't think you realize how sorry you're going to be that you didn't accept his offer."

Kyle stared into the deputy's eyes, wondering if she had just threatened him. Her level gaze revealed no malice, but the cold certainty she projected reminded Kyle again that a demon lurked behind those bright blue contact lenses.

Thanks, but no thanks. I'd rather take my chances with Amanda.

"I appreciate your concern, Deputy. But didn't the doctor say that the invitation doesn't expire? I may decide you're right after all."

Deputy Arpin tilted her head back and gave Kyle a considering look. A slow smile crept across her lips. "Sure, Kyle. You're welcome any time. Well, I should be going." She turned and headed back toward her car.

Kyle resisted the urge to sigh in relief when she left the porch. He waited while she got into her car and backed out of the driveway, and he returned her wave as she drove off.

As soon as she was on her way, he went to his Explorer and got in. His hands were shaking so badly in reaction to the encounter that he had trouble sticking the key into the ignition. Once he had the rig started, he took several deep breaths and rested his head on the steering wheel.

For the moment, they were off his case. But he doubted that would last long.

~

Kyle shivered and closed his window part way as he threaded the Explorer through residential back streets. Being on the boat all day had given him a sun-baked feeling, and the tree-shaded avenues were chilly by comparison. The day had been blustery and cool, perfect for sailing, but it also carried the first hints of fall. He sighed, thinking that North Idaho's six weeks of genuine summer were nearly over. The thought that this could be his *last* summer crept into his mind, turning his mood dark.

The sail with Greg had distracted him enough to give him a brief respite from his worries. Now that he was left to his own thoughts again, he had to tell himself to breathe and loosen his grip on the steering wheel. A child played with a ball in the front yard of a home up the street, reminding Kyle of the danger in letting his attention stray. *Relax. Concentrate on your driving.*

In spite of his admonishment to himself, Kyle couldn't help thinking about what Amanda might be doing at that moment and how Dr. Rutlinger was going to react when Deputy Arpin told him of Kyle's decision.

With his mind on other things, he started to pull into his driveway before he registered that a car was already parked in it.

He hit the brakes and his front tires skidded across the concrete sidewalk, stopping barely short of the other car's bumper. He backed up and cranked the wheel so he could go around the familiar Subaru and park in his usual spot on the grass to the right of the driveway.

What the hell was Sherry doing here?

Sherry had emerged from her car and was checking out the skid marks. "Wow, that was close. Didn't you look before you turned in?"

Kyle didn't have time for this. Too much was going on, and he needed to cut off any Sherry drama before it began. "What are you doing here, Sherry?"

She frowned and her eyes showed how his question had hurt. "Hey, that's not a very nice way to greet your fiancée." She clutched her forearms, holding them tightly against her torso.

Kyle's knuckles went white where they gripped his dry bag. "I could say the same of you. And that's *former* fiancée. Why are you here?"

Sherry came forward and stood close, looking up with an insistent expression. A gust of wind whipped by, tousling her hair and raising goose bumps on her arms. "Don't be like that. I came to talk to you. Can we go inside? I'm getting cold."

Part of Kyle wanted to fold her into his arms and warm her, but the image of her giving the engagement ring back helped him resist the temptation. "I'm surprised you didn't let yourself in. You still have a key, don't you?"

She looked down. "Yes, but it didn't feel right."

Kyle's voice softened. "I appreciate that. I guess we can go in and make some tea to warm you up. I'm sure there's still a box of your favorite herbal tea right where you left it."

She gave him a tentative smile and started to reach out to him, but arrested the motion and went back to the open door of her car. She retrieved her purse, locked the Subaru, and met him on the front porch.

Kyle unlocked the door and let them in. The house was cozy and warm inside. Sherry took a seat at the tiny kitchen table next to a window that let in the afternoon sun. Kyle put the kettle on and added a teabag to each of their cups. He snorted to himself when he realized that he had inadvertently grabbed a pair of photo mugs featuring images of Sherry and him during happier times. He hoped she wouldn't read anything into that.

Kyle used the tea preparations as an excuse not to look at her. She had broken his heart and run out on him. It didn't matter why she was here because there was no way he was taking her back. He had been stupid to let her come in. He should have told her to shove off.

By the time he carried the two steaming mugs to the table, he'd worked his anger up to the point where his hand was shaking when he set the mug down in front of her.

He sat down opposite her and finally looked into her face.

Sherry's expression was contrite and a little frightened. She'd been with him a long time and could probably tell how mad he was. Putting both hands around her mug, she blew across the hot tea to cool it. She was delaying.

Kyle didn't want to drag this on any longer than necessary. "Well, you said you wanted to talk. I'm listening."

She took a deep breath and let it out. When she looked up from her tea, her eyes were glistening with unshed tears. "I screwed up. I threw away a great relationship and a great guy for a fantasy. I thought getting away from North Idaho would free me to do all the things I've dreamed of doing. I thought being in the city would be more exciting and give me better opportunities."

She paused as a tear rolled down each cheek. Kyle continued to sip at his tea, watching her. He already knew all this.

Sherry looked down at her tea and spoke quietly. "I was wrong. I had more opportunities, but not better ones. The city *is* exciting as long as you have money. I looked for work, but all I could find were crap jobs like the one I left here. By the time I burned through my savings, I was sick of the traffic, the attitudes, and the crowds. I realized it was time to come home."

She took a tissue from the box Kyle kept on the table and wiped her eyes and nose. Tissue in hand, she watched Kyle, waiting for him to speak.

"Sorry it didn't work out. What are you going to do now?"

Sherry shrugged. "I'm going to try to get my old job back. If that doesn't work, I'll look for something else."

"Have you considered Spokane?" Sherry's parents were in Spokane and although it wasn't a huge city, it would offer many of the things Sherry thought she wanted.

Sherry took a sip of her tea and then answered. "I considered it. But that's not where I want to be. Mom offered to let me stay with them. It was sweet of her, but she knows it would be a bad idea. We'd kill each other within a week."

Kyle thought he saw where she was heading, and he wasn't going to make it easy for her. If she thought she was going to walk right back into the life she'd thrown away, she was about to be disappointed.

Kyle stood and carried his mug to the opposite side of the kitchen. He turned and leaned against the counter, looking at her over his mug as he took another sip. "Well, I wish you luck whatever you decide to do. If you don't mind, I need to shower off the sunscreen and then take care of some things."

Sherry looked down into her mug and her shoulders began to shake. She closed her eyes and tried to hold back the sobs that were building. When she got herself under control, she looked at Kyle with pleading eyes and a tear-streaked face.

"Please, Kyle, I need your help. You used to love me. Can't you let me stay with you for a little while? I'll sleep on the couch. I'll pay you back for rent and food as soon as I get work."

Kyle's annoyance grew with each tear that fell. Some guys would do anything to stop a woman from crying, but it just pissed Kyle off. Crying was frequently a huge manipulation, particularly when the woman wanted something. By the time Sherry stopped begging, Kyle had to clench his jaw to keep himself from shouting at her.

When he had settled himself down, he said, "No. You can't stay here. There's too much going on right now, and I can't have you in the way." *Damn. Shouldn't have said that.*

Sherry looked surprised and then puzzled. "Really? What's going on?"

Her question was mildly insulting, even if it was true that he rarely had anything unusual "going on." Kyle grimaced at having piqued her curiosity.

"It doesn't matter. You need to find someplace else to stay."

Sherry let her shoulders slump in defeat. She picked up her mug and carried it to the sink, right next to where Kyle was standing. After setting down the mug, she turned and put her arms around him, pressing her face into his shoulder. The familiar feel of her embrace made Kyle think back on how it had once been so good. She was right—he *had* loved her once upon a time.

Kyle set down his mug as well, but didn't return the hug. He kept his arms at his sides and waited for her to let go. But she didn't let go. More warm tears dripped onto his shirt.

"Please let me stay just a little while. I promise I'll get out as soon as I can. I have nowhere else to go. I know you don't love me anymore, but please don't hate me."

Kyle tilted his head back and groaned at the ceiling. He didn't hate her. He still loved her, even with a broken heart. He could give her a few days to find another alternative. Hell, she could have the whole house to herself in another couple of weeks, if things didn't go well.

He sighed in exasperation at himself. "Okay. But only for a few days. You need to find something else fast."

She leaned back, smiling. "Thank you!" She gave him a quick, tight hug. "You've always been my hero." Her kiss of gratitude was salty from tears and a bit sticky from her wet nose, but her soft warm lips made him sad for what had been lost.

Sherry went back to the table for two more tissues and brought one to Kyle. "Sorry. That was probably pretty gross."

"Don't worry about it."

She was all perky and sweet, now that she had gotten her way. "You go ahead and shower. I'll get my stuff out of the car and set up camp in the living room. Thanks again for letting me stay. I promise not to make trouble. I'll even make dinner for you tonight."

"Sounds good," Kyle said to her back as she scurried out the front door.

Trudging up the stairs, Kyle was certain he'd made a big mistake. The only positive aspect of this new disaster was that Sherry might distract him from constantly thinking about his little lycanthropy problem.

~

The next day at work went exceptionally well. Kyle ran a final test of his database scripts and was able to tell Vanya that he was ready to go whenever the data warehouse guys were ready. She was pleased with his progress and praised him for it.

"Good work, Kyle. I've got another project waiting that I think will be perfect for you. It has high visibility, which means there will be a lot more pressure, but it will also give you a chance to show what you can do. How long do you think it will be before the data warehouse project is completely wrapped up?"

Kyle hated giving estimates when the timeline was not fully under his control, but Vanya hated it when her subordinates were vague about schedules. The only solution was to be optimistic and specific, and to qualify everything.

"Assuming the data warehouse guys make it a high priority, the new scripts could be in production by Wednesday."

She beamed. "Excellent. I'll make sure the data warehouse manager understands the urgency."

True to her word, Vanya made the right calls and Kyle was pulled into an implementation meeting with the data warehouse group before lunch. By the end of the day, things were looking good for a Wednesday rollout, exactly as he had hoped.

Vanya called him into her office late in the day to fill him in on the new project. It promised to be challenging and interesting. He would be the team leader and the tasks would cross several business disciplines. Vanya was putting a lot of faith in his abilities to give him that much responsibility.

Driving home that evening, Kyle realized that he had been so wrapped up in his work that he had hardly thought about his other problems. Having normal conversations with normal people doing normal things made the events of the past weekend seem like some kind of bad dream or elaborate hoax. He hadn't actually seen anyone turn into a werewolf, nor had he seen Amanda do anything "witchy" or magical. As for the tarot reading, there was nothing mystical about a deck of cards with pretty pictures. It could still all be some kind of scam, or he could be dealing with several people who shared a weird delusion.

Arriving at home, Kyle pulled into the driveway, easily maneuvering around Sherry's car this time, and parked in his usual spot. Seeing the Subaru reminded him of the new problem that awaited him.

As soon as he opened the front door, Sherry voice exclaimed from the kitchen, "You're home!" She ran to the entryway and startled him with an unexpected hug. "I've got great news! I got my old job back today."

Kyle shared a grin with her. "That is great news."

So, when will you be leaving?

She took his hand and led him back into the kitchen. She must have spent part of the day cleaning because the kitchen looked better than it had in weeks. "I start tomorrow. I'll catch the end of the pay period, so I should get my first partial check next Friday."

That's nice. Next Friday, I'll be a demon.

Kyle forced himself to keep the smile on his face. "Cool. Hey, thanks for cleaning up in here. It looks great."

Sherry looked around the room proudly, admiring the results of her efforts. "I wanted to do something to thank you for letting me stay here. I don't want to be too much trouble."

Too late for that.

Kyle started loosening his tie. "That's sweet. Look, I'm going to go change out of my work clothes. Then maybe we can think about what's for dinner. I'm starving."

Sherry stepped forward and helped him pull off his tie, just like she used to do. "How about we order a pizza to celebrate? I'll call it in, if you want."

The familiar intimacy of her undressing him felt both comfortable and wrong. He stepped back and took the tie from her hands. "Yum. I'm up for pizza."

She clasped her hands together and smiled sheepishly. "Sorry. Old habits."

Meeting Kyle's eyes again, she squinted and leaned forward. "That's weird. I don't remember your eyes being that color."

As much as he tried to ignore them, the physical changes Kyle was experiencing mocked his mass-delusion theory. He should have planned a response in case anyone noticed the amber in his eyes. Time to think fast.

"Yeah, I noticed a change too. My doctor says it's not uncommon and that it's nothing to worry about."

Sherry stepped closer for a better look, and Kyle leaned back from her scrutiny. "I think it's kind of sexy," she said in a husky voice.

Uh-oh.

She seemed to realize his discomfort and backed up. "Oops. Too soon for that sort of talk, I guess."

Kyle frowned. "It's always going to be too soon."

Sherry let out a quick breath of frustration. "Don't be that way. It's not like I cheated on you. Can't you forgive me?"

Kyle folded his arms, his tie dangling from his hand. "You wouldn't be here if I hadn't forgiven you. But that doesn't mean I'm ever going to trust you again."

She looked down with a shamed expression. "Okay. I guess I deserved that. All I'm asking for is a second chance."

Kyle was tired of the conversation, and he wanted to get out of his work clothes. It was odd how he could wear slacks, a dress shirt, and a tie all day without thinking about it, but as soon as he got home, he was overwhelmed with a desire to change into something more comfortable.

"We'll see," Kyle said as he turned to the stairs and went up to the bedroom. On his way up the stairs he realized that his comment had probably given her false hope when all he was really trying to do was shut her up. *Oh, well.*

As frustrating as it was to have Sherry show up while he was dealing with so many other issues, it was nice to not be alone. He had talked himself into thinking that he was enjoying his bachelor lifestyle, but an empty house could be a lonely place. Maybe he could trade Sherry in for a dog.

Chortling at his own joke, he decided he'd try to enjoy the evening. It had been a great day at work, and Sherry's job would give her the money she needed to get back on her feet and out of his life for good. There was no point in worrying about things he couldn't fix right now. Besides, maybe things were finally changing for the better.

CHAPTER 9
Ultimatum

The phone rang at Kyle's desk, interrupting his concentration. He growled as he reached for the handset, hating to lose his train of thought while he was in the middle of a detailed data analysis. After a bit more tweaking, the script he was working on would handle the few anomalies that had cropped up in testing.

"Hello. This is Kyle."

"Hey Kyle, this is Bob Daily."

Kyle's next-door neighbor and landlord had never called him at work before. The old guy and his wife kept to themselves, but he always smiled and waved when Kyle saw him puttering around in his front yard.

"Hi, Bob. What can I do for you?"

"I'm afraid I have bad news. I saw smoke coming out of your upstairs window a little bit ago and called the fire department. The firemen put it out, but the bathroom is in pretty bad shape. You should probably come home and have a look."

Kyle closed his eyes and put his forehead in his hand. *Just what I need.* "Okay, Bob. I'll head over as soon as I can. Did they say what started it?"

"Yep. It looks like an electrical fire. Some appliance was left on. The firemen think it was probably a curling iron."

Kyle flushed with embarrassment. "Oh my God, Bob. I'm so sorry. Sherry came back over the weekend and she started a job today. She must have been so excited that she forgot to turn it off."

"Don't worry about it, Kyle. I'm just glad no one was hurt. I'm sure the insurance will pay for the repairs, but you'll probably want to stay somewhere else during the remodeling."

Damn. Talk about bad timing.

The small old house had only one bathroom, so if the damage was severe enough to make it unusable, he'd have no choice but to stay somewhere else. And for the short term, he had to deal with Sherry as well.

Kyle ended the conversation with Bob and made a few notes so he'd remember what he was working on when he'd received the call. He told Vanya about the emergency, and since it was nearly three o'clock, explained that he'd probably be gone for the rest of the day.

During the drive home, his anger at Sherry grew. How could she be so stupid? She wasn't *that* excited about returning to her old job as a legal secretary. She'd gone back for the money and not much else.

Pulling into his driveway, Kyle looked up at the front of the house and shook his head in disgust. The tiny bathroom window was broken out and soot stained the siding above it. He didn't have much hope for what the inside would look like. Thank goodness Bob had seen the smoke, or the whole place might have gone up.

Bob tottered around the hedge between their houses and stood next to Kyle, looking up at the bathroom window. "I talked with the insurance company. They should have someone out to take a look tomorrow. Even putting a rush on things, it could be a couple of weeks, maybe a month, before it'll be fixed up again."

Kyle shook his head and sighed. "I don't know what to say, Bob."

Bob patted him on the back. "You've been a good tenant, Kyle. Accidents happen. I'm happy that you and your girl are okay, and that I caught it before it went too far."

"Thanks, Bob. I appreciate your being so cool about this. If there's anything I can do to help, please let me know."

Kyle went inside to assess the damage. It was pretty bad. Everything was coated with fire-extinguisher powder and the entire exterior wall was singed and peeling. The wooden sink base was charred and the rug that had been on the floor was a powdery mess. The shower curtain had melted onto the bathtub. Sitting on the counter was the culprit responsible for this disaster. The soot-covered metal parts of a curling iron were stuck to the countertop by a blob of plastic, which was all that remained of the handle. The blob had trapped a few crispy strands of fabric that came from the soggy, charred towel that was in the sink.

The smell was the worst thing of all. The odor had spread throughout the house, but the bathroom and the hallway absolutely reeked of smoke and burned chemicals. The hallway ceiling showed smoke damage as well, but luckily it didn't extend far enough to reach the bedroom. His clothes *might* still be salvageable.

Kyle was still staring in dismay at the wreckage when he heard Sherry's car pull into the driveway. A few seconds later, the door banged open and Sherry pounded up the steps.

"Oh my God! What happened?"

Kyle waved at the curling iron. "You happened. Apparently you left the curling iron on this morning, sitting on top of a towel, no less."

Sherry looked at the curling iron with confusion and shook her head. "No, I didn't."

Kyle snorted. "Well, somebody did."

When she met Kyle's eyes, her expression was confused, not guilty.

"Kyle, I swear to you that I distinctly remember unplugging it before I left the bathroom. And I have *never* set a curling iron on a towel or anything else made of fabric. I've read too many horror stories about that sort of thing."

Sherry seemed sincere. Whatever faults she might have, being careless wasn't normally one of them. But still ....

"Okay, so how do you explain this?"

She made a face of dismay and said, "I can't. It's like someone came in here after I left and used my curling iron. But who would do that?"

No one. Unless it was someone trying to send a message.

Kyle's hands clenched into fists and his eyes grew wide. His breathing became rapid and shallow.

Sherry misread his fright and stepped back with a wary expression. "I swear I didn't do this, Kyle."

Kyle focused on her again and made his hands relax, realizing how threatening he must look. "Sorry. I believe you. This is just too much on top of everything else that's going on."

Sherry stared at him for a minute. "What *else*? Did you hook up with someone while I was gone? Some girlfriend who's jealous that I'm staying here? Tell me the truth, Kyle."

Kyle shook his head with a sardonic twist to his mouth. "I have no jealous girlfriends." Yes, he had hooked up with someone while Sherry was gone, but Clarissa was dead. Sort of.

For a moment, Kyle wondered if the demon inside him had made him do this without his conscious knowledge. But the timing didn't work. He had showered first and left for work before Sherry brought her things up to the bathroom.

The more he thought about it, the more solid his suspicions became. If Sherry hadn't done it accidentally, someone else must have done it intentionally and with the goal of making it appear to be her fault. Because of the fire, he needed some other place to stay. Would the Pack actually burn his house down to force him to stay with them? The flesh of his neck tingled when the distinct impression of mocking smugness floated across his awareness, as if the demon were indirectly answering his question. *Whoa. That was creepy.*

The house was no longer safe. He would be vulnerable if he stayed, and he was putting Sherry in danger as well.

"Grab your stuff. We're going to check into a hotel while they work on the house. We can't stay here without a bathroom."

Sherry was initially surprised by his declaration, but nodded as she thought about it. "I guess we don't have a choice. It might be a while before I can pay you back for my share though."

"Don't worry about that now. Let's get out of here. This place is giving me the creeps."

Kyle packed up a week's worth of clothes and underwear, relieved that they smelled only faintly of smoke. He guessed that most of his toiletries had been destroyed by the fire, and he had no intention of digging through the wreckage for whatever might have survived.

Sherry had been living out of her suitcase, so she was ready to go when he came downstairs. As he closed the door behind them and locked it, he wondered if he'd ever see the place again.

A slow burn of anger began to grow in the pit of his stomach. He was tired of being manipulated. As soon as he found a room, he needed to let Amanda know how to get in touch with him and ask her what kind of progress she was making. His time was running out. Somehow, he had to get his life back under his own control.

~

With the prospect of a long stay, Kyle chose the least-expensive hotel he could find that had a vacancy and wasn't a dive. Sherry followed him around from place to place in her Subaru, letting him handle the negotiations. They also dropped by a grocery store so they could get replacement toiletries. By the time he opened the door to their hotel room, they were tired and ready to settle in.

Kyle handed Sherry the second key and a twenty-dollar bill. "I need to call work and let my boss know what's going on. Would you mind getting us some take-out for dinner?"

Sherry took the key and the money, giving him a sidelong glance. "No problem." She looked around the room and her eyes settled on a refrigerator in the corner. "We have a fridge, so I can get us some sodas or beer too, if you want."

"Sure. That sounds good. We'll probably be here for a while. If I can stomach the idea tomorrow, I might swing by the house and grab a few more things from the kitchen."

Kyle went over to the bed and sat down next to the nightstand that held the phone. He looked up to see that Sherry was watching him with an unreadable expression. "Do you think you'll need more money?" he asked pointedly.

She picked up her purse and opened the door, seeming reluctant to leave. "No. This should be enough. I'll be back in a few."

After the door had closed, Kyle pulled a slip of paper from his pocket and dialed the number he'd written down under Amanda's name. He got voicemail.

"Amanda, this is Kyle. I'm at the Ponderay Hotel, in room 236. There was a fire at my house and I don't believe it was an accident. I think a mutual acquaintance was trying to send a message. Anyway, I haven't heard from you, and I need to know how things are going. Please call me here or at work as soon as you can."

Kyle hung up and then called work so he could tell Sherry he had done so. It was almost six o'clock by then, but Vanya often worked late. Kyle filled her in on what happened and reassured her that he didn't need more time off to deal with it.

In truth, he *did* want to take the next week off and figure out some way to help Amanda. He couldn't keep waiting and hoping someone else would save him. Somehow, he had to save himself, or it wouldn't matter whether or not Vanya took away that great new project opportunity.

Phone calls handled, Kyle started putting his clothes away. After he'd emptied his suitcase and tucked it into the closet, he lay back on the bed and waited for Sherry's return.

The bed was comfortable enough, but there was one big problem: there was only the one bed. Kyle had asked for a room with two, but none were available. He didn't want to pay for two rooms, and he knew Sherry would object to the additional expense as well.

When they'd first entered the room, Kyle had seen the brief smirk on Sherry's face when she spotted the single queen-sized bed. Keeping his distance from her would be a challenge if they had to share it. Unfortunately, the room offered no decent alternatives. The two chairs weren't big enough to fully relax in, and the floor had thin, industrial carpet.

Kyle was sitting in one of the chairs reading a book when Sherry returned with the food and drinks. She had gotten take-out from a nearby Thai restaurant, and they shared it at the room's tiny round table.

Sherry was suspiciously quiet during the meal. Kyle appreciated her silence because he had a lot on his mind; however, he caught her watching him every time he glanced at her. Kyle had the uncomfortable suspicion that she was plotting something.

After dinner, they watched television for a while, and then Kyle got ready for bed. He normally slept in the nude, but with Sherry there, he opted for boxers and a t-shirt. He brought his book to the bed and got under the covers while Sherry brushed her teeth.

When she came out of the bathroom she was still wearing the clothes she'd changed into after work. Kyle had expected her to change into the long nightshirt she preferred to wear in summer. He was even more surprised when she started stripping off her clothes and laying them on one of the chairs. Down to nothing but a pair of panties and a bra, she turned and smiled at his open-mouthed stare. Without a word, she unclasped the bra and pulled it away from her breasts. She dropped the bra behind her on the chair and then slowly pulled her panties down, stepping out of them and adding them to the pile. Her eyes never left his face, and his eyes didn't miss a second of her performance. He blinked away a distressing moment of *déjà vu* from Clarissa's similar striptease.

When she was finally standing there wearing nothing but a smile, she cocked her hips to the side and cupped her breasts in her hands. "Remember these?" she said in a teasing tone.

He remembered, although the refresher was certainly appreciated. Back when they were together, he'd felt fortunate to be engaged to such an attractive woman and when she left him, he knew that their compatibility in bed would be hard to replace.

Kyle put his book down and sat up as she moved toward the bed. Part of him wanted to resist her, but a different part of him was reacting right then. She stopped with her breasts within inches of his nose, her body heat calling out for his touch. He looked up at her, a deer in the headlights, so to speak. She looked down at him with a smug smile that said, *Like shooting fish in a barrel.*

Kyle's objections to rekindling a relationship with the woman who had left him evaporated the moment his hand made contact with her soft, warm skin. She wasn't aggressive about her victory and didn't push him, but she didn't have to. He was a willing participant in all that transpired.

Later that night, Sherry was snuggled up under his arm with her head on his chest and one leg over his. Her steady breathing and occasional muscle twitches told him she had fallen asleep. Under the sheet, his hand softly caressed her arm and the length of her side down to the swell of her hip. She felt so good.

And he felt so guilty. He had no right to get Sherry mixed up in this mess he was in. Even if Amanda succeeded in curing him somehow—which was looking less likely with every passing day, could he trust Sherry not to break his heart again? Maybe all she wanted was a physical relationship this time. But one of them would eventually want more, possibly with someone else, and that would lead to more heartache down the road. Never mind what would happen if he turned into a demon-possessed werewolf.

He had to talk to Amanda as soon as possible.

~

Kyle caught himself whistling while he made coffee the next morning at the hotel-room sink. When he realized what he was doing, he stopped abruptly and glanced at Sherry in the reflection of the mirror. She was sitting up in bed watching his progress, with her arms wrapped around her legs and the covers discreetly pulled up around her chest. She burst into laughter at his embarrassment.

"Someone feeling a little more relaxed and happy today?" she teased.

Kyle punched the coffee maker's "on" button and turned around.

"There's no denying it, you're as sexy as ever," he answered.

She smiled at him and gave him an air kiss. "Thank you for not denying it. We might even have time for another relaxation exercise this morning before work."

"That sounds like fun, but I've already showered, and I need to get to work early today. My boss is giving me a new project, and I still have a couple of minor things to wrap up on the old one."

She pouted and wiggled so the covers fell away. "You weren't so reluctant last night."

Kyle pointed toward her chest. "You cheated by doing *that*. I never stood a chance."

She shrugged and grinned wickedly. "That explains the first time, but the second time you were so energetic I thought we'd wake the neighbors."

Kyle's breath caught. *What second time?* Tentatively, he said, "I hope you enjoyed yourself too."

Sherry sighed wistfully. "Oh, I did. I thought you were having a bad dream and was about to wake you, but I learned you weren't asleep after all. Some parts of you were *very* awake," she added with a giggle.

Kyle remembered none of this. Was the demon becoming capable of taking over his mind? He would be in big trouble if it contacted the Pack and warned them of Amanda's efforts to find a cure. What if it knew it was in danger and tried to move to a new body?

Kyle couldn't see any marks on Sherry, but he had to ask. "I didn't … hurt you or anything, did I?"

"No, it was fine, really. It's okay to be a little rough once in a while."

That was confirmation enough. Kyle didn't like mixing sex and violence in any way, so "rough" wasn't in his comfort zone. He knew from personal experience that Clarissa's demon was far less restrained.

Sherry kicked the covers off and lay back on the bed. "Sure you aren't up for another round? I'll bet I can change your mind."

Kyle made a show of blocking his view of her, but then spread his fingers so he could see her through his hands. "I'm sure you could, but please don't try. This new project could be a career-maker." *Or breaker.*

She slipped out of the bed and padded over to him, mincing in a way that made all the fun parts bounce and sway enticingly. She put her arms around him and gave him a peck on the lips. "Okay, I'll be good." She released him and bumped her hip against him. "But I could have been *really* good."

Kyle patted one bare butt cheek as she slipped into the bathroom and closed the door with a giggle.

He shook his head at himself. *Man, what am I doing?*

It was so easy to fall back into the comfortable patterns he'd had with Sherry in their prior life together. The longer he stayed with her, the harder it would be to separate later. Adding sex back into the mix sure as hell wasn't going to make matters any easier. He had to put an end to this somehow, before she got seriously hurt.

While Sherry took her shower, Kyle got dressed and poured himself a cup of coffee. In the past, he'd always prepared Sherry's cup for her too. He considered not getting hers ready just to break pattern, but he realized the gesture would be a hollow one. It would only hurt her feelings if she caught on to what he was doing.

He frowned while he poured her coffee, knowing that at some point her feelings were going to get hurt anyway.

By the time Sherry exited the bathroom with a towel wrapped around her head and another around her torso, Kyle was dressed and almost ready to leave.

"Wow. You *are* in a hurry," she commented as she let her hair down and used the towel to squeeze the last bit of water from it.

Kyle stood at the door with his hand on the knob. "I guess I'll see you here tonight. I'm not sure what time I'll be back because of this new project, and I plan to stop by the house."

Sherry stopped fussing with her hair and came toward him. "What? No good-bye kiss?"

Kyle leaned forward and gave her a brief but tender kiss on the lips. "Have fun at work today," he said, opening the door.

Sherry rolled her eyes. "I'll try. You know those lawyers—they're a hoot and a half."

Kyle chuckled as he pulled the door closed behind him and hustled along the walkway to the stairs that would take him down to the parking lot.

～

Although Kyle did plan to get to work early, what he really needed to do was get away from Sherry for a while so he could think. The next full moon was only a week away, and he still hadn't managed to get in contact with Amanda. Where was she? What was she doing? At lunch, he might shoot over to Butterflies and Rainbows to see if Lucille could tell him anything.

He was so wrapped up in his thoughts that he didn't notice that the car parked next to his Explorer was occupied, until the dark-tinted window rolled down as he came alongside.

"Good morning, Kyle."

Kyle jumped and took a step back. The face behind the sunglasses belonged to Fenris Kellen, the Foundation's lawyer. "What's up, Fenris?"

"Skyler saw the report of the fire at your house, and we were all concerned. Are you okay?"

"I'm fine." Kyle waved toward the hotel. "I'm staying here until the repairs are finished."

Fenris glanced toward the building with a smirk to show his opinion of it. "You know that isn't necessary. Our offer to stay at the Foundation still stands. I can guarantee you'd be a lot more comfortable there, and you'd save a lot of money. It would be safer too."

A spike of anger over the implication that choosing *not* to stay at the Foundation might be unsafe pushed aside Kyle's sense of caution. "I felt perfectly safe until I told Deputy Arpin that I didn't want to stay at the Foundation. Now I'm wondering what the next *accident* will be."

The lawyer frowned. "I hope you aren't suggesting that we had anything to do with the fire. That kind of slander would be actionable if you repeated it to anyone else."

Kyle rolled his eyes. Leave it to a lawyer to go straight to the threat of a lawsuit. "It isn't slander if it's true," he retorted.

The lawyer spoke in a bored voice. "If you find evidence that it's true, let me know and I'll take care of it. In the meantime, it would be in your best interest for you to part ways with the young lady and stay with us for the next week."

Of course they knew about Sherry. If they had started the fire, the curling iron would have been a giveaway as well as a convenient tool for arson. And now they were here, lying in wait for him. Kyle had never spotted them following him, but the Pack seemed to have eyes everywhere. He could add paranoid glances in the rearview mirror to his list of distractions. But to be fair, it wasn't paranoid if they really were out to get you.

"I told Deputy Arpin that I would let you know if I changed my mind about staying at the Foundation. I haven't changed my mind."

The lawyer stared at him for a moment. "Kyle, let me be blunt. We are concerned about your well-being and the safety of your companion. If you do not place yourself in our care, you will jeopardize both." He glanced around furtively and lowered his voice. "The one time you cannot control your transformation is at your first full moon. Your girlfriend will be in great danger. You must be in a secure location."

That was new information. Without thinking, Kyle asked for verification. "I can't control the transformation at First Moon?"

The lawyer tapped his fingers on the car door. "So, the witch *has* been telling tales."

Shit. They've never used the term First Moon with me. I'm sorry, Amanda. I did it again.

It was time for Amanda's emergency plan. "You people said you'd answer my questions, but you danced around a lot of details. Amanda helped me understand what I'm getting myself into."

The lawyer's face colored slightly and he leaned forward. "As I told you before, the witch has an agenda. You should stay away from her. If she told you about *Erst Mond*, you know there is nothing you can do to stop what is happening.

You *will* come to us one way or the other. If you come now, you will avoid causing pointless danger to those around you."

So Amanda had been telling the truth all along. She apparently didn't know about the involuntary transformation, but it was unlikely that a human had ever witnessed First Moon and lived to report it. It was also possible that Fenris was lying.

A wave of hopelessness sapped Kyle's strength, making him stumble backward and bump against the door of his Explorer. He almost gave up and agreed right then to go along with Fenris. He'd heard nothing from Amanda. Sherry would be confused and hurt, but she'd stay safe. He could call in to work from the Foundation and give them some excuse to be gone for the next week. It didn't matter what he told Vanya—he wouldn't be going back to work there anyway.

The lawyer sensed victory and smiled. He nodded at Kyle encouragingly. "You know I'm right. We can go to the Foundation right now."

Amanda's words from their discussion on Saturday rose to the forefront of his mind. *Don't give up on yourself. And don't give up on me.* It was true that he had only a week left, but at least he had that one week. He couldn't give up as long as there was even an infinitesimal chance of being cured.

But how would he justify his continued refusal to Fenris? He had to buy more time without tipping Fenris off to the *real* reason he needed more time.

"Fine, but I'm not going to simply disappear right now. I need to wrap up a few things first. Give me a couple days."

The lawyer's smile turned to a frown and a glare. "Don't mess with me, Kyle. We can take care of anything you need. You don't even have to drive. I can take you up there with me."

Kyle didn't doubt that Fenris's dark-blue sedan would become his hearse if he got in right then. That image gave him an idea for a way to deflect Fenris from the truth.

Kyle straightened himself up and unlocked the door of his Explorer. "That's not going to happen. I don't trust whatever *comfort* you may be offering. I have one week left of my life, and I'm keeping it."

The lawyer started his car's engine. "You're making a terrible mistake," he stated flatly as he put the car in gear and drove off.

Kyle got into his rig and took a deep breath to slow his pounding heart. His hands shook in reaction to the confrontation, and he beat his fists against the steering wheel to make the shaking stop.

When he drove out of the parking lot toward work, his frustration turned his stomach into knots. Where in the hell was Amanda?

Chapter 10

Pagan Origins

Kyle was getting settled in at his desk when his phone rang. It wasn't eight o'clock yet, so he considered letting the call go to voicemail. But what if Amanda was calling? He picked up the handset and answered.

It was Sherry. "Who the hell is Amanda? I thought you said you didn't hook up with anyone while I was gone."

Kyle's mind reeled. "What are you talking about? I didn't hook up with Amanda. What's going on? Is she there with you? Let me talk to her, please."

"She's gone now. Who is she, Kyle?"

"She's just a friend who is helping me with … a project. What did she say?"

"She said she needs to talk to you. She said she had news. What *news*? Like maybe she *isn't* pregnant with your child?"

Kyle couldn't help laughing, which only made Sherry angrier.

"Don't you *dare* laugh at me. I want to know who she is."

"Sorry. I laughed because the idea of Amanda carrying my child is ridiculous, since we've never had sex. You are way off-base on this one, Sherry. Please stop assuming the worst."

The line went quiet, but Kyle could still hear Sherry breathing. "Okay. I have to go to work now, but I want to talk about this later."

Kyle hung up the phone and stared at it. Great. Another complication.

The phone rang again and Kyle shook his head. Sherry wasn't going to let go of this easily. He picked it up and answered with a resigned, "Hello."

"You sound glum."

"Amanda! I am so glad to hear from you. I've been trying to get in touch with you for days."

"I know. Sorry about that. Some of my research took me out of town."

"Sherry said you have news."

The line was quiet for a moment. "She already called you? No wonder I couldn't get through a minute ago. Sorry if I caused any trouble. I didn't know you had a live-in girlfriend."

"She's not my girlfriend. Well, she used to be. I'm not sure what she is now. It's a long, complicated story that I'd rather save for a time when I don't have a week left to live."

Amanda chuckled. "I understand. Well, the good news is that I've been able to run down more information about the successful *lupusdaemon* exorcism. It was performed by a Navajo medicine man. I couldn't get anyone from the tribe in Arizona to talk to me about it, but while I was down there, I found a record of an eyewitness account from a trader who was visiting the tribe at the time. After correlating that account with the other information I've gathered, I have a working theory."

The line went quiet just when she was getting to the good part. Kyle motioned her to continue even though she couldn't see him. "Which is what? Don't leave me hanging here."

The reluctance in her voice was clear. "Well, it's still only a theory, but the one thing that stands out about this exorcism is that it *wasn't* performed by a priest. According to ancient legend, *lupusdaemons* entered the world through pagan magic. It might take a similar form of ancient magic to remove them from the world as well."

Kyle's spirits sank. "So what can we do if the tribe won't talk to you and a priest can't help me?"

Amanda responded with a terse and mildly offended tone. "Pay attention, Kyle. I'm a witch. Pagan magic is kind of my specialty."

After an embarrassed silence, Kyle got his vocal cords working again. "Sorry. You can probably tell that I know absolutely nothing about magic."

"That's okay. I'm sure most of this seems ridiculous to you, but if you want my help, you're going to have to trust me."

"I *do* trust you. You're the only one who hasn't been lying to me."

"Okay, good. I think we can try an exorcism on Saturday. I need a few more days to gather some things I'll need for the ceremony and work up an incantation. I have to warn you that I've never created a spell this powerful from scratch before. There are risks to both of us if it goes wonky."

"Wonky?"

"That's a technical term we witches use for spells that don't work out as anticipated."

For a moment, Kyle thought she was being serious. Then he got the joke. "Oh, ha-ha. Be careful saying stuff like that. I know so little about what you do that I can't tell when you're kidding."

"Sorry about that. So, other than the complicated situation with that girl in your hotel room, how have things been going?"

Kyle sighed, knowing he had to fess up about the conversation with Fenris that morning. "I hate to tell you this, but the Pack knows about our little chat."

"How much do they know?" she said in a tight voice.

Someone coming into the office walked by Kyle's cubicle right then, so Kyle lowered his voice.

"They don't know about the cure, but they figured out that you told me about the demon."

With relief in her voice, she said, "I expected that. Just not so soon. Anything else?"

Yes, there was something else, but Kyle was reluctant to bring it up due to his growing interest in her. He really didn't want to talk to her about Sherry or what had happened with Sherry last night, but Amanda's safety was at stake too, so he *had* to tell her.

"I think the demon is gaining more control," Kyle said.

"In what way?"

"Sherry told me that last night I ... we did something I don't remember doing."

"Did something?" Amanda laughed. "I can imagine. It was Clarissa's demon, after all. *Lupusdaemon Horndogus*."

Kyle's face went hot. "Yeah, you get the picture. Anyway, I'm worried it might take over while I'm asleep again and contact the Pack. I'm also worried it might feel threatened by our plans and try to switch to Sherry."

"It can't. Transference can only happen during a full moon. Remember? I told you about *Vollmondritus*."

"Right. Right. Sorry, but none of this stuff makes much sense to me."

"Keep it together a little bit longer, Kyle."

"Okay. I'll try."

"Listen, I'm going to leave something with Lucille that might help keep the demon at bay. I've never heard of one manifesting before *Erst Mond*, or I'd have given it to you sooner. It won't taste good, and it might upset your stomach a little, but take it before you go to sleep."

"Thank you. When should I pick it up?"

"I'll make sure it's there by lunchtime today."

"Thanks again, Amanda. I don't know how I'll ever repay you for all this."

"Don't worry about that now. Let's focus on getting rid of that demon. I need to go. I'll talk to you later."

They said good-bye and Kyle hung up the phone. He stared at the handset for a moment, wondering what she meant by not worrying about paying her back *now*. He couldn't quibble with whatever she might ask of him because she was saving his life, but he hated trading for an unknown debt. Who knew what kind of favor or favors a witch might demand?

Amanda was doing a lot of work for him and even spending her own money on things like airline tickets to the Southwest. She seemed to be a nice person, but charity had its limits. What was she hoping to get out of all this?

On his lunch break, Kyle drove over to Butterflies and Rainbows, hoping Amanda had remembered to drop off the medicine she'd promised. He opened the front door with a lot less trepidation than the last time he'd been there. So much had changed in just a few days.

Lucille was in the front of the store this time, and the tinkling bells on the door alerted her to his presence. She stepped into the center aisle holding a couple of books in her hands.

"Hello again, Kyle. I have the tincture Amanda prepared for you."

Kyle appreciated that the incense inside the store was much milder this time. His eyes weren't even watering. "Hi, Lucille. Thanks for holding it for me."

The older woman retreated to the back of the store. Kyle followed her slowly, taking a moment to get a closer look at the items she sold. He could see a pattern with regard to their placement. The most decorative, inexpensive, and frivolous items were near the entrance. Those shelves held things like polished stones, glass bead necklaces, incense, and decorative incense burners. The deeper he went toward the back of the store, the more mystical the items became. The aisle with books seemed to demarcate some kind of transition. The back shelves held figurines, herb packets, candles, bells of many shapes and sizes, and other things that were obviously the more esoteric and expensive wares in the shop.

By the time Kyle reached the cash-register counter, Lucille had placed a tiny brown bottle of tincture, whatever that was, into a small paper bag. Lucille held up a folded note. "Be sure to follow Amanda's instructions." She slipped the note into the bag and passed it to Kyle.

Amanda didn't tell him how much the tincture would cost. If the stuff worked, it would be worth whatever price she asked. "Should I leave money for her?" he asked.

"That won't be necessary. Not everything has a value that can be measured in dollars and cents, young man."

Kyle blushed. As with the tarot reading he hadn't wanted, he had offended Lucille again by offering her money. How could these people pay their bills if they didn't charge him anything? He sobered when he thought about his earlier conversation with Amanda. *Not now.* He would have to pay later, and probably not with dollars and cents.

Wanting to help out in some way, Kyle pointed to a dream catcher that dangled from the ceiling above Lucille. "How much for that?" The fluffy white feathers that hung from the bottom of the hoop were attractive. Sparkling red and blue beads had been worked into the strings that crisscrossed the hoop, leaving a hole at the center. The artwork slowly shifted in response to a passing draft.

Lucille narrowed her eyes at him. "Do you even know what *that* is?"

Kyle shrugged. "Sure. It's a dream catcher. I've been having bad dreams lately. Maybe it will help."

The woman folded her arms. *Damn. I can't win with her.*

"What do you see when you look at the dream catcher?" she asked.

Kyle stared at the hanging artwork and tried to understand what she wanted from him. "I see cool webbing with pretty beads and feathers. It looks to be higher quality than the ones I've seen at street fairs." The look she gave him told him she wasn't interested in compliments on the construction of the object. A belligerent edge crept into his voice. "Why? What do you see?"

She looked up at the dream catcher and said, "Tradition. Generations upon generations of tradition. That is the artwork of a spiritual craftswoman. She entrusted her creation to me, and I will ensure that it goes to someone who respects it and will benefit from it. You, dear boy, are not that person. Your spiritual self cowers within you, isolated and unaware. That dream catcher cannot help you."

While it was true that Kyle had never had much interest in spiritual matters, Lucille's words stung. She hadn't spoken with a superior tone, but the words came across as if she had.

Kyle held up the paper bag and shook it. Anger tinged his every word. "Then what about the tincture? Will *that* help me?"

Lucille raised both her eyebrows. "You tell me. Do you trust Amanda? Do you believe in her? That tincture isn't like some chemical brew you would pick up in the pharmacy.

It's more than that. It was crafted specifically for *you*, and Amanda put a bit of herself into it."

Kyle looked at the bag dubiously. *Eww. That sounds disgusting.*

Lucille saw his expression and rolled her eyes. "Oh, dear Lord. I didn't mean a literal piece of herself. Amanda put a bit of her *spiritual essence* into the making of that tincture, and she did it with you in mind. That makes it more than the sum of its herbal components. For lack of a better word, it's magical."

Kyle's anger drained away. A month ago, he would have laughed and walked out the door, throwing the tincture away in the nearest wastebasket. But the past couple of weeks had changed him. He couldn't deny what had been happening to him, as much as he tried to do so. The term "magic" still made him shudder, but he was willing to admit that the world *might* be driven by more than he could see.

And he *did* believe in Amanda. He knew the tincture would work because she told him it would. He looked Lucille straight in the eyes and stated with confidence, "It will work."

Lucille gave him the first smile of their encounter. "Yes, it will. There's hope for you yet, young man." She came around the counter and shooed him toward the door. "Now, quit trying to throw money at me, and let me get back to work."

"Yes, ma'am."

Kyle carefully wrapped the paper bag around the tiny bottle inside and clutched the package tightly in his hand. If Amanda had gone to the trouble of making a magic potion specifically for him, he wasn't going to take any chances with it. He just had to make sure that Sherry didn't find out who had given it to him.

CHAPTER 11

Sanctuary

At work the next day, Kyle was going over the requirements specification for the new project when his boss appeared at his side. Kyle looked up to see that Vanja was frowning and her forehead was creased with concern.

"You okay?" he asked. "You look disturbed."

She nodded and raised an eyebrow in a *you could say that* expression. "Could you join me in my office?"

"Sure," Kyle said, getting up from his chair.

While Vanya led the way back to her office, Kyle wondered what could possibly be the problem. He had spoken with the data warehouse group and the new code had moved into production smoothly the night before with no incidents. That project was complete and labeled a success, as far as he knew. As for the new project, he hadn't even had it long enough to screw something up. Had they canceled it?

In spite of his personal issues, he hadn't been skipping much work, and he'd made up for the little time off he had taken. Thanks to Amanda's tincture, he'd slept solidly for the first time in days, so he was alert and ready to go that morning.

Vanya sat at her desk and said, "Close the door and have a seat."

Kyle did as instructed and waited while Vanya stared at him with a confused expression.

"Kyle, did you do something I don't know about that might have caused trouble with someone in upper management?"

131

Uh-oh. No conversation starting with *that* question could end well.

"Not that I'm aware of," Kyle answered. "Why? Have I been taken off the new project?"

"In a manner of speaking. I've been instructed to let you go."

Kyle's mouth dropped open and his heart skipped a beat. "Why? What have I done wrong?"

A look of frustration flashed over Vanya's features. "I don't know. They won't tell me. I told them you've been doing great and that the team needs you, but they wouldn't listen."

"Do I have any recourse? Is there someone I can talk to?"

"Believe me, I've already tried talking to someone else. The decision makes no sense. When I tried to find ways around it, I was told to drop it or follow you out the door."

A dark suspicion swelled in the back of Kyle's mind. "Do you know who is behind the decision?"

"No. Only that it was someone at a V.P. level or above. My boss, the department director, didn't understand either. But the mantra all the way down has been, 'Leave it be; it's done.'"

Kyle looked down at his hands. "Well, thanks for trying."

Vanya sighed and shook her head. "I wish I could have done more."

Kyle suspected he already knew the answer, but he asked anyway. "When do I have to leave?"

Vanya's reluctance told Kyle his suspicions were correct. She shrugged and let out a frustrated sigh. "Right now. I have to take your identification badge, watch you pack up your desk, and escort you to the door."

Kyle groaned.

"I know. But listen, they didn't say I couldn't give you a good letter of recommendation. I'll put something together and send it to you."

Kyle nodded and gave her a sad smile. "Thanks, I appreciate that."

⁓

Packing up his desk with his boss standing at the cubicle doorway with her arms folded and his co-workers looking on was every bit as humiliating as Kyle had anticipated. Everyone was shocked by the sudden termination and some even seemed angry on his behalf. But with Vanya standing there, no one spoke to him or tried to interfere.

Shaking his hand at the front door, Vanya said, "If it's ever possible, I'd take you back in a heartbeat. Best of luck to you."

"Thanks. It looks like I'll need it."

The glass door to the building closed with a click of finality. Three years at Northern Peaks Sports Equipment was over just like that, for reasons no one understood.

As Kyle turned and walked to his rig, he was pretty sure he *did* understand what was going on. The Rutlinger Foundation had influence somewhere high in the company. The executive in question might even be a member of the Pack himself.

The Pack had raised the stakes. With no source of income and no place to stay other than a hotel room, they were pushing him hard to move into the Foundation.

But the Pack had miscalculated. Their efforts to demoralize him had only made him more determined to stay out of their clutches. And now he had plenty of free time to figure out some way of stopping what was happening to him.

He was tired of waiting on the sidelines while Amanda held his life in her hands. He was going to help her somehow, whether she wanted him to or not.

~

Sitting in his Explorer, Kyle tried to figure out what to do next. The Pack was systematically stalking him, and so far, he had made himself an easy target. That had to change. They undoubtedly knew he was going to be fired today, so he could expect another visit from one of the Pack members any time.

He needed to disappear. But how? The Pack was everywhere. He had to either find a safe place to hide or leave the area. Leaving wasn't an option if he wanted Amanda's help. Could he hide with her? She said the Order had an agreement with the Selkirk Pack. Could she protect him from them?

Kyle started the Explorer and drove to his house. He parked on the street because a work truck was blocking the driveway. The sooty bathtub insert was sitting out on the front lawn with the melted shower curtain tossed haphazardly into it. He was happy to see that someone was already at work on the place.

He went inside, calling out to the workmen. He greeted them and explained who he was before going about his business. He set aside the box of personal items from his office at Northern Peaks, and after a quick check to make sure the construction men had gone back to work, he opened the small safe he kept at the back of the closet. The safe held important papers he didn't want damaged or lost. Considering the suspected break-in and the fire, he concluded it was worth the money he'd spent on it.

In addition to papers, the safe held some emergency cash. He put the cash in his wallet and locked the safe.

After bidding farewell to the workers, Kyle got back into his SUV and planned his next move. Anxiety tugged at him, urging him to keep moving. It was particularly important to get away from all the places the Pack could expect to find him.

His heart jumped into his throat when a police car turned a corner up the street and headed his way. But it wasn't a sheriff's cruiser, it was a city patrolman. Kyle raised a hand in greeting as the officer drove by. He took a deep breath and released it as the adrenaline rush slowly faded.

Kyle checked his watch. It was ten thirty. Sherry would be at work. That was good because he had to go back to the hotel room and pick up his stuff, and he had no idea how he could explain to her what was going on. He started the Explorer and headed toward the hotel.

Would it be right to simply disappear without telling her why? He could leave her a note, as lame as that sounded. After all, she had ditched him without warning, so why should he feel guilty about doing the same?

A realization dawned. Kyle hadn't even considered taking Sherry with him. More than anything, that told him how he really felt about rekindling a relationship with her. He still didn't trust her, and he couldn't see that changing. The sex and the comfort of familiar companionship had blinded him to that truth.

Looking at the situation honestly, he knew Sherry hadn't come back because she loved him. She came back because she'd run out of money. He didn't owe her anything.

By the time he reached the hotel, he'd come up with a plan. He went to the front desk first and paid for another two weeks. Sherry had that long to find a new place to stay, or she could continue to pay for the hotel room herself, since she would be getting paychecks by then.

Next, Kyle went up to their room and packed his things. He sat down at the tiny table and left a brief note to Sherry saying an emergency had come up and that he needed to leave town for a few weeks. He let her know that he'd covered the room for a couple of weeks, so she wouldn't panic. She'd be angry, but maybe that would help her move on.

Using the room's phone, Kyle called his landlord and told the old fellow the same story about an emergency. Bob wished him well and promised to keep an eye on the construction progress.

At that point, he had done what he could to tie up the loose ends of his life and was free to do whatever he wanted with his last days.

He headed out the door thinking that it was time to push his luck and see how far Amanda would go to help him.

~

Kyle had a phone number for Amanda, but no address. He tried to look her up in the phone book, but he couldn't remember her last name. He didn't think she'd ever told him what it was. His only option was to go to Rainbows and Butterflies and ask Lucille for help.

Kyle checked his rearview mirror a lot more often than he normally would, expecting to see Fenris's dark sedan or Deputy Arpin's cruiser appear behind him at any moment. They might have someone else following him instead, so he watched every car for suspicious behavior. His distracted state made him nearly rear-end the car in front of him more than once.

The thought of walking from the downtown parking lot to Lucille's shop was unappealing; he'd be too exposed. He decided to try finding a spot along the street near the shop, which would be tricky so close to lunchtime. But he was in luck. An elderly man pulled his gray boat of a sedan out of a spot one door down from Butterflies and Rainbows. Kyle put on his blinker and parallel parked the Explorer in the vacated space.

Entering the shop, Kyle rushed forward until he found Lucille thumbing through a pile of receipts at the back counter. She narrowed her eyes and looked him up and down.

"Hello, Kyle. You look distressed."

Lucille wasn't who he was looking for, but she was the only person other than Amanda who knew about his situation. He was so relieved to have someone he could talk to that he blurted out everything that had been on his mind.

"I'm fine for now, but I need to talk to Amanda right away. They're moving in on me. They burned my house and got me fired. I don't know what to do. Amanda said she has some kind of truce with them. Can I hide with her? If I stay at the hotel, I'm a sitting duck. And I can't put Sherry in the middle of this."

Lucille dropped the receipts and waved toward him in a *settle down* gesture. "Stop and catch your breath." She came around the counter and led him over to where she had done the tarot reading.

"Are you sure the Pack is behind the house fire and you losing your job?"

Kyle nodded vigorously. "There's no doubt in my mind. They are trying to force me to stay at the Foundation."

Lucille sat down and her brow wrinkled in thought. "We didn't expect them to be so aggressive," she mused. "They know you will come to them eventually."

"So you don't believe there's a cure?"

Lucille looked Kyle straight in the eye. "I won't lie to you about it. Amanda is the only hunter who truly believes there is a cure. The Order has been indulgent with her so far, but the rest of us expect that you will be eager to join the Selkirk Pack after First Moon."

Kyle was stunned. Amanda was the only person who was interested in helping him because she was the only one who believed he *could* be helped. Her own Order didn't believe in her.

I'm doomed.

Kyle's thoughts spiraled into visions of a demon taking over his mind, of changing into a wolf and prowling the forest, and of a headstone with his name on it. He blinked several times and a tear spilled out of his eye, spotting his pant leg.

Lucille's voice grew tender. "I'm sorry, Kyle. But I don't want to give you false hope."

Kyle's moment of self-pity twisted into frustrated anger. "What about Amanda?" he snapped. "She's been willing to give me false hope. So what am I supposed to do? Let the Pack win without a fight? What if Amanda is right and the rest of you are wrong?"

Lucille gave him a hard look in reaction to his tone, but he didn't care. She had no stake in this. It was his life that was at risk.

"I admire your spirit," she said. "If you are willing to trust your life to Amanda's cure, you deserve a chance to see if it will work. But this is not a decision to be made lightly. Requesting sanctuary with the Ternion Order has consequences. You must follow certain rules, or sanctuary will be revoked."

"It sounds like witness protection."

She considered his remark. "That's not a bad comparison. We can go over the details later, but for now you need to understand that the Order will control your movements. You'll also need to turn your finances over to us, so you can't be traced through your accounts. All contact with your family and friends must go through the Order as well."

She paused, giving Kyle a chance to respond. He shrugged. "What choice do I have? It's either the Pack or the Order."

"All right then. As a hunter myself, I can sponsor your request for sanctuary immediately."

Kyle waited for a moment to see if Lucille was going to seal the deal by doing something special. She merely sat there with her hands in her lap.

"That's it? No signing in blood? No fairy dust to mark me as a ward of the Order?"

Lucille chuckled. "Sorry to disappoint you. Signing in blood is too unsanitary. Fairy dust would be expensive and obvious. We'll have to make do with paper contracts and an ink pen once we get you to the refuge."

"Where's that? Will I be close enough to help Amanda?"

Lucille gave him a wry grin. "Oh, yes. You'll definitely be close enough to help Amanda. You'll be living with us."

"Us?"

"Amanda rents space at my farmhouse outside of town. The property is also one of the local refuges. You'll be quite safe there."

Living with Amanda? Sherry would be livid. Not that he cared much about what Sherry thought right then.

"Thank you. That's very generous. When should I go?"

Lucille reached to pick up the phone under her counter. "You stay here for now. This place is a refuge as well. I need to make a few calls, and then we'll move you to the farm."

"That sounds like a lot of trouble. Can't I just drive there?"

"Remember what I said about the Order controlling your movement? If you want sanctuary, you need to sit back and let us take care of you for now."

While Lucille made calls, Kyle grew frustrated at sitting and doing nothing. His leg bounced on the footrest of the bar stool until a significant glance from Lucille made him stop. He got up and walked around the shop just for something to do.

The bells on the front door jingled, and Kyle stepped behind a bookshelf, peering down the main aisle toward the door. Two teenage girls dressed entirely in black had entered the shop. One of the girls was heavily pierced and wore her dark hair in a style that could only be termed "modern rat's nest." Her chubby form pushed her tight top into rolls over her hips and her cleavage was squished together, mounding the soft pale flesh to just below her chin. Blood-red nails tipped each finger.

The second girl was as nondescript as the first was flamboyant. Her mousy blonde hair fell in stringy strands past her shoulders, obscuring most of her face. Her matchstick figure and pencil-thin arms made Kyle suspect she had some kind of eating disorder.

The two girls disappeared into one of the aisles at the front half of the store. Kyle glanced at Lucille, but she was still talking quietly on the phone and writing something down, seemingly unaware of her new patrons. He considered keeping an eye on the girls, but this wasn't his store, and it wasn't his responsibility to prevent shoplifting.

Kyle occupied himself by browsing some of the books sitting on the shelf in front of him. A colorful cover caught his eye and he picked up a book on crystals and gems. He thumbed through it, enjoying the photographs of the various minerals. The book claimed that specific gemstones had various magical properties associated with them. Hematite was supposed to promote healing? He scoffed quietly to himself. *Who makes up this crap?*

He peered around the corner again when he heard one of the girls say something about leaving. They were headed toward the door when the dark-haired girl came to a sudden stop and looked up.

A sign above the door said, "Please don't steal from me." He couldn't tell if it was a trick of the lighting or if the sign was illuminated somehow, but he thought he saw a glow pass over it from left to right.

The girl turned around, a doubtful frown on her face. Her skinny friend turned quickly to keep up, seeming surprised by the change of direction. As the girls came toward Kyle, the heavy one slipped two fingers into her cleavage and lifted out a tiny sculpture of a fairy. She glared at Kyle, daring him to make a comment, but he just stared.

"What's *your* damage?" she asked in a snotty tone as she strutted past.

Kyle watched the girls approach the checkout counter. Lucille used her shoulder to keep the phone to her ear while she rang up the sale. When the girls turned to leave, Kyle stepped back and pretended to be absorbed in the mineral book.

He peered around the corner again after they passed and watched them leave. The sign didn't flash that time. *Interesting.* Kyle tried to imagine a theft-deterrent system that was so small it could fit on that tiny sculpture, but the solutions all seemed too high-tech for such a small shop.

As an experiment, Kyle carried the book he was holding toward the exit. He watched the sign carefully and took one deliberate step at a time. Nothing happened. Standing almost directly under the sign, he craned his neck around, looking for wires or sensors, but saw nothing obvious. Thinking maybe Lucille had triggered the sign manually, he looked for surveillance cameras. Again, nothing.

Giving up with a shrug, Kyle went back to see how Lucille was coming with her phone calls. On the way, he put the book back on the shelf where he'd found it.

Lucille was off the phone and was writing in a small black leather notebook. She closed the notebook as Kyle walked up.

Kyle hooked a thumb over his shoulder in the direction of the door. "I think that girl was going to steal the figurine. She seemed to change her mind at the door."

Lucille gave no indication that she had been aware of the situation. "I'm glad her conscience led her to a better choice." She put the black book under the counter and picked up the receipts that were still sitting next to the register.

"I think your 'don't steal' sign convinced her to do the right thing." Kyle added.

She responded with an exaggerated nod. "That *is* why I put it there."

Kyle was curious about the sign, but didn't want to come right out and ask her if it was magical in some way. If it wasn't, he'd feel like an idiot.

"Is there anything *special* about that sign?"

Lucille looked up at him. "Yes there is. I made it myself."

She was holding a straight face, but her eyes were smiling. She probably knew what he was really asking, but she wasn't going to make it easy on him. "What's the matter? Does the sign bother you?"

"No. It's fine. I thought I saw it flash earlier when the girl almost left without paying."

Lucille put the receipts down, and the teasing look left her eyes. If anything, she appeared to be surprised. "You did? That's…"

"What?"

She paused and pursed her lips before continuing. "Unexpected."

Apparently, not everyone saw the sign flash. Was that because the effect was so subtle? He'd doubted his own eyes right after he'd seen it happen. Maybe it was supposed to be a subliminal thing, and he happened to be watching it from the right angle at the right time.

Whatever the case, Lucille wasn't forthcoming. Kyle was satisfied with his own explanation, so he let it go. Lucille could keep her secrets.

Putting the receipts away behind the counter, she changed the subject. "I'm sure you'll be interested in knowing that the director has provisionally accepted your request for sanctuary. An escort should be here in fifteen to thirty minutes."

Kyle imagined himself driving out of town bracketed by huge black SUVs with flashing red lights. "Is all this really necessary?"

"Probably not, but the director insisted that the escort include someone from our tactical discipline."

"The Order has disciplines?"

"Ternion means three, Kyle. The Order's three disciplines are tactical, technological, and transcendental. The director insisted on tactical assistance because we take a request for sanctuary very seriously."

"So I see."

Lucille gestured toward the tarot counter. "Shall we do another reading while we wait?"

"No thanks."

The store's door chimes rang again and Kyle turned to see who was coming into the shop this time. His heart nearly stopped when he saw the cold face of Fenris Kellen. The lawyer's eyes darted around and his body shivered, as if the shop were chilly.

Kyle eased around the counter to stand next to Lucille, keeping his gaze on Fenris the whole time.

The lawyer moved toward the counter in a slight crouch, as if he were trying to move silently, even though he could clearly see that Kyle and Lucille knew he was there. When he came alongside the last aisle, about six feet from the counter, he stopped and straightened. He rolled his shoulders and tugged his jacket into position.

"Hello, Kyle. I'm glad I found you. Good day, Ms. Hayworth."

Kyle was paralyzed with fear. He couldn't have spoken at that moment to save his life, but fortunately Lucille had no such problem.

For the first time since he'd met her, her confidence seemed to slip. She greeted the lawyer with a cautious tone. "I'm surprised to see you here, Mr. Kellen."

Fenris's jaw clenched and he glanced around the room again. He answered in a bitter voice. "My purpose is strong, and your wards are weak."

Lucille muttered, "I'll have to do something about that." She narrowed her eyes at the lawyer. "What can I do for you?"

Fenris's feral gaze pinned Kyle in place; Kyle could barely breathe under the weight of it. "I'd appreciate a moment of privacy while I speak with Kyle."

Lucille slowly shook her head. "I can't do that. Kyle has requested sanctuary, and the Order has granted it."

The lawyer's nostrils flared and a growl emerged from deep in his throat. "Pointless," he grumbled. He addressed Kyle directly. "What do you hope to gain from this foolishness? If the witch has told you there's a way out, she's lying to you."

Kyle tried to speak, but his vocal cords wouldn't respond. He cleared his throat and rallied his courage. "I think *you* are the one who has been lying to me."

The lawyer let out a sinister chuckle. "What can I say? I'm a demon."

The blatant admission caught Kyle off guard. An urge to get far away from Fenris nearly made him turn and run through the rainbow curtain behind him. Did the store have a back exit? If it did, where would he go? Lucille said her shop was a refuge. He was undoubtedly safer there than he would be running through the streets, but it didn't seem like much of a refuge if demons could walk in the front door.

At that moment, the rainbow curtain billowed toward the back room in response to a door opening at the rear of the shop. Kyle jumped in alarm at the surreal coincidence of timing. Lucille crossed her arms and a smug expression settled on her face. A moment later, two people stepped through the curtain—a big man and a well-dressed woman. Both went still when they saw Fenris.

The lawyer's eyes went wide, and he smiled. "My, my. You should be honored, Kyle. They brought out the big guns for you."

The man certainly looked like he could qualify as a "big gun." He was tall and had an athletic build. His sun-bleached hair and tanned skin indicated that he spent a lot of time outdoors. Kyle was barely able to make out the words Pesce Marina printed on his faded orange t-shirt, but it confirmed Kyle's guess that he might be a boatman. His tan cotton jams and worn deck shoes reinforced the motif.

The woman also gave the impression of strength, but not in a physical way. Her salt-and-pepper hair had been twisted into a fancy braid that came forward over her shoulder and touched her folded arms. Curly wisps escaped the braid at her temples and at the end where it had been tied off. Her outfit was the color of purple iris and included an embroidered vest covering a loose-fitting, long-sleeved blouse. She wore a matching skirt made of heavy linen. Her tense posture and dark, focused eyes indicated readiness to strike. Kyle half expected her to raise her arms and nod her head like the genie from that old television show, turning Fenris into a frog or a newt.

She looked down her nose at Fenris and then turned to Lucille. "Who let the dogs out?"

Fenris barked out a laugh. "That was a cheap shot, Noreen." The lawyer shook his head and gave Kyle a bemused smile that said this was all a futile waste of time. "Okay, Kyle. Have it your way. I can see there's no reasoning with you." The lawyer turned and walked toward the exit. "I'll see you next Friday," he said over his shoulder with a wave. With one last dark glance toward the new arrivals, he exited and closed the door a little harder than necessary.

"That one has *never* had any manners," the woman said with a sharp shake of her head.

The man grumbled in a deep voice, "He is a lawyer and a demon," as if that were explanation enough.

Lucille put a hand on Kyle's shoulder. "This is Kyle Nelson, our sanctuary applicant. Amanda is expecting him at Hayworth Farm. Kyle, this is Noreen Thornquist and Jonathan Pesce. They will escort you to the farm. Follow whatever instructions they give you."

"What about my rig and my things?" Kyle asked.

Noreen held out her hand, palm up. "Give me your keys. Your vehicle will be delivered to the farm by the end of the day."

Kyle was about to object, but Lucille's hand tightened on his shoulder, reinforcing her command to follow their instructions. "Okay, here." Kyle unclipped his keys from where they hung on his belt loop and handed them to Noreen.

Noreen gazed at him dubiously as she accepted the keys. "So this is the subject of Amanda's bold little project. Is he going to be trouble?"

Lucille gave Kyle's shoulder a supportive squeeze and then let go. "He'll be fine. He just doesn't know much about us or what we do."

Noreen arched one thin eyebrow. "He knew enough to ask for sanctuary."

"I suggested it, once he explained his situation. The director accepted the request."

Noreen looked at Lucille for a moment. She pressed her lips together and nodded once. The director's acceptance was evidently good enough for her.

Lucille wasn't quite finished. She narrowed her eyes at Noreen and said, "As for her *little project*, Amanda may be young and ambitious, but she's also a talented hunter."

Noreen shrugged. "Of course. She was *my* apprentice." With that, she turned and walked through the rainbow curtain into the back room.

Jonathan looked at Kyle and tilted his head toward the curtain, indicating that Kyle should follow Noreen.

Kyle took a deep breath and let it out. He glanced at Lucille before he went through the curtain, and she gave him an encouraging smile.

Kyle stepped out the back door of the shop, blinking in the bright sunshine. When he saw what awaited him in the parking area behind the building, he almost laughed. Noreen was standing by the open back door of a large, dark-green SUV. The vehicle didn't have flashing red lights, but otherwise it was a lot like what he had imagined earlier.

Kyle clambered into the backseat of the Toyota Sequoia, noting that it still had that new-car smell. He observed his silent companions while they got into the front and wondered if he was making a terrible mistake.

But then movement out of the corner of his eye caught his attention. A familiar dark sedan was parked along the street with a view of the parking lot. Kyle couldn't see clearly through the tinted windows, but he was certain Fenris sat inside the car, watching the proceedings.

Maybe it was a mistake to ask for sanctuary, but he'd rather take his chances with the Ternion Order than with the Rutlinger Foundation.

Chapter 12
Hayworth Farm

On the way to the farm, Jonathan struck up a conversation with Kyle, making him feel a lot more comfortable about his decision to go along with them. As he suspected, Jonathan was into boats. He owned and operated the eponymous Pesce Marina referenced on his t-shirt.

Jonathan seemed like such a normal guy that Kyle was tempted to ask him how he got involved with the Order, but he couldn't figure out a polite way to do it. In truth, Noreen intimidated him, and he didn't want to say anything that might offend her.

For her part, Noreen was silent for most of the trip. She asked Kyle what kind of vehicle he drove and where he'd parked it so they could retrieve it later, but that was the end of her contribution to the conversation.

About ten minutes outside of town, they turned off the highway onto Farm-to-Market Road. Most of the homes along the route were farmhouses with enormous barns and an abundance of acreage. The fields were in various states of use. Some had been hayed for the season and looked like endless tidy lawns. Others were fallow, and most of these were filled with colorful wildflowers and weeds. In late summer, small white daisies with yellow centers dominated, forming a blanket of white across the abandoned fields. Sprays of yellow goldenrod filled the margins.

After several more minutes of travel, Jonathan slowed and turned off the main road. The gravel driveway was blocked by a livestock gate, so he stopped the SUV and got out to open it.

Kyle checked out the place that would probably be his home for the next several days. He wasn't impressed. The wooden fencing along the road desperately needed paint. The farmhouse was surrounded by trees, but from the road, the structure looked dark and forbidding. The barn had a decidedly disreputable look as well. It had a substantial lean, and the door to the hayloft hung at an angle by its one remaining hinge.

Jonathan got in, moved the rig forward, and then got out again. Kyle watched him close the gate, thinking it would have made a lot more sense for Noreen to have opened the gate for them, but she didn't seem inclined to leave the air-conditioned comfort of her front seat. Kyle would have been happy to do it himself if he'd had the presence of mind to make the offer instead of gawking at the farm.

When Jonathan started driving forward, pressure briefly pushed at Kyle's sinuses. He reflexively yawned his jaws open and his ears popped. It was as if he had suddenly dropped in elevation. As they rolled down the driveway, Kyle did a double take at his surroundings and reconsidered his first impressions. The bright white fence line they drove alongside was actually in *good* repair. Kyle tilted his head side to side when he noticed that the barn looked sturdy and straight from this angle. The loft door did hang open, but both hinges were intact after all. The farmhouse wasn't as gloomy as he'd first thought, either. The driveway curved toward the house, and the trees opened up to reveal a cheerful, two-story home painted pale yellow with dark-blue trim.

Kyle was beginning to feel as if he were in a scene from the *Wizard of Oz*—the one where Dorothy leaves the black-and-white dullness of her house and steps out into the wonderful Technicolor experience of Oz. At any moment, Munchkins, or perhaps fairies, would dance out from behind the trees onto the front lawn. *I've a feeling I'm not in Kansas anymore.*

As the SUV approached the house, Amanda opened the door of the screened porch and came down the front steps to meet them. Kyle was surprised at how happy he was to see her. If he had a tail, it would be wagging. He hoped he'd never find out what *that* felt like.

Kyle got out as soon as the vehicle came to a stop.

Amanda had reached the driveway by then and looked Kyle up and down. "Are you okay? Lucille said you might be in danger."

Kyle appreciated her concern, but felt bad about worrying her. "I'm fine. But the Pack won't leave me alone. They're doing everything short of kidnapping me to get me to stay at the Foundation."

Her eyes widened with alarm. "We can't let that happen."

"I know. That's why I'm here."

It was sweet that she seemed to care about him, but he still wasn't sure why. The only spark they had between them was when she touched him, and he didn't think static charge counted in relationship matters. Maybe he would learn more about her motivations now that they would be under the same roof.

Jonathan came around the front of the rig, which he'd left running. He and Noreen were apparently not sticking around.

Noreen rolled down the window. "Hello, Amanda."

Amanda bowed her head and shoulders. "Greetings, Master Thornquist. I hope things are well with you."

The woman smiled for the first time Kyle had seen since he'd met her. It was a tight smile that showed little warmth, but it softened her stern visage. "*Noreen* is fine, Amanda. I'm no longer your master."

Amanda answered with her own tight smile. "As you wish, Noreen."

Kyle didn't understand the byplay between the two women, but got the distinct impression they weren't on the best of terms. He figured it would be a bad idea to get in the middle of a fight between them and hoped that he wasn't already.

Jonathan cleared his throat. "We're heading out. Kyle, it was good to meet you," he said, shaking Kyle's hand. Jonathan turned and went back to the driver's side of the SUV. "We'll be back in a bit to drop off Kyle's Explorer," he called over the hood.

Amanda and Kyle watched as Jonathan backed around and drove off. The SUV's tires crunched in the gravel, and a thin gray cloud of dust swirled in its wake.

Kyle looked over at Amanda to find her staring at him. It wasn't an unfriendly stare, but she had the look of someone who was trying to solve an unexpected problem. *That problem would be me.*

"This will be interesting," she said in a musing voice. "Come on inside and relax for a while. I have a project for work I need to finish today, but I can give you a full tour in a couple of hours."

Kyle followed Amanda through the screen door and onto the porch. To his right, a cushioned porch swing looked like the ideal place to kick back with a beer and have a relaxing conversation. Kyle also looked forward to enjoying a meal at the round glass-topped table and wrought iron chairs that had been arranged on the left side of the porch.

Rich, musty smells enveloped Kyle and soothed some of his tension the moment he entered the house. The place was old, but someone had nicely renovated it. Most of the lighting fixtures, electrical outlets, and wall switches looked relatively new. The living-room walls were white-painted plaster above natural wood wainscoting that had become dark with age. Kyle had a thing for wood, so he immediately appreciated the design sensibilities of the person who chose the mahogany furniture. Everything was mission style, dark and sturdy, with thick cushions covered in maroon or pine green.

Amanda poured each of them a glass of lemonade and suggested that Kyle sit on the porch and enjoy what was left of the cool morning. He could help himself to anything in the refrigerator or cupboards if he got hungry.

Kyle took a sip of his lemonade. "Mmm. This is good. What is it you do for work?" he asked, reluctant to let her leave him alone.

"I'm a marketing copywriter. I write sales copy for web pages, e-mails, brochures, stuff like that."

"Cool. And you can do that from home?"

"That's the beauty of it. I can make my own hours, which is almost a necessity for anyone who is active in the Order. Every once in a while, like now, I have a deadline to meet, but I can usually spend a lot of time working on whatever I want."

"Nice. As a beneficiary of that freedom, I'm glad."

Amanda chuckled. "Like I said, I do have a deadline right now, so I'll be back down in a bit. If you want, you can explore the grounds by yourself. Just be sure to stay back from the fence."

"Electrified?"

"Not exactly. Let's just say it's a protective barrier and leave it at that."

More mystery. "No problem," Kyle said with a sigh.

Amanda gave him a wink and left the kitchen. A few seconds later, her feet pounded up the stairs to the second floor.

Kyle went back out to the porch and sat on the swing for a few minutes. He closed his eyes and listened to the chickadees peep and robins chirp. The swing was as comfortable as it looked.

After a few minutes of sitting alone, his thoughts turned back to the predicament he was in. The Order had granted him sanctuary. Now what? He had made it to the farm, but Amanda was busy working on a copywriting project. That seemed so ordinary, after everything that had happened. Part of him wanted to go up the stairs and try to talk her into putting everything else aside so she could work on *his* problem. How could some web page possibly compete with the fact that he would be dead in a week?

A strange creaking sound came from the thick acrylic tumbler that held his lemonade. Kyle relaxed his grip, realizing he had nearly cracked it. Unable to stay still any longer, he got up and went into the front yard, taking his drink with him. He spotted the barn and decided to start his explorations there.

As soon as he stepped into the sunlight, the sun's intense glare replaced the morning cool hoarded by the trees near the house. His skin welcomed the sun's warmth, but after only a few steps, sweat beaded on his forehead along his hairline.

A blue tractor squatted under an overhang on the right side of the barn. The odor of diesel and oil floated on the air. The tractor and the implements stored behind it were rusting where the paint had worn off.

The barn door was partially ajar, so Kyle peered into the gloomy interior. It took a moment for his eyes to adjust to the dim lighting afforded by the grimy clerestory windows up in the loft. Horse stalls lined both sides of the barn. Most of the stalls were given over to the storage of old junk, but the last two on the left were clean and thoroughly stomped by hooves.

Tubular fence panels formed a generous corral alongside the barn. Sandy ground churned up by hoof prints indicated regular use, but no horses were present.

Next to the corral, goats milled around in a large fenced area. Their little tails wagged and their mouths were in continuous motion. A goat resting on the ground stretched its neck forward, looking like it was about to throw up, but then settled back and started chewing. Not knowing much about goats, Kyle made a mental note to ask Amanda if they chewed a cud.

Across from the goats and behind the house, Kyle found a tidy garden with a tall fence around it to keep out deer. He wasn't much of a gardener, but he recognized corn stalks, and he spotted green and yellow summer squash growing under plants with enormous spreading leaves.

The garden shared a fence with a chicken yard of equal size. A big chicken coop straddled the two areas, but the garden side was closed up so the chickens couldn't molest the crops. Upon consideration, Kyle thought he understood the arrangement. The chickens and the garden were rotated between the two areas. Each year, a ready supply of chicken manure would be waiting to help the new plants grow. Meanwhile, garden waste could be thrown over the fence to the chickens.

Continuing past the garden, Kyle found the horses in a fenced pasture. He rested his arms on the gate to watch them. The brown-and-white equines cropped the grass near a cluster of pines along one edge of the pasture. They were pintos or paints, or whatever the correct term was for horses with big white patches.

Both horses eventually turned their heads his way and started walking toward him. When they reached the gate, he put his hand out to let them sniff, keeping his fingers curled under in case either one tried to bite. The bigger one nuzzled his hand and pushed at it, probably wanting a treat of some kind.

"Sorry guys. Maybe next time I'll bring something for you."

The horses lost interest quickly and went back to grazing.

Kyle watched the horses for a while, enjoying the bucolic peacefulness of Hayworth Farm. The sun was intense out in the open, but a light breeze kept him cool. He tipped up his glass to suck down the last of his lemonade and wondered when Amanda would be finished with her work.

The horses raised their heads in tandem and perked up their ears when the goats started bleating. Kyle looked over to see all of the little animals scampering toward the near side of their pen. Something in the tall grass on the other side of the property fence had apparently spooked them. He walked over to take a look.

Kyle tried to calm the goats with a soothing voice, but they mostly ignored him. He walked along the outside of the pen toward the property fence to see what made them so agitated. He'd heard that North Idaho had no poisonous snakes, but the goats probably didn't know that.

The flutter of a colorful but faded ribbon tied to one of the fence posts caught his eye. The ribbon held several plant sprigs tight against the post. The odd decoration reminded Kyle that Amanda had told him to stay back from the fence.

The breeze picked up at that moment and blew the grass back to reveal a black nose and gray furry muzzle. Amber eyes glared at him through the fence, and Kyle took an involuntary step backward. The plastic tumbler slipped from his hand and hit the ground with a clatter of ice cubes. The huge wolf bared its teeth and growled, ending the growl with a sharp admonishing bark. Having delivered its message, the wolf faded back into the tall grass. Kyle tried to track the wolf's movement, but the fitful breeze randomly shifting the heavy seed heads made that impossible.

So much for secrecy. The Pack knew he was here.

Kyle reached down to pick up the tumbler with a shaking hand. He dumped out the remaining ice and wiped off the dirt that had stuck to the condensation on the outside. Walking back toward the house, he figured he should tell Amanda right away about what had happened. But Amanda was already at a second-story window, staring toward the grass beyond the goat pen. She had probably heard the goats through the open window. She looked down at Kyle and motioned for him to come inside.

Amanda met him at the front door. "What happened? I heard the goats and saw you drop your glass. I thought I heard a bark too. Did a dog scare the goats?"

"It wasn't a dog. I think it was Reggie."

Amanda gasped and covered her mouth with her hand. "Are you sure?"

"Not really. It could have been any huge wolf, but it seemed to know me. Sorry, but I think they know I'm here."

Amanda scrunched her face and waved away his concern. "Don't worry about that. It wasn't much of a secret. The Order has only a few refuges in this area. The Pack would have guessed we'd bring you to this one."

"Then why the gasp? Do you know Reggie?"

With a preoccupied expression, Amanda took the dirty tumbler from Kyle's hand and carried it into the kitchen. He followed her, wondering why she wasn't answering the question.

She rinsed the remaining dirt off the glass and left it in the sink. Then she turned and leaned against the counter, facing Kyle. She stared at the floor, obviously debating what she was going to say.

"I do know Reggie. Well, I *used* to know Reggie. Before he became … one of *them*."

A new puzzle piece spun in Kyle's mind, trying to fit into what he already knew. "Was he a boyfriend or something?"

The eyes that met Kyle's were haunted with painful memories. "He was my brother."

Kyle was stunned speechless for a moment. The puzzle piece stopped spinning, but he still couldn't make it fit. "Is what happened to your brother the reason you are helping me?"

She swallowed hard and nodded. "Yes."

Something more hid within her eyes. Reggie was a full werewolf, well past his first moon, so he couldn't be saved. Or could he?

"So, what—you don't want to see someone else suffer the same fate as your brother?"

"Exactly," she answered a little too quickly.

Kyle didn't trust the way she latched onto the explanation he had dangled in front of her. There was something else she wasn't telling him. He had never fully believed that her motivation was pure altruism. Did she have something more to gain? Kyle blinked a couple of times when a possible answer came to mind.

"You think you can save him."

She looked at the floor again and said nothing. Her silence was answer enough.

"But you told me that the demon would take over and I'd be gone after First Moon. Was that a lie?"

Amanda straightened up and took a step forward, her hands clasped together at her waist. "No! It wasn't a lie. That's what everyone believes."

Kyle thought he was finally beginning to understand. "Everyone except you. I'm your test subject. If you can help me, you might be able to help your brother."

Her shoulders sagged and she wouldn't meet his eyes. "I know it's a foolish hope, but I have to try." When she looked up at Kyle, her eyes were brimming with tears. "I miss him so much."

She reached up to wipe her eyes and then covered her mouth when a sob broke free. When Kyle stepped forward and wrapped his arms around her, she didn't resist. She rested her head on his shoulder and fought to control her grief.

Once she stopped crying, she squeezed Kyle's shoulder and eased back from him. She took a step into the living room and yanked a tissue from a box that sat on a side table. After wiping her eyes and nose, she spoke quietly. "I'm sorry I didn't tell you everything. I didn't think it mattered, and this is hard for me to talk about."

Amanda was right. The full explanation for why she wanted to help him didn't matter. But knowing the truth about her motivations gave Kyle a comforting sense of clarity that he'd lacked before.

"I think I understand. I'm sorry I opened an old wound, but I feel better knowing where we stand. If helping me helps you get Reggie back, I'm more than happy to be your guinea pig. Just don't keep me in a cage or make me run any mazes."

She laughed and gave him a quick hug. "I promise. Thank you for not being mad at me. How about I give you that tour, and then maybe we can have lunch. I have a little more work to do before I can send off the files for my writing project, but later on, we can sit on the porch with a couple of beers, and I'll explain what I've got planned for Saturday."

Beers on the porch. She's a girl after my own heart.

"Sounds good. But since I'm here, should we try for tonight or tomorrow?"

"We can't do it tonight because I won't have everything I need until tomorrow. And tomorrow's bad because of the celestial alignments."

Kyle scoffed. *Celestial alignments?* "Are you telling me that we have to wait until the stars align?"

Amanda looked annoyed for a moment, but then took a deep breath. "It sounds stupid when you put it like that, but essentially, yes. Planetary influences are subtle most of the time, but I don't want anything working against us. Exorcism is not a simple spell. We'll need all the help we can get."

Kyle hung his head. "Sorry. I'll have to take your word for it."

"Thank you." Amanda put one hand on her hip and wagged a finger at him with the other. "And it would help if you stopped making fun. I know you are struggling with all of this, but considering everything that has happened, you really should try to be a little more open-minded. It will help us both on Saturday."

Kyle's voice took on a defeated tone. "Amanda, I don't understand much about what's going on, and the more I learn, the scarier it is. I'll try to tone down the snark, but sometimes I think it's the only thing keeping me sane."

Amanda's expression softened. "I understand. The paranormal has a way of enveloping you. It will be hard to simply walk away once you've seen what's behind the curtain."

She'd touched on one of Kyle's biggest fears. His life had been torn to confetti over the past few weeks. He'd never be able to pick up all the pieces, just as he was no longer the blissfully ignorant software developer he had once been.

What did that mean for his future? Who, or what, was Kyle Nelson going to become?

~

Late in the afternoon, Kyle helped Amanda lead the horses back to the barn where they would spend the night. Jonathan and Noreen came by with Kyle's Explorer and his luggage, but they didn't stay. Kyle unpacked his things in a small but serviceable bedroom upstairs.

After dinner that first night, Kyle relaxed with Amanda on the porch swing. Lucille sat at the table, quietly knitting a scarf from several shades of red yarn. The sun was barely above the horizon, the last rays warming the side of Kyle's face as the heat of the day rapidly dissipated.

Kyle closed his eyes and enjoyed the scents flowing around the porch. The occasional whiff of horse manure added its tangy odor to the earthy scent of hay and the perfume of summer's last wildflowers. The occasional bleat of a goat or snort of a horse punctuated an otherwise peaceful evening of birdsong and the whisper of aspen leaves.

When he opened his eyes, he glanced at Amanda and found she was staring at him. "What?"

She smiled. "You seemed so relaxed there for a minute. You've had a clenched look from the moment I met you, and I think this is the first time you've loosened up."

Kyle nodded and took a deep breath, noting with satisfaction that he could inhale without his chest feeling restricted. "I think this place is good for me."

Lucille gathered up her knitting and stuffed it into a floppy cloth bag at her side. She levered herself up from her chair and said, "I'm running out of light, so I'm heading in."

She picked up the bag and went over to the swing. "Do you have anything special planned for this evening, Amanda?"

Amanda glanced at Kyle. "All things considered, I think it's a good idea to strengthen the wards."

Lucille nodded. "I agree. Will you need anything from me?"

"No, thanks. I still have plenty of herbs left over from last time."

"All right, dear. I'll be inside reading if you change your mind."

Amanda thanked her and bid her goodnight. Kyle wished her a pleasant evening as well and thanked her for letting him stay at her farm.

After Lucille went inside, Amanda checked the sun's position. It was below the horizon, but there was still plenty of light. She got up from the porch swing and went out onto the front lawn. She looked up at the sky for a moment and then came back.

Amanda went to the front door of the house and paused with her hand on the doorknob. "I'm going inside to get some things. I'll be right back."

As the evening darkened, the breeze picked up and grew cooler. Kyle was thankful for Amanda's suggestion that he bring out a flannel shirt, and he slipped it on.

Several minutes later, Amanda came out onto the porch carrying an aromatic cloth bundle, a battery-powered lantern, and a glass carafe of what appeared to be water. "This is going to take me a while, so if you want to go inside and watch television or something, feel free."

Television didn't sound appealing, and neither did sitting alone on the porch while she was out "strengthening the wards," whatever that meant. The idea of watching Amanda perform witchcraft was both unnerving and fascinating. "Do you need help?" he asked spontaneously.

"No thanks. I've done this a few times before."

Her answer was more of a disappointment than a relief. In two days, he was going to be at the center of a magical ceremony, so it would probably be a good idea to get a feel for what he could expect. He tried again. "May I come with you and observe? It might make things easier on Saturday."

Amanda pursed her lips in consideration. "Only if you promise not to interrupt or make fun of me. If you have questions about anything you see me do, save them for while we are walking the property line. I've got eight ward points to set and only a few hours of moonlight left, so I can't have you slowing me down."

Kyle agreed to her terms and offered to carry the heavy water container.

"We'll start with the one that was most recently compromised," she said, leading him around the house toward the goats.

Kyle hesitated when he reached the corner of the goat pen, remembering the amber eyes that had glared at him from the other side of the fence. He shook off the trepidation and caught up to Amanda, not wanting to look like a coward.

Amanda unrolled the fabric bundle and set it on the ground. A strong grassy smell rose from it, mixed with the distinct aroma of licorice. About a dozen pockets were sewn into the roll, with bundles of herbs poking out of eight of them. A coil of string or twine was stuffed into one pocket, and another held a hunting knife in a leather sheath. Kyle hoped she wouldn't be using that knife to draw blood from anything, including herself.

Amanda took the carafe from Kyle and set it next to the other items. She checked the position of the moon, which was about a quarter of the way between mid-sky and the western horizon. She then turned to Kyle.

"Any questions before I begin?"

Kyle had been hoping she'd ask. "What are the plant bundles?"

"Each bundle has a small sage smudge with a sliver of licorice root. The sage purges negative energies from the grounds and reinforces the protective nature of the ward. Licorice reinforces the psychological aspect of the ward, helping make the farm uninteresting to passersby."

Kyle remembered his arrival and how unappealing the farm had looked then. Could that have been the ward at work?

"That it?" she asked and Kyle nodded. "Okay, then." Amanda pointed to a spot where Kyle could observe but where he'd be out of her way. "Stand right here and don't move around or say anything until I'm done."

Kyle positioned himself where she indicated and nodded enthusiastically.

Amanda chuckled and shook her head. She took a deep breath and closed her eyes. She placed her hands together in front of her face, as if in prayer. After a moment, she bent down and drew the hunting knife.

"I release this ward and the protection it grants." She cut the old twine from the fence post and let it fall to the ground.

Kyle half expected something to happen when the old ward was released, and he was a little disappointed when it didn't. Maybe this was all hocus-pocus after all.

Amanda poured a small amount of water onto the knife blade and said, "Spirits of water, purify this instrument and purge it of negative energies." Using the sharp blade, she cut a length of new twine and then set the knife aside. Amanda tied the twine around the fence post. Wrapping her hand around the post, she faced north and bowed her head. "Spirits of the north, anchor and support these protections."

Amanda picked up the carafe of water, wet the twine with it, and poured a trickle that flowed down the post. "Spirits of water, purify this space," she intoned. When the water reached the bottom of the post, she stopped pouring.

The moment the water touched the ground at the base of the post, something shoved Kyle hard enough that he stumbled forward and had to cling to the fence to keep from falling. Amanda sent an annoyed glance his way, but then her eyes widened. She motioned him to flatten himself against the fence. Pressure like a strong wind helped him do as she indicated. He spread his arms out at his sides for stability as something he couldn't see buffeted him. The hair on the back of his neck rose when he noticed that the grass was bending away from him. The evening breeze was blowing in the opposite direction from the unseen force that pressed him against the fence.

Amanda watched Kyle for a moment and then closed her eyes briefly. She shrugged and continued with the ritual. Or spell. Whatever it was.

She squeezed the bottom of a pocket in her kit and pushed out an old flip-top lighter. Facing south, she lit one of the sage bundles. "Spirits of fire, lend strength to these protections." She then turned east, blew out the burning sage leaves, and waved the smoking herbs in a circle. "Spirits of air, protect this space from prying eyes and all who would do us harm."

Amanda carefully tucked the herb bundle under the twine that encircled the post. She reached down to the kit and extracted two metal rods.

The metal rods turned out to be a striker and a chime. She suspended the chime by putting her finger through a metal ring that was attached by a thin chain. After checking the herb bundle to make sure it was secure, she said, "With these tokens, I invoke the illusion of wretched despair. May all who gaze upon these protections turn their attention elsewhere." She then rang the chime once.

When Amanda struck the chime, a faint, shimmering wave of greenish light floated from her toward the post. As the light approached the post, the ward charm sucked it in like smoke being drawn into an exhaust vent. The breeze suddenly shifted and blew in the same direction as the force that was pushing on Kyle, but after a few seconds, it returned to normal.

Amanda reached toward Kyle with her hand open. He pulled one hand away from the fence, and the moment his hand touched hers, the odd pressure that had been pushing on him stopped. He tipped forward and she grabbed his shoulder with her free hand to steady him.

Once he got his feet back under him, he released her hand and looked at her questioningly.

She nodded. "Yes, we can talk now."

"That was weird. What was pushing me?"

"Given the timing, I'd say the water spirits. It happened when I called upon them to purify the grounds."

"So I'm ... an impurity?"

"Not you. The demon."

"But it stopped when you touched me," he mused.

"I invited you to be here."

Kyle didn't care much for that answer. It made him sound like some kind of vampire. "Is that going to happen every time?"

"It might. You should stand next to the fence from the start. It would probably be best if you followed along *outside* the fence, but I'd like to avoid that."

With Reggie lurking about, Kyle preferred to stay inside the ward as well. His doubts about whether or not the protections were real had evaporated when something tried to shove him out. He was also certain that the wards had inspired his initial impressions of the farm when he'd arrived that morning.

Amanda packed up her kit and let Kyle carry the water again. Before tucking the knife back into its sheath, she wiped the blade carefully with a wet cloth she had brought with her. The cloth had been stuffed into a plastic sandwich bag so it wouldn't get her pocket wet. When she noticed his curious expression, she anticipated his question about what she was doing.

"The holy water has a trace amount of salt in it, which doesn't do the knife any good in the long run. I wipe it down with plain water so salt won't rust the blade or build up in the sheath. I'll rinse it more thoroughly when we get back inside."

The next fence post was the property's northwest corner post, located behind the barn. While Amanda was setting up for the new ward, Kyle looked toward the first post and realized they had quite a bit of walking to do.

"How big is this place?" he asked.

"The original homestead was a full section, but most of it has been sold off. All that's left now is this quarter-section piece."

"How big is a section?"

Amanda gave him a teasing smile over her shoulder. "Come on, Kyle. How long have you lived in Idaho now? You gotta get with the lingo."

Kyle snorted as he handed her the carafe. "Hey, I'm a city dweller, not a farmer."

Amanda set the carafe down and rolled out her kit. "A section is a square mile, or six-hundred and forty acres. The farm is one-hundred and sixty acres—a square half-mile. So the perimeter we have to walk will be two miles total."

Amanda appeared to be nearly ready, so Kyle stood next to the fence. "It's cool that you know this stuff."

She shrugged one shoulder and stood. "To tell the truth, I asked the same question the first time I set the wards. I wondered how far I had walked, and Lucille was kind enough to enlighten me."

"Aha," Kyle responded, and they shared a laugh.

Amanda went through the same ritual that she had with the previous ward. The pressure to push Kyle off the property never arrived. Amanda surmised that her first invitation was necessary to allow Kyle inside the new ward, but since the subsequent points were extensions of the same ward, the invitation covered them as well.

By the time they reached the fourth post, full dark had fallen and their only light came from Amanda's lantern and the half moon above. Kyle cast a few nervous glances at the waxing moon, thinking about how the remaining dark segment was a measure of the time he had left. In exactly one week, the full moon would rise and he would become a werewolf.

That is, unless Amanda could cure him. For the first time, Kyle truly believed in that possibility. He no longer doubted her abilities, and he didn't care if she had personal motivations for helping him. If she succeeded, she'd save his life.

On their way to the last post, Kyle was overwhelmed with gratitude for what she was doing for him. "Amanda, thank you. I haven't been very cooperative, and I'll try to do better. I want you to know that I trust you, and I have faith in you."

Amanda gave him a sidelong glance. "Where did that come from? Don't get me wrong, I'm glad to hear it, but that was quite a change of heart."

Kyle waved his hand to encompass the property. "All this … ward stuff. It's real. I may not understand what you do, but I can't deny that it works. Everything I've heard about magic has always been so unreliable and unverifiable. I've just watched you repeat a process and get consistent results. That, I can believe in."

Amanda patted him on the back. "I'm glad I made a believer out of you. That will be a big help to me on Saturday. But I have to warn you. Not all magic is reliable."

Kyle mentally kicked himself for daring to have a moment of hope. "I thought, since the wards work so well, I had reason to be optimistic."

"Optimism is good, but this ward has been tested and refined over several decades … maybe centuries. What I'll attempt on Saturday doesn't have that history."

Kyle sighed. "I understand."

"Sorry, I didn't mean to bum you out. We have a real chance of making it work, but I can't promise anything."

Amanda checked the position of the moon, as she had been doing all evening. It was not far above the horizon and would probably set within the hour. Her interest piqued Kyle's curiosity.

"Why do you keep checking the moon? Does it affect the wards somehow?"

She shook her head. "Not directly. I'm strongest when I work in moonlight. In my coven, I'm known as a moon witch because of the affinity."

"Why the moon?"

"No one knows. Some of us work best in daylight, others at night. Some when the moon is high in the sky and others when it is on the opposite side of the world. When I first started practicing, I tried every condition I could think of. My best work has always been in the moonlight between first quarter and last quarter."

Amanda being a moon witch trying to exorcise a werewolf demon had a certain symmetry to it that appealed to Kyle. "Somehow, that seems like a good omen. The moon has special meaning for me too now."

Amanda laughed, "I'll say. But I suppose you're right about it being a good omen." She went quiet for a moment, then added thoughtfully, "I'll be at my strongest on the full moon, but unfortunately, we can't wait until then."

No, they couldn't. It would be too late.

Their heads turned in unison toward an odd noise to their left. Tiny sparks were crackling along the perimeter fence, keeping pace with them. Amanda raised the lantern to get a better look and stopped with a gasp. A pair of eyes reflected back at them out of the darkness.

Amanda dropped her ward kit and took a step back. With the lantern farther into the periphery of his vision, Kyle was able to make out the long lean shape of a huge gray wolf. "Reggie," he blurted. The wolf nodded its head once and then sat down.

Amanda's eyes were wide, and the lantern shook in her hand. Her other hand was closed tightly into a fist while tears pooled in her eyes. She was repeating something. At first Kyle thought she might be casting a spell, but then he made out the words: "Please, don't," she was saying, over and over.

Don't what? Kyle wondered. But then he looked back to Reggie and understood. The wolf was going to transform.

The part of Kyle that wasn't about to soil his pants looked forward to witnessing a genuine werewolf transformation. At the same time, he understood how awful it must be for

Amanda to see her brother this way. But there was nothing he could do to stop it.

Kyle expected Amanda to turn the lantern away or avert her eyes, but she continued to stare in horrified fascination as the tears streamed down her cheeks.

The transformation was not what Kyle expected. It didn't involve any of the bone-stretching, facial morphing, fur-sprouting, or screaming in pain they showed in the movies. Instead, a roiling black cloud that crackled with violet arcs of energy enveloped the wolf. Kyle gagged on the stench of death that permeated the air as the opaque cloud twisted and shifted with the buzz of a million flies drawn to a rotting corpse. After an eternity of several seconds, the cloud swiftly expanded and dissipated with a whoosh, and Reggie stood on the other side of the fence where the wolf had been. He was, of course, completely naked.

"Hello, Kyle," he said.

If Reggie wasn't concerned about his nudity, Kyle wasn't going to make an issue of it. It was nothing he didn't see in the mirror every day. Well, Reggie might have a few superior attributes, but nothing to be jealous of. Much.

"What do you want?" Amanda asked.

"You know what I want. I want Kyle to come with me to the Foundation."

He addressed Kyle. "You're running out of time, and you're putting every living thing on the farm at risk by staying here. Come with me now, and we'll make your last days pleasant. You can have anything you want. Deputy Arpin has been disappointed by your absence and looks forward to getting reacquainted with you."

Kyle shook his head. Talk about making a deal with the devil. "As tempting as that sounds, I think I'll hang with Amanda for a while longer."

Reggie turned his attention back to Amanda. She swallowed visibly and blinked the last remaining tears from her eyes, but she stood straight and faced him.

"You know that your plans for Kyle will never work, little witch. You don't have the knowledge or the power. You will fail, and it might be the end of you."

Amanda narrowed her eyes at him. "So you admit it can be done."

"In the entire history of our kind, it happened *once*, long ago, by a powerful and determined man who got lucky. You may be determined, but your power is a fraction of what his was, and luck is ever a fickle companion."

Kyle's despair returned full force as his hope waned. He should go with Reggie and be done with this. But then he looked at Amanda. He saw the determination in her eyes and had felt her power first-hand. Reggie was trying to erode her confidence in herself, but he wasn't succeeding. Her defiance reminded him of something Fenris had said. This was a demon talking. Everything he said could be a lie.

Amanda seemed to realize what he was doing too. She squared her shoulders. "Be gone, demon. You aren't welcome here."

Other than rolling his eyes, Reggie ignored her. Addressing Kyle again, he said, "This is your last warning, Kyle. If you insist on endangering your friends, it is out of our hands. But if you decide to do the right thing, you know where to find us."

With those words, the black cloud returned with all its noise and stench. The wolf had already disappeared into the brush by the time the cloud cleared.

Amanda swiped the last remaining tears from her face and snatched her kit from the ground. "Let's go. We have one more ward to set." She marched off without waiting for a reply.

Kyle followed her, distracted by his own thoughts. So the Pack knew what she was up to after all, and they didn't believe she would succeed. Her own Order didn't believe she'd succeed. That left only him and her. For her part, Amanda seemed to believe in herself enough to try.

What did he believe? If everyone else was right and Amanda was wrong, he was a dead man. He would put his faith in Amanda to the bitter end. He hoped that end would not include him turning into a wolf and tearing her to pieces.

CHAPTER 13

Moon Shrine

Friday morning dawned gray and overcast. The clouds had trapped the heat of the previous day, and the fitful rainfall dried almost as soon as it hit the ground, adding a heavy mugginess to the air. The weather in mid-August was a time of transition between summer and fall, with everything from hot days and swift violent thunderstorms to cold days and long soaking rains.

It was strange not going to work, but Kyle decided that making money was the least of his worries right now. Unfortunately, being at loose ends gave him too much time to think. He spent most of the day trying to distract his mind by reading on the porch while Amanda worked on one of her writing projects. He was only partly successful.

No matter how hard he tried to suppress it, Kyle kept picturing the noisome scene of the previous night. If he ever had any doubt about the dark nature of the werewolves, watching Reggie's unholy transformation had eliminated it. The black cloud had reeked of evil, and he wanted nothing to do with it.

At lunch time, Kyle rummaged around in the kitchen and put together a sandwich for Amanda and himself. A bowl of salsa and a bag of chips completed his culinary masterpiece. On his way out to the porch with two glasses of lemonade, he called up the stairs to let her know the food was waiting.

In response to the warm and humid weather, Amanda wore a light sundress with a faded flowery print, wide shoulder straps, and a scoop neck. When she came out to the porch, she flapped past him in a pair of flip-flops, her knee-length dress showing off a nice pair of legs.

"Thanks for fixing lunch," Amanda said, sliding her chair up to the table.

"It's the least I could do," Kyle replied.

She picked up her sandwich and took a bite, and Kyle took notice of her toned arms and shoulders. This was the first time he had seen so much of her at once, and he liked what he saw.

"Something wrong?" she asked after swallowing.

Kyle realized he was staring and shifted his eyes to his plate. "No. I just noticed that you changed your clothes."

She picked up a chip and dipped it in the salsa. "Yeah, the house has no air conditioning, and my office can be uncomfortable when it gets this humid. I see you dressed down today too."

Kyle wore a t-shirt and shorts, his favorite weekend attire when the weather permitted. "Hey, I'm living the life of the unemployed. Might as well take advantage of it."

"Good for you. What have you been up to all morning?"

Kyle finished his bite and said, "Reading and trying not to think."

Her eyes sparkled with mirth. "Is it working?"

"Not really. I'm trying to make sense of what's happening, but so much of it seems contradictory."

"In what way?"

"One thing that confuses me is that you're using witchcraft to fight demons. But isn't witchcraft supposed to be demonic in nature?"

Amanda sat back, a hurt expression on her face. "What gave you that idea? Has anything I've done seemed evil or harmful in any way?"

Kyle waved his hands and shook his head. "No! See, I don't know what I'm talking about. I don't even know how to ask about this stuff without potentially offending you."

She went back to her sandwich, looking disappointed and a little miffed. Kyle didn't want to risk making her angrier, but he wanted to understand what he was getting himself involved with.

"Can you maybe tell me a little about how your magic *does* work?"

Amanda gave him a considering look while she finished her sandwich.

"First, tell me what *you* believe in, Kyle. You don't strike me as a devout … anything."

Kyle shrugged. "I went to church with my parents when I was young, but never really connected with the whole Christian-fellowship thing. I guess I'm agnostic. I have no idea if God exists or not. If He does exist, I've seen no evidence that He demands worship. I consider myself to be a Wyld Stallynist. We should all be excellent to each other and party on."

Amanda stopped in mid-reach for a chip. "Wait … was that a *Bill and Ted* reference?"

"Got it in one," Kyle said with a grin.

Amanda chuckled. "Okay, that's good to know. There's no point in talking to you about this if your mind has been shaped and closed by years of doctrine."

Kyle tapped his head with his fingertip. "Nope. No doctrine in here. Just confusion."

Amanda brushed her hands over her plate and sat forward. "Here's what I believe. Some witches do practice a form of religion based on pre-Christian pagan beliefs and gods. My coven believes in something more basic. More elemental. In simple terms, there are dark forces and light forces. Dark forces are used to manipulate and harm, and light forces are used to protect and heal. The term 'worship' is defined as reverence and adoration for a deity. I don't believe the light forces are deities, and when I petition them for help with my works, it's more about respect and gratitude."

"If they aren't deities, what are they?"

"I don't know. I don't think anyone living *can* know. All I know is that they have the ability to help or to hinder, and that they respond to people who have personal power."

"But you said the werewolves are some kind of demon. Where do demons and Hell fit in?"

"Some of the forces, both light and dark, exhibit awareness and a sense of personal identity. We call those forces 'spirits'. We use the term 'demon' for powerful dark spirits."

"So, does that make angels powerful light spirits?"

"Exactly. Spirits can be exorcised or banished, but we don't pretend to know where they go. 'Away' is usually good enough for our purposes. Personally, I think Hell is an analog—it's any place you don't want to be."

"I can relate to that. I've been there many times."

"Haven't we all."

Engine noise distracted Kyle from the conversation and he turned to see a package-delivery truck rumble through the gate and roll down the driveway toward the house. He tilted his head toward the truck. "What does the driver think about the wards?"

Amanda shrugged. "Once you've been through the wards, you see the place for what it really is. Most people dismiss their initial impressions as an optical illusion, but the ward sticks with you enough that you don't want to talk to others about what you've seen."

Kyle watched the brown truck pull up to the house and come to a stop. "That's so cool. But I can imagine how tempting it would be to abuse that kind of power."

The driver went into the back of the truck, and Amanda lowered her voice. "That is why the Order exists. One of my tasks as a hunter is to watch for abuses of power."

Kyle lowered his voice to match hers as the driver reappeared and leaped out of the side door of his truck, hitting the ground at a jog. "So the Ternion Order is the supernatural police?"

Amanda held her finger up to her lips in a shushing gesture, but answered his question in a whisper. "More or less." She rose from her seat and met the driver at the screen door.

"Hi, Pete. Need a signature?"

The delivery man smiled and held out a clipboard. "Hi, Amanda. Line eighteen, please." He checked her out while she signed and then noticed Kyle on the porch. He nodded a greeting, and Kyle raised a hand in response. After signing, Amanda handed back the clipboard, and the driver eased the package toward her. "It's heavier than it looks," he warned, and she took it from him carefully with both hands. Kyle could tell from the way her arms dipped that it was indeed heavier than one would expect for an eight-inch cardboard cube.

"Have a good day," the driver said before turning and jogging back toward his truck.

"Thank you," Amanda called to his retreating back.

By the time she reached the table with her package, the delivery man had turned his truck around and was speeding toward the gate.

Amanda set the package on the table and said, "Be right back." She went into the house and came back a moment later with an old serrated kitchen knife, which she used to cut the tape holding the box closed. When she opened the box flaps, several packing peanuts swirled out and floated to the top of the table and the floor.

"I hate this stuff," Amanda said as she scooped up the wayward pieces of foam. She cautiously extracted a rounded object that was wrapped in brown paper, brushing more clinging peanuts back into the box.

She pulled off the wrapper, revealing a shiny brass pot about four inches in diameter with a deep rounded bottom. She held the pot up by a thick wire handle that arched from a tab on one edge of the rim to another on the opposite side. She inspected it for a moment and then put it on the table, where it rested on three stubby legs. Astrological symbols had been etched in a band along the rim, and a Celtic knot decorated the side.

"It's beautiful," Kyle commented.

Amanda's growing smile spread to a full grin. "I know. It's much nicer than I expected. The pictures on the web site didn't do it justice."

Kyle looked at her in surprise. "You found this on the Internet? Where? The Witch Warehouse?"

"Ha, ha. Celtic symbolism is popular, so it isn't hard to find things like this if you know where to look."

Kyle leaned forward to get a closer look at the designs. "I'll keep that in mind the next time I need some eye of newt."

Amanda put her hand on her hip. "Oh, you're full of humor today, aren't you? I thought you weren't going to make fun."

Kyle flopped back in his chair and rolled his eyes. "Sorry. I was only joking." She gave him a look as if she were deciding on the sincerity of his apology. "I didn't mean to be disrespectful."

Amanda seemed mollified and sat down again. When she leaned forward to pull up her chair, the neck of her dress fell forward, revealing a white lacy bra and moderate but respectable cleavage. Kyle quickly brought his eyes back to her face before she looked his direction. If the *Wizard of Oz* was any kind of guide, she was definitely a good witch. She was way too hot to be a wicked witch.

Kyle cleared his throat and tried to get past the awkward moment. "What is it for?" he asked, putting as much interest in his tone as he could.

When she answered, she seemed to be over her annoyance. "It's technically a cauldron, but I prefer to call it a crucible. The term *cauldron* is so, 'double, double, toil and trouble.'" Kyle couldn't help but smile, and she wagged her finger at him. "Which I *never* say, in case you were wondering. Anyway, it's for you, partly. I need it for the ceremony tomorrow."

Kyle sat forward again, genuinely interested now. "I'm surprised you don't already have one."

When she didn't answer immediately, he looked up and realized she was blushing. She met his eyes and raised her shoulders in a sheepish shrug. "My old one was ceramic, and I broke it last week. That's why it's only *partly* for your ceremony."

Kyle knew better than to tease her about something that was probably an important piece of equipment for her work. He tapped the crucible a couple of times with his fingernail, making it ring. "You shouldn't have any problems with this one breaking."

Amanda brightened and sat up. "That's what I was thinking. Plus, brass complements the kind of spell I'll be casting tomorrow. It's a win for both of us."

After everything Kyle had seen over the past few days, he was getting a sense for how certain aspects of magic worked. This brand-new crucible was going to play a significant role in the exorcism tomorrow. Frowning at the lustrous object, he thought it seemed incomplete somehow. "Doesn't it need to be consecrated or something?"

Amanda's eyebrows rose in unison. "I'm impressed. You're catching on. Yes, I'll need to put a little extra effort into purifying it tomorrow before we get started because I don't know who might have handled it." She picked up the heavy pot and cupped it in her hands. "In time, we'll become more attuned to one another."

Kyle wasn't sure what it meant to become attuned to a metal bowl, but he guessed it would be better if that had already happened. His fate rested in the efficacy of a spell that depended, at least in part, on this new, unproven addition to Amanda's toolkit.

Kyle sipped his drink to calm the sudden burning in his stomach. It didn't help much, the lemonade being fairly acidic itself. Tomorrow night, Amanda would try to rid him of this hitchhiker he had unwittingly taken on board. If she succeeded, he would find some way to pay back Amanda and the Order for helping him. If she failed, he might have to find a cliff and jump off. Everybody dies sometime, and he refused to hand his living body over to a demon.

~

Friday afternoon and Saturday passed quickly. Amanda tried to keep Kyle distracted by having him help her and Lucille with the chores around the farm, but as Saturday evening drew near, he started to get twitchy. Although his superhuman strength was helpful at times, it also underscored his situation and reminded him of the exorcism to come.

Late Saturday afternoon, they went for a horseback ride in the horse pasture that occupied the southwest quarter of the property. The fenced-off area included a copse of tall pine trees along the western edge that offered shade for the horses.

The horses were named Buck and Edna. After Amanda saddled Buck for Kyle, he stood hesitantly at the horse's side.

"What's wrong?" Amanda asked.

"How did this horse get his name?"

Amanda laughed. "Don't worry. He was named Buck because he's a buckskin paint, not because of the way he treats riders."

"Good to know." Kyle got into the saddle and followed Amanda's instructions for how to hold the reins.

Friday's gray overcast had broken up into distinct fluffy white clouds that floated across the sky and blocked the sun often enough to keep the riders from getting too warm. They followed a trail around the perimeter of the horse pasture, enjoying the views of the farm, the nearby mountains, and the neighboring properties.

While they were riding through the trees, the horses startled once at a loud rustling near the fence. Something swished away through the grass and then was silent. Kyle stared through the fence, fully expecting to find a glaring wolf, but all he saw was grass waving in the stiff breeze.

"Probably a coyote," Amanda said in a reassuring tone.

They finished the ride without further incident and went inside after unsaddling the horses and rubbing them down.

Lucille had prepared eggplant lasagna for dinner, which filled the house with a rich, mouth-watering aroma. But Amanda insisted that they wait until after the ceremony to eat so they could be fully alert. For the first time, Kyle started looking forward to the exorcism. His growling stomach turned out to be a powerful motivator for getting it over with. To take his mind off his hunger, Kyle got permission to check up on Sherry and his house.

His first call was to the hotel where Sherry was saying. The room was in his name and he had paid for it, so the man at the front desk was happy to answer his questions.

"Yeah, she's still here. Son, you'd best be hiding someplace good, 'cause she came down here madder than a wet hen asking after you. Only contact info I got is for your house in town."

Kyle gave the man the number at the farm in case he needed to get in touch.

"Ain't none of my business, but you might consider wearin' a steel athletic cup next time you see that little gal."

Kyle chuckled, although he didn't think the man was far off the truth. "Thanks for the advice. I'd appreciate it if you didn't mention this call to her or give her that new number."

"No problem. I don't need that kind of aggravation."

Kyle ended the conversation and called his landlord. Repairs on the house were progressing well and the place would probably be habitable within a week. After he hung up the phone, Kyle sighed in relief. Sherry was okay and it looked like he'd have a house to go home to. Assuming he survived another week.

"Everything okay?" Amanda asked.

Kyle shrugged. "As well as can be expected. Sherry is pissed at me, but that's nothing unusual."

Amanda put her hand on Kyle's shoulder and looked into his eyes. "Are you ready to do this? It won't be full dark for another hour, but it will take some time to get prepared. The moon will be at meridian around nine o'clock, and that would be an excellent time to begin."

Kyle nodded as his heart rate increased. It was almost time. "What do I need to do?"

"Get into some comfortable clothes. The moon shrine is in the attic. It can be a bit warm up there, so keep that in mind."

Kyle changed out of the jeans and light flannel shirt he had worn riding, and switched to cargo shorts and a t-shirt. He grabbed a clean flannel shirt in case it got cooler later on.

He went back out into the upstairs hall, but Amanda's door was still closed. He was trying to decide where to wait when Lucille opened the door and peeked out. She slipped a hand through the opening and pointed toward the door next to Amanda's. "Go on upstairs and turn on the ventilation fan that's on the wall to the left. Don't touch anything else. Amanda will join you in a minute."

Kyle opened the indicated doorway, revealing the attic stairwell. The area above was fairly dark, so he flipped a switch just inside the door. Lights came on and he started up the stairs.

The room was warm and stuffy as predicted, but the ambiance made Kyle shiver anyway. The sconce lights in the four corners of the room produced plenty of soft yellow light, but they didn't improve the brooding heaviness of the space. Perhaps the green and blue wall hangings were responsible.

He spotted the ventilation fan high on the wall. Presumably, the switch positioned lower on the wall controlled it. Kyle crossed the room, carefully skirting a concrete pad that lay on the floor immediately below a hexagonal cupola. Kyle glanced up as he went around. A large picture window dominated each of the cupola's eight sides, letting in the last glow of the setting sun.

Kyle flipped the switch and the ventilation fan quietly ramped up to speed. Air instantly started flowing into the room from the stairwell, drying the sweat that had started beading on his forehead.

He inspected the concrete pad. The six-foot square was about two inches thick and had a five-foot-diameter circle engraved into the surface. The purpose of the two beams he'd seen straddling the bearing walls in the hallway below suddenly became clear. What he'd thought was an odd decorative addition or repair was, in fact, reinforcement.

The edges of the pad weren't precisely aligned with the walls, leading Kyle to conclude that it had been oriented to true north. Corresponding with each point of the pad's square, four circular depressions, each about five inches across, shared a tangent with the main circle. A copper tube exited the western corner of the pad and entered a lever valve before disappearing into the floor.

Amanda's voice came from the doorway, startling him. "What do you think of my moon shrine?"

He hadn't heard her come up the stairs over the soft hum of the fan. Plus, she was barefoot, adding to the stealth of her arrival. She wore a belted, midnight-blue kimono over loose-fitting pants of the same color and silky material. It looked like something she might wear to bed. Although it covered everything except her head, hands, and feet, the flowing outfit was incredibly sexy.

Getting no reaction from Kyle but a stare, Amanda glanced down at her attire and said, "I suppose it looks like I'm wearing pajamas, doesn't it?"

"You look ... nice," he said. Wondering about his own attire, he asked, "Should I remove my shoes in here?"

"You don't have to, but you might be more comfortable. We'll probably be here for a while."

Kyle followed her suggestion and kicked his shoes off by the doorway while she bustled around the room. He followed her progress, noticing that, as loose-fitting as her clothes were, the silky material draped in ways that revealed her curves. With her dark hair tied back in a tight braid, nothing obscured the view.

He shook his head and tore his eyes away from her. Sure, she was attractive, but his growing fascination with her seemed unusually intense. Was this simply normal horny male behavior, or could it be the influence of the demon? He imagined an evil cackling in his mind, enjoying his self-doubt.

Amanda glanced over her shoulder at him. "You okay?"

Kyle resolved to focus on what she was doing rather than watching her do it. "Yeah, fine. Just a little distracted."

"That's understandable. I know this is probably scary for you, but don't panic. I'm not expecting anything spectacular to happen. I'll either succeed or I won't. I doubt we'll have any spinning heads or projectile vomit."

Kyle's stomach grumbled in spite of the unsavory reference, reminding him that he had eaten nothing to throw up. At least he had one less thing to worry about.

Amanda stood at a waist-high table covered with an indigo cloth. Silver stars of varying sizes decorated the skirt of the cloth. The brass pot that had arrived the previous day sat at the middle of the table. On a shelf above the table rested three rounded glass pitchers with gracefully curved handles. All of them had been filled with a clear liquid. Several other items that looked like they might have come from Butterflies and Rainbows were positioned along the wall at the back of the table surface.

"Could you please turn off the fan and have a seat in that chair?" She pointed toward a straight-backed spindle chair in one corner of the room. "I'll need you to be quiet while I work. I have to consecrate the crucible first, and then it will be your turn."

Kyle did as she asked. The fan had already pulled the stuffiness out of the room and brought the temperature down to a comfortable level. He sat in the chair and watched silently while Amanda began her preparations.

Amanda carefully centered thick colored candles in each of the depressions he'd noticed earlier around the circle. Kyle suspected that she chose candles of different colors for a reason, since she seemed to be selective about which candle she put where. He took a moment to orient himself and concluded that she had placed the green candle to the north, the yellow candle to the east, the red candle to the south, and the blue candle to the west.

Next, she carried several items to the concrete pad. She made multiple trips to her table and retrieved some herbs from the storage cabinets along the west wall. Kyle noticed that she set each item as far as she could reach into the circle, but never stepped onto the pad. By the time she stopped to survey her collection, she had the herbs, a pitcher of water, her old-fashioned lighter, a feather fan, a rather nasty-looking double-edged dagger, a bell, and the new crucible.

Apparently satisfied with her efforts, Amanda lit a couple of the candles on her table and turned off the sconce lights. Although the room became much darker, the moon augmented the light of the candles through the cupola. She returned to the north corner of the pad and turned around to look up at the north wall above the table.

Kyle leaned forward in his chair and craned his neck around to see what she was looking at. He hadn't noticed it before, but the wall had two dark-gray vertical lines painted on it. No, that was wrong. One of the lines was painted on the wall, and the other was a shadow. Tracking the angle with his eyes, Kyle realized that someone had painted a thin black line on the south-facing window of the cupola. The shadow line on the wall was cast by moonlight, and Kyle guessed that the lines would join when the moon reached meridian.

Amanda placed her hands palms-together in front of her face. Bowing her head, she swept her hands to the side until her arms were straight out and then slowly dropped them to her sides. She turned around and stepped into the circle. Moving to the center of the circle, she folded her legs under her and sat cross-legged. She arranged the dagger, herbs, and other items in a semi-circle with the new crucible directly in front of her.

Kyle's chair was positioned in a corner of the north wall, and since Amanda was facing north, he was able to see everything she was doing. The whispers of her clothing as she moved and the silvery half-light of the room blended to give her an air of strength, beauty, and mystery.

Amanda used her lighter to burn the sprig of herbs. As soon as the tips flickered with flame, she blew them out. The bundle smoldered, producing an aromatic smoke. She waved the sprig in a circular motion and called for the spirits of light to help her push dark forces away.

Kyle was pushed back into his chair by a pressure on his chest. After a moment of disorientation, he recognized the sensation as similar to what he'd experienced when Amanda refreshed the wards. Once again, the spirits were reacting to the presence of the demon. The part of him that still had trouble accepting magic posed the possibility that this was all in his head. Psychosomatic or not, it *felt* real enough.

By the time Amanda set the sprig down, it had nearly stopped smoking. She picked up the bell, which had squared-off corners like a cow bell, and she rang it once with a metal striker. Although the sound wasn't that loud, it was almost painful to hear. A force slammed Kyle back in his chair so hard that it knocked the wind out of him and bumped his head against the wall. It shoved his chair the last couple of inches until it too was pressed against the wall. It was as if he were seated in a race car and someone had popped the clutch, pushing the pedal to the floor. So much for the psychosomatic theory.

The pressure eased and Kyle rubbed the back of his head. Amanda ducked her head in an apologetic shrug.

Amanda put down the bell and picked up the pitcher of water. Rising to her feet, she stood in front of the blue candle, holding the pitcher with both hands. She called to the spirits of water to purify her circle and keep dark spirits at bay. She kneeled and slowly poured water into the depression around the blue candle, which was now lit and flickering in response to her movements. The water flowed into the main circle and made its way around the entire ring, filling the other candle depressions along the way. When she stopped pouring, her liquid circle shimmered silver in the moonlight.

An oddity struck Kyle, making him furrow his brow. When had she lit the candle? Her position had partly obscured his view, so he hadn't noticed when it happened. *How* intrigued him even more than *when*. She was holding the pitcher with both hands the whole time. Had she used her toes to light the candle? He resolved to watch more closely when she came around to a position that gave him a better view.

Amanda crossed the circle and traded the nearly empty pitcher for the feather fan. Facing the yellow candle, she held the fan across her chest as if she were about to dance. She called to the spirits of air to protect her working. Kyle watched closely this time, and nearly gasped when the candle lit without her touching it. Amanda took the flame as her cue. She swept the feathers in a continuous up-and-down curve, painting an invisible cylindrical wall above the circle of water. As sensuous as any dance, her graceful movements were captivating.

A shimmering in the air disrupted Kyle's focus when Amanda had nearly completed her circuit. Distortion followed her fan motions around the circle, like heat waves rising from a desert highway. The invisible wall wasn't so invisible after all.

Amanda put the fan down and stood facing north toward the green candle. Her position gave Kyle the best view of her activities. Kyle leaned forward to check the moon's shadow line on the wall above him and observed that it had moved from the left side of the painted line to the right. The moon was now past meridian.

While he watched, the line grew fainter and disappeared as the room grew noticeably darker. Kyle's pulse quickened at the ominous sign until he realized that the moon had merely gone behind a cloud. The light from the candles on the table and in the circle seemed to grow brighter with the loss of moonlight, shifting the spectrum of illumination in the room from silver to gold.

Amanda stood still for a few moments behind the wall of distortion, and Kyle thought she might be waiting for the moon to come out from behind the cloud. But then she reached into her pocket and withdrew a necklace with a pendant set with some kind of dark stone. She put the necklace around her neck, and wrapped her hand around the pendant. She called to the earth spirits to anchor her protections and give her a strong foundation for her working. The green candle lit spontaneously, even though Amanda hadn't moved.

Kyle glanced around the room, wondering what sign he might be missing. Then it came. A deep boom, more felt than heard, rattled Kyle's lungs. It was like the sonic boom of a jet airplane, but much more visceral. The spirits of earth had spoken.

Apparently, this was the sign Amanda had been waiting for. She crossed the circle to the red candle, picking up the dagger as she passed. She held the dagger at arm's length with both hands, pointed toward the ceiling, and called to the spirits of fire to lend her power and strengthen her working.

Kyle had a poor line of sight to the red candle from where he was sitting, but the moment it lit was obvious. The fire spirits seemed to be showing off as the wick burst into flame and flared nearly a foot before subsiding to match the other candles.

The flickering light from all four candles sparkled on the steel blade of Amanda's dagger. Her hands were glowing, and for a second Kyle thought her sleeves might have caught fire. He started to rise from his seat, but the glow left her hands and flowed up her arms, where it briefly enveloped her from head to foot before fading. Kyle slowly reseated himself, shaking his head in stunned amazement.

Amanda returned to the center of the circle and sat cross-legged again. Her ritual for consecrating the crucible seemed to involve more water and calling on spirits, but Kyle was too distracted with his own thoughts to pay much attention.

What he had witnessed was disturbing on a primitive level. He had a strong urge to run out of the house, jump into his Explorer, and drive as fast and far as he could. He started to get up out of his chair to go, but then he remembered the reason he was there. Running away would only lead to one unpleasant conclusion. Was the desire to run coming from the demon? He ground his teeth in frustration at having to second-guess his every emotion and impulse.

He gripped the arms of the chair and closed his eyes, taking a deep breath to calm himself. It didn't work. Nausea struck hard, and he swallowed convulsively to keep from gagging. It was a good thing they hadn't eaten before coming up to the moon shrine.

In a few minutes, all of this strange power would be focused on him. Amanda was clearly a powerful witch who knew what she was doing. Having observed her abilities, his concerns about the new crucible fluttered away like leaves in a fall wind. If she believed that she had the knowledge, the tools, and the power to pull off the exorcism, then he believed it as well.

But what would it feel like to have a demon torn from your mind?

He hated going to the dentist, for goodness sake! At least with a tooth extraction, you got anesthesia. Was there a magical anesthetic for demon extraction?

Kyle forced himself to sit still, keep his eyes closed, and breathe slowly while Amanda worked. He could still hear her, but not seeing the things that his brain said were impossible helped tremendously.

After several minutes, Amanda unexpectedly rang the bell again. Kyle jumped and reflexively opened his eyes. As with the ward spell, a green shimmer flowed from Amanda to the crucible, which sucked it in and glowed with a white aura that faded quickly. From that point, it sounded like she was finishing up the casting.

Amanda addressed each candle again, releasing the spirits and thanking them for their assistance. The candles went out each time without a trace of smoke, as if she had pinched each wick with wet fingers. Kyle resisted the temptation to close his eyes again, determined to deal with what he was witnessing. He'd be in the middle of it all too soon.

She released the spirits in the opposite order that she'd called them. When she was done, the column of distortion had disappeared. She leaned over and turned the valve Kyle had seen earlier, letting the water drain from the circle.

Amanda's new crucible was filled nearly to the rim with water when she carried it toward the table. She dumped the water into an empty black trash can next to the table.

She held up the crucible proudly and said, "All set. We can safely use it for your ceremony now."

"Awesome," Kyle said without much enthusiasm.

"Are you okay? You look a little pale."

"I'm freaking out here a little, but I think I can hold it together."

She looked up at the wall. The clouds had passed for the moment and the moonlight drew the moon's position line well past the meridian. "Maybe we should wait until tomorrow. I could use a break, honestly. I think I underestimated how much energy the consecration would take. Also, the moon will be up later tomorrow, so we can time the critical part of your ceremony with the meridian."

Kyle collapsed back into the chair, not realizing until that moment that he had literally been on the edge of his seat. "You've convinced me." The last thing he wanted to do was push her limits, given what was at stake. "My nerves are kinda shot anyway."

Amanda finished wiping out the crucible with a dark towel and set it on the table. "Then tomorrow it is. Let's go get something to eat. I'm starving."

Kyle followed Amanda out of the moon shrine and down the stairs. He was both thankful for the reprieve and disappointed that he would have to live with the demon for another day. Maybe by the following night, he'd be able to absorb what he'd experienced and reconcile it in his mind somehow. He was pretty sure that Amanda would think it was poor form to puke inside the circle.

CHAPTER 14

In the Circle

Kyle made himself useful around the farm Sunday morning by helping Lucille in the garden. She set him to work tying up tomato plants that had started to tip over and picking green beans from a tall trellis.

He had no idea that pole beans could be so prolific. He laughed when Lucille set out a five-gallon bucket for him, but an hour later, the bucket was full and he was starting to think he might be able to fill a second one.

"That will do for today," Lucille said. She had a basket on her hip filled with summer squash and a half-dozen fresh herbs.

"How are you going to eat all these?" he asked.

"One bite at a time," she answered, shuffling off toward the house.

Kyle picked up the bucket and followed.

At the screen door, Amanda took the bucket from him and said, "You have a call. It's the front-desk guy from the hotel."

Kyle thanked her and ran inside to pick up the receiver. "This is Kyle."

"Hey, this is Earl down at the Ponderay Hotel. That little lady of yours checked out this morning, and I've got folks who'd like the room if you're willing to give it up. I'll give you a refund for the unused days, of course."

"She checked out already? Did she say where she was going?"

"Nope. Didn't ask. None of my business. She just turned in her key and left. So how about that room?"

"Sure, you can have it back."

"All righty then. Come on by when you get the chance and I'll cut you a check for the balance. You have a good day, now."

"Thanks, same to you."

Kyle hung up the phone with smile on his face. Sherry must have found another place to stay already. Good for her. The sooner she moved on with her life, the sooner she could forget about him.

Amanda peeked her head out of the kitchen doorway and saw that he was smiling. "Good news?"

"Yep. I think I may have one less complication in my life. Sherry checked out of the hotel this morning."

Amanda stepped fully into the room, a look of concern on her face. "Are you okay with that?"

"Absolutely. I didn't want to kick her when she was down, but if she's ready to move on by herself, I'm thrilled for her."

"Cool. Well then, let's get to canning."

"Canning?"

"You didn't think we were going to eat all those beans tonight, did you?" Amanda said with a wink.

For the next few hours, Kyle helped Lucille and Amanda prep and preserve the green beans. "Canning" was a bit of a misnomer because the jars were made of glass, but the result was the same. They pickled about half of the beans as "dilly beans," which Amanda assured him were delicious. Kyle was surprised to discover that he enjoyed himself and gained a new appreciation for gardening and self-reliance.

They were cleaning up in the late afternoon when Amanda suggested to Kyle that they go for another horseback ride.

"I'd love that," Kyle responded. He set aside the pot he was cleaning and turned to face Amanda and Lucille. "You know, I want to thank you both for letting me stay here and share your lifestyle for a while. I'm having a great time. Much better than I expected."

Lucille smiled and nodded. "You're quite welcome. I appreciate your willingness to lend a hand. This *lifestyle* can be a lot of work, particularly this time of year."

The phone rang and Amanda left the room to answer it. Kyle went back to his cleaning, but then Amanda yelled his name, saying the call was for him.

Kyle went to the phone expecting it to be the hotel guy again, since few other people even knew he was at the ranch. But the disturbed look on Amanda's face told him it was someone else. She put her hand over the receiver and whispered, "It's Sherry," before handing the phone to him. She left the room to give him some privacy.

Kyle hesitantly put the handset to his ear. He hoped Amanda was mistaken. "Hello?"

"Just tell me one thing. Are you sleeping with her? Miranda, or Sandra, or whatever her name is."

Amanda was not mistaken. How had Sherry gotten this number?

"That's a hell of a greeting, Sherry. And the answer is no, not that it's any of your business."

"How can you say that? We were engaged to be married. I thought we were working things out. Until you ditched me at the hotel."

Sherry's voice sounded *off* somehow.

"What's the matter with you? Have you been drinking?"

"I've had a glass of wine or two. Who cares? It's Sunday and I don't have to drive anywhere."

Well, that explained it. Sherry didn't hold her liquor well.

"Where are you, anyway?" Kyle asked.

"I'm where you should be. That's why I called. You need to get your butt up here and be with people who care about you and can help you instead of hanging out with that dark-haired whore."

Kyle fell, more than sat, in a nearby chair. The blood drained from his head so quickly that he saw stars in the corners of his eyes.

She had indirectly answered his question, but he had to hear her say it. "Tell me where you are."

"I'm at the Rutlinger Foundation. Dr. Rutlinger and his friends told me about your illness and how stubborn you are being about getting treatment. I told them I wanted to help, and they offered to let us use a spare room while you're in recovery so you won't have to keep paying for the hotel room."

"Sherry, listen to me. I want you to start drinking water and coffee right now and make up an excuse to leave when you think you can drive safely. Get out of there as soon as you can. Those people are not what they seem."

Sherry sighed noisily into the phone. "They warned me you'd react this way. You can't play around with this degenerate nerve stuff, Kyle. Let them help you. Let *me* help you."

Kyle assumed she meant *degenerative* nerve disease. That was apparently what Dr. Rutlinger had told her was wrong with him. She clearly wasn't getting his message. Kyle couldn't come right out and tell her the truth about them because she'd never believe him. Anything he told her would sound like an excuse to avoid "treatment."

Dr. Rutlinger's deep, cultured voice came on the line. "Hello, Kyle. We were hoping Sherry would be more persuasive. Perhaps giving her the wine was a miscalculation."

Kyle stood up, clenching his free hand into a fist. "Let her go. She has nothing to do with this."

"Relax. Sherry is free to leave whenever she wishes. But she wants to help you, Kyle. I think it's commendable that she is so dedicated to you after the poor way you've treated her."

Kyle put his head in his hand. The Pack had taken the standoff to the next level. They said Sherry was free to go, but Kyle wasn't fooled. She was a hostage. He had no choice. He couldn't leave Sherry in their hands.

"If I come up there, will you let her go?"

"Whether she stays or leaves is up to you and her."

Bastard.

Kyle shook his head. "Fine. I'll be there within a couple of hours."

The line went quiet for a moment. "I'm glad to hear it, but it won't be quite as easy as that."

Kyle blew out a breath in frustration. "What are you talking about? What do you want now?"

"It's not about what *I* want. You have taken sanctuary with your friends. They will feel obligated to talk you out of coming. You must convince them it is for the best."

With Sherry listening in, the man was careful with his wording, but his message came through loud and clear. If Kyle wanted to leave, he would have to release himself from the protection of the Order.

"Okay, so it might take a little while, but I'll be there. Please don't hurt Sherry."

"This paranoia is a symptom of your illness, Kyle. We have no wish to harm anyone. Everything will be fine if you let us take care of you."

Yeah, right. More doublespeak.

If only Sherry knew what she dealing with. She'd run away screaming, like he wished he could.

"Goodbye, Dr. Rutlinger." Kyle hung up the phone without waiting for a response.

Kyle went into the kitchen and sat heavily at the table. Lucille and Amanda looked up from their cleaning efforts, but both waited for him to speak.

He got right to the point. "They have Sherry."

Lucille wiped her hands on a towel and turned to face Kyle. Her face had the predatory glare of a raptor. "Are you saying that they are holding her against her will at the Foundation?" Her voice was cold and laden with implication.

"Not exactly. They've convinced her that my unusual behavior is caused by some disease. She believes she's helping them bring me in for treatment. They claim she is free to go, but I'm not convinced that's true. I have to go up there and get her away from them."

Lucille took a step forward and pointed a finger at him. "You will do no such thing. You will stay in sanctuary and let the Order handle this."

Amanda had been standing silently throughout the exchange. Before Kyle could respond, she held up a hand and spoke. "Wait. Think about this. Why would they kidnap a normal, knowing that the Order wouldn't stand for it? Even if Sherry *is* free to go, involving her was risky."

Kyle shrugged. The answer was obvious. "They want me at the Foundation before First Moon."

Amanda's thoughtful expression didn't change, but she subtly shook her head, rejecting Kyle's answer.

Lucille watched Amanda closely. "What are you thinking?" she asked.

"I'm thinking this is more about getting Kyle away from me than it is about getting him to the Foundation."

The room went silent while everyone digested the possibility.

Lucille frowned, giving Amanda a concerned look. "If that's true, and they believe you may have figured out a way to free Kyle, your knowledge will become a terrible danger to them."

A chill ran down Kyle's spine. It was bad enough being a target of the Pack when they wanted you *alive*. Both Sherry and Amanda were in grave danger, and it was all because of him.

Kyle stood and squared his shoulders. "Look, I'm not trying to be a hero or anything, it just doesn't make sense for everyone else to pay for my mistake. I'm the one who slept with Clarissa and got myself into this mess. Let me go to them and end this." Amanda started to protest, but Kyle spoke over her. "I'm sorry you won't have the chance to test your theory, but it would be a lot safer for you to accept that nothing can be done."

Amanda narrowed her eyes at him. "Never," she said between clenched teeth. "I won't let a bunch of demons scare me into giving up on you or my brother. The Order may not share my faith in finding a solution, but all of the other hunters have my back. Don't you dare give up on me."

Kyle's shoulders slumped. "But what are we going to do? I can't leave Sherry with a bunch of werewolves."

Lucille came forward and gripped Kyle's shoulder with one strong hand. "Listen to me. Sherry will be fine. They don't dare hurt her, and when they figure out that their plan has failed, they will send her on her way. To make sure that happens, I will speak with our Director of the Hunt, the man who oversees Order activities in this region. The werewolves defy *him* at their peril."

Amanda gave him an encouraging smile. "Trust us, Kyle. Sherry is not in any real danger, but you still are. The best way to end this is for us to be successful tonight. You'll get your life back, and they won't have any reason to bother you."

"Okay, I'll stay if you promise the Order will get Sherry away from them." He glanced at both women, who nodded solemnly.

Amanda went over to Kyle and gave him a hug, patting him on the back as she released him. "I'm glad that's settled. Let's get the rest of this cleaned up and take Buck and Edna for a spin around the pasture."

While Kyle helped with the cleanup, he continued to worry about Sherry. By the time he walked out to the stables with Amanda, he had decided to trust his new friends and their faith in the Ternion Order. Besides, the best revenge against the Pack would be to rid himself of this *lupusdaemon* that had destroyed his life. All he had to do was survive the exorcism.

~

When Kyle emerged at the top of the stairwell on Sunday night, the moon shrine didn't intimidate him nearly as much as it had the night before. Then, the room had seemed dark and heavy and every object in it was mysterious and potentially dangerous. He commented on the change in atmosphere as Amanda entered the room after him.

"It does tend to get that way if I'm away from it for a while. The nature of the work I do attracts both light and dark spirits. Sometimes the shadows are so thick in here that the lights barely push them back."

Kyle shivered, thinking about how he had tromped around the shrine the prior night, oblivious to the reason for his unease.

"Are the dark spirits dangerous?"

Amanda went around him to the covered table, or her "altar" as she called it, and started moving items to the concrete pad. "They aren't dangerous so much as meddlesome. They mess with your head by exaggerating your dark emotions. If I don't banish them, they'll interfere with my work."

"Can't you permanently consecrate the shrine?"

"You mean like a church? No. This is too private a space. A church remains consecrated because it's in almost constant use by the clergy and the congregation, and that continually refreshes the wards. But even a church quickly loses that protection if it's desecrated or abandoned."

Kyle relaxed in the chair to stay out of the way while Amanda prepared the circle. Unlike the night before, she put everything outside the circle. After placing the colored candles, she surveyed her collection with her hands on her hips.

She beckoned Kyle. "Would you please move the chair to the center of the circle?"

Kyle picked up the chair and carried it to the pad. He stopped at the edge, reluctant to step up onto it.

"Go ahead," Amanda said. "Cross between the candles."

He stepped up into the circle and set the chair down. He leaned back and adjusted it a couple of times until it was as centered as he could make it.

He looked at Amanda for approval and she nodded once. "That's fine. It doesn't have to be perfect." He was about to leave the circle when she added, "Have a seat."

Kyle sat down and wiped his clammy palms on his shorts. The demon surged from the shadows of his mind and struggled to exert control, and Kyle held his breath while he fought against the surprise attack. It clawed forward into his consciousness so far that Kyle nearly echoed its growl of frustration when he finally pushed it back into its dark corner. Nervous sweat trickled down the nape of his neck, and Kyle calmed himself with the thought that anything the demon disliked was probably a *good* thing for him.

Even though the concrete pad was only a couple of inches thick, the higher elevation made him feel like he was on stage. The circle seemed much smaller from his new vantage point, and the claustrophobic impression made his flesh crawl. If Amanda intended to join him, she wouldn't have much room to work. Glancing down at her tools sitting outside the ring, he suspected she had other plans.

He started to ask a question, but the first word came out as a squeak. He cleared his throat and tried again. "Why am I inside the circle?"

Amanda seemed to notice his distress for the first time. "Sit back and relax, Kyle. The circle will protect you while we cast out the demon. If we can get it out, it won't be able to go back."

Kyle was relieved to hear that, but if the circle was protecting him, what was protecting Amanda? Rather than distract her with the question, he decided to trust that she knew what she was doing.

Amanda checked the moon's position using the lines on the north wall. The moon line was about a foot from the meridian line. She gave Kyle an encouraging smile. "Are you ready? Once I get started, don't speak unless I ask you a question, okay?"

Kyle nodded and clenched his hands together in his lap. "Ready."

Amanda started by putting on a strange necklace that had a loop and pendant at both the front and the back. She asked the spirits of the light to shield her, and a glowing nimbus spread from the pendants until it encased her entire body.

Amanda moved on to perform a ritual that was similar to the one she'd used the previous night to consecrate the crucible, but she went around the outside of the circle instead of the inside. She had her back to him when she called to the spirits of each element, but the candles lit exactly as they had the night before. The wording of her spell was significantly different, asking the spirits to prevent the demon from escaping.

When she began painting the shimmering wall of force with her feather fan, a headache bloomed in Kyle's head. By the time she had completed the circle, the pain had grown so strong that he pressed his hands to his temples. The demon was trying a new tactic. It strummed his fears and doubts like an instrument, triggering an urgent desire to leave the circle. Kyle fought the impulse, certain it would unravel all of Amanda's work.

Amanda sat cross-legged, facing Kyle, with the brass crucible in front of her. She poured a small amount of what appeared to be sand into the vessel and lit a chunk of charcoal, which continued to glow when she blew it out. She appealed to the spirits again, burning small amounts of pungent herbs on the charcoal.

"Spirits of the light, I call you to help save this mortal soul known as Kyle Nelson from the dark spirit that seeks to possess his body. Bring the power of light to bear on this dark shadow and drive it forth. Send it back to its origin and let it plague the living no more."

Kyle gasped as the pressure in his head intensified. His vision narrowed until all he could see was Amanda against a backdrop of shadow. He touched his nose in response to a tingling sensation in his nostrils and glanced down to find blood on his fingertips.

A long, mournful howl broke the stillness of the night and penetrated the windows of the cupola, causing Amanda and Kyle to both look up. Amanda's face settled into a determined mask. She picked up the double-edged blade she called an "athame" and pointed it toward the circle; her eyes widened when she noticed the blood on Kyle's face, but she didn't stop. She called to the spirits again, using the same words.

The pressure in Kyle's head suddenly relented, but it was like pushing against a door that suddenly gave way. Reeling disorientation took the place of the pain. He gripped the chair arms tightly to stop the room from spinning, but it was no use. His heart was pumping so hard that his pulse pounded in his neck.

And then he was falling. It was as if the concrete pad had dropped open like a trap door and dumped him into a black chasm. But there was no sound and no rush of air. He had no mouth to scream with and no arms to wave in panic. The entirety of his experience was total darkness and the sensation of falling into an abyss.

He mentally cringed, expecting to crash-land any second. The fall continued. He couldn't feel his arms or legs, but he tried to reach out tentatively anyway. He found nothing. After another few moments, the falling sensation faded. Had he been floating the whole time? It was impossible to tell. But even falling was better than the total sensory deprivation that had taken its place.

He tried to call out to Amanda, but he couldn't hear his own voice or feel his lungs taking a breath to shout. Where was he? How did he get there? Why was he disconnected from his senses?

That was when it hit him. The demon had shoved him aside. Kyle was learning what it felt like to be fully possessed.

He could look forward to that kind of existence for the rest of his body's biological life if the exorcism failed. Would the death of his body free him at last, or would his awareness be trapped in the darkness forever?

He doubted that he'd ever know the answer, since he would probably go insane within a few days.

He couldn't let the demon win. He had to retake control of his body. But how? Mentally probing the darkness that surrounded him, he found the same nothingness in every direction.

Then he heard a voice calling his name. It was Amanda! A tiny fuzzy light-blob appeared in front of him. The blob grew and slowly resolved into an image. It was Amanda, still seated outside the circle. Tears streamed down her face as she repeatedly called his name and begged him to answer her.

Kyle's awareness slammed back into his body with such force that every nerve ending tingled. It was as if the circulation to all his limbs had been constricted and then released. He rolled his head back and took deep breath, reveling in the simple act of drawing air into his lungs.

Amanda had brought him back. Was the demon gone?

No. Its lurking presence still crouched and growled from the shadows of his subconscious.

She gulped and stared, her chest heaving while she tried to catch her breath. "Kyle, say something. Are you all right?"

As good as it was to be back in his own body, Kyle was so exhausted that he could barely hold his head up. He nodded and managed to whisper, "Been better."

Amanda immediately launched into her ritual for ending the session and releasing the spirits. After she drained the water from the circle, she kneeled next to the chair and took his hand in hers.

"I'm so sorry," she said.

Kyle closed his eyes and bowed his head. "It didn't work."

She squeezed his hand. "The demon manifested. It said … unpleasant things. I couldn't drive it out."

Kyle squeezed back. "Thanks for trying. Can we talk later? I need to lie down."

She stood and held out a hand to help him up. "Of course. You should try to eat and drink a little something first. Let's go downstairs."

Kyle accepted her help and rose from the chair. His fatigue made the trip downstairs seem like part of a dream. He was famished, but only managed to swallow a few bites before his head was nodding over his plate. Lucille and Amanda helped him to his room, and the last thing he remembered that night was falling onto the bed.

CHAPTER 15

The Totem

Kyle woke up the next morning feeling rested, although a mild headache reminded him of the prior evening's failure. Hunger pangs gnawed at his stomach, encouraged by the aroma of coffee and cooking food filtering into his room through the door.

He levered himself out of bed and put on the shoes that someone had been kind enough to remove for him. He was still wearing his clothes from the previous day, but decided not to worry about that until after he'd investigated the inviting smells.

As soon as he appeared at the kitchen doorway, Amanda poured him a cup of coffee and put it into his hands. She looked over her shoulder at Lucille. "You were right. As soon as you started making breakfast, he appeared like magic."

Lucille flipped a couple of pancakes out of the pan and onto a plate and then winked at Amanda. "Most men respond positively to regular feeding."

Kyle sat at the kitchen table with a sigh and sipped his coffee. Amanda brought two plates of pancakes to the table and set one down in front of him. Taking a seat in the opposite chair, she joined Kyle in spreading butter on the cakes and taking turns with the syrup.

Kyle started feeling better as soon as he had consumed a few heaping forkfuls. He stopped only long enough to thank Lucille and compliment her cooking. He was eating the last bites of the first three pancakes when Lucille came by with another stack on her spatula. Kyle dug in, thanking her again.

Amanda accepted one additional pancake and told Lucille she'd take care of the cleanup.

Lucille took off her apron and washed her hands. "Thanks, dear. I should get down to the shop. I'm expecting deliveries today."

After Lucille left the kitchen, Kyle and Amanda ate in silence. Amanda finished first and sat with her hands wrapped around her coffee cup. Her gaze landed everywhere except on Kyle. For his part, Kyle focused on his plate until he had mopped up the last bit of syrup with his final forkful of pancake.

Kyle sat back and patted his stomach. He took a gulp of his coffee, now lukewarm, and stared at Amanda over the rim of his cup. Her eyes met his and then dropped.

"So what's next?" he asked.

Amanda eyes were sorrowful when they met his. "I don't know. My bag of tricks is empty. All that research and preparation was apparently for nothing."

Kyle kept his voice even. "So you're giving up?"

Her voice took on an annoyed edge. "Is it *giving up* to stop when you've done all you can and have no way to move forward?"

He couldn't deny that she had been working hard on the project. But she'd had to do everything by herself. Maybe she needed an outsider's perspective.

"I want to help."

Amanda's gaze softened. "Kyle, you keep telling me that you know nothing about what I do."

"That's true. Maybe you need to go over everything with someone who will ask stupid questions. Someone who will make you challenge your assumptions. Maybe you know *too* much about this stuff and your knowledge is creating blind spots."

Amanda didn't look like she was buying his suggestion. She rotated her cup in her hands.

Kyle decided to press his argument. "Amanda, when the demon took over last night, it pushed me into a place I never want to visit again. I'm not being melodramatic when I say I'd rather die. Please let me help you figure out what went wrong so we can try again."

Amanda stared at Kyle, her eyes wide. "Reggie has been in that place for nearly two years."

Kyle shrugged. "Maybe. Who knows if the same thing happens at First Moon." He hated to say his next words, but she needed to understand what was at stake. "I don't think I could remain sane if I stayed in that limbo for any length of time."

Amanda blinked away tears and pressed the heels of her hands to her face. She sniffed and took a deep breath. Tipping her cup to check the contents, she drained the last bit of coffee and set the cup down with a thump of finality.

"Okay, why not? If we don't come up with anything, we'll be in no worse shape than we are now."

It wasn't quite the enthusiastic response Kyle was hoping for, but it would have to do. He finished his coffee and then helped Amanda straighten up the kitchen.

~

Later that afternoon, Amanda and Kyle were at a small square table in one corner of her office. She had laid out all of the materials she'd collected relating to lycanthropy and the legendary ritual that cured it.

They had disappointingly little to work with.

Amanda worked at her computer while Kyle read the account of the Navajo medicine man's ritual. It took a while to work through the odd phrasing and spelling common to the period. It was obvious from the start that the ritual described by the observer was substantially different from what Amanda had done. When he asked her about that, she said she couldn't duplicate the medicine man's ritual because she didn't have his exact wording and the ceremony was based upon his own belief system. In a sense, she'd had to re-write the recipe using her own ingredients. Unfortunately, her recipe hadn't been close enough to produce the same outcome.

He glanced at her as Amanda started typing a message. "I can move to the porch if you need to get some work done," he offered.

"No, that's okay. I took the week off, and I'm just making sure no emergencies or questions have come up. I have a couple of messages to send and I'll be done."

He was humbled by how generous she was being with her time. "I'm grateful for the sacrifice you're making. I hope I'm not making your life difficult financially."

Amanda laughed. "Don't worry about it. My expenses are low and I've got plenty of savings. I haven't had a vacation in too long anyway."

Kyle harrumphed. "Some vacation."

Amanda stopped typing and sat back in her chair. She looked at Kyle through serious eyes. "If we succeed, it will be the best vacation ever."

Kyle smiled and patted the pages in front of him. "Working on it."

Amanda returned his smile and went back to typing.

To eliminate the mental translation he had to perform every time he read the Navajo ritual, Kyle started rewriting a translation in his own words. The process turned out to be more valuable than he'd anticipated because it helped him highlight parts of the account that were vague or confusing.

He reasoned that if something was wrong with Amanda's ritual, it was most likely to be in one of the parts that was poorly described.

He was finishing up his translation when Amanda joined him at the table. He handed the original documents and his translation to her. "What do you think? Did I get it right?"

Amanda went through the pages. About half-way through, she looked up at him with respect. "This was a good idea. I wish I'd thought of it earlier. I was too focused on formulating my own ritual."

"It may not make any difference," Kyle said. "But I got tired of the convoluted language. The narrator seemed to back up a couple of times, so I rearranged everything to put it in the right order."

Amanda handed the pages back to him. "Looks good to me. What's next?"

Kyle was approaching the problem similar to the way he solved programming challenges. After all, they were essentially debugging Amanda's exorcism ritual. The Navajo ritual was like an old program that had to be rewritten in a new language, and they had to be careful to support all of the operating assumptions that were inherent in the old code.

Kyle gave Amanda an apologetic glance. "Just so you know, this could take a while and it may try your patience." He paused and Amanda nodded for him to go on. "I now know *what* the medicine man did, but I need to understand *why* he did it. I want to go through every step of his ritual and have you explain what it means. Then we can review what you came up with and see how it matches up."

The look Amanda gave him was dubious. "How will you be able to criticize my work without a background in what I do?"

Kyle was used to hearing that question. Many of the subject-matter experts he'd worked with in the past didn't understand that he only needed them to explain their process, not justify it. Kyle's job as the programmer was to make their job easier by automating the parts that were the most tedious, repetitive, and prone to error.

"I'm not going to criticize your work, I'm going to question it. You'll have to handle all the critique yourself. This will be the dumb-question phase of the analysis that I warned you about earlier."

Amanda chuckled and nodded. "Okay, that actually sounds useful."

Kyle shifted his chair next to Amanda's and they went through the Navajo ritual one step at a time. Kyle kept notes as they went along, and he started to appreciate how much time she had already spent researching Navajo symbolism and mysticism. They found only a couple of places where she'd had to make a questionable judgment call, and that was mostly due to a deficiency in the narration.

At first, Kyle was disturbed that some guesswork was involved.

Amanda reassured him. "These rituals aren't as rigid as you might expect. Two different medicine men, even from the same nation, might approach it differently. The main thing we need to do is understand the mechanisms they used to achieve the purpose of the ritual. Every belief system wraps its own 'noise level' of symbolism around that fundamental purpose. Like you said, *why* is more important than *how*, particularly when we are trying to separate the noise from the core elements."

That made sense. Analyzing any process often revealed aspects that were irrelevant or had become obsolete over time. Calling it noise level was a good analogy.

By the time they were done, Kyle felt like he had a good understanding of the medicine man's ritual. The core elements were surprisingly logical, and the Navajo mysticism that enveloped it added an elegance that inspired awe.

"It's like some kind of performance art," Kyle observed.

"It is!" Amanda agreed. "When I perform a ritual, it's almost like a dance with the spirits. The more focused and engaged I am, the smoother it becomes and the better it feels. A ritual that goes perfectly can leave me feeling euphoric for hours."

Kyle took her hand in his and looked into her eyes, smiling at the excitement he saw there. "That's so cool." His breath caught as he stared into the depths of her pretty hazel eyes. The two of them were practically shoulder to shoulder, so their faces were only inches apart. Amanda returned his stare, her head tilting slightly in a quizzical way. His eyes went to her lips, and he wondered what it would be like to kiss her. He turned away and released her hand. "Sorry."

She patted his hand. "That's okay. Maybe we can continue that conversation when this is over and the demon is gone."

Kyle gave her a lopsided grin. "I'd like that. Particularly the 'demon is gone' part."

"Then let's get busy. We still have to go over my interpretation."

They spent the next hour going over Amanda's version of the ritual. Kyle was able to follow Amanda's rationale for every decision she had made to translate the Navajo exorcism to her own. All of the core elements seemed to be present.

"It should have worked," Kyle concluded.

Amanda rested her forehead on her hand and didn't bother responding.

"What exactly did the demon say when it … took over?" Kyle asked.

Amanda gave him an incredulous look. "You think the demon would have given me a clue for improving the ritual?"

"Not intentionally. Tell me what it said."

"It said I was wasting my time. It said it could not be exorcised, and better mortals than me had tried and failed. I argued that a mortal *had* succeeded before and that I would do it again. It laughed at me and said I didn't have what it takes."

Kyle thought for a minute. Maybe the demon *had* given them a clue. An idea began to form, but before he pursued it, he needed more context.

"When did you first feel like things were getting out of control?"

Amanda got a distant look while she considered his question. "I hate to say it, but as soon as I started on the exorcism itself, something was off." She put her finger down on the first page documenting the steps of her ritual. "All of the stuff up to here is common to nearly every spell I cast. The exorcism itself happens from here to right before I release the spirits."

Her answer didn't help much from a diagnostic perspective. It was like a program throwing a general error message. But it showed they were missing something fundamental.

"When did the demon start talking?"

Amanda flipped through the pages of her ritual. She pointed to a step on the third page and said, "Right here. The moment I called it forth to draw it out of you, it manifested in your body and spoke to me instead."

Kyle shuddered at the memory of what that moment had been like for him. He quickly turned his attention back to what Amanda had experienced.

An idea continued to tickle the back of his mind. They were missing something fundamental. Sometimes programs failed in strange ways because of a problem in their environment. Like when they lost their connection to a database or were missing a configuration file. The program could be perfectly fine, but if it wasn't installed correctly, it would fail, and often with confusing or even misleading side effects.

Amanda was watching him think. When he glanced at her, she raised an eyebrow in query.

"What do you suppose the demon meant by, 'You don't have what it takes'?"

Amanda shrugged. "It was an insult. The demon thinks I'm incapable of performing the exorcism."

Kyle picked up the pages he had written documenting the Navajo ritual. Not seeing what he wanted, he went back to the original text.

"The medicine man walked forward and put his hands over the wolf-man's head. Gripping the wolf skull, he called forth the demon. He then raised his hands high and cast the demon into the abyss."

Amanda had been reading along with him. Her voice took on an edge of impatience. "Okay. We have that part. That's where I called forth the demon. And it *came* forth. Like I explained before, I don't need to physically touch you for a ritual involving spirits. All that would do is put *me* at risk of possession."

"What if we've been reading this wrong? We assumed he gripped the skull of the wolf-man. What if he literally had a wolf skull in his hands instead?"

Amanda frowned and sifted through the original account. "I don't see any other mention of a wolf skull."

"True, but everywhere else, the narrator calls the victim the wolf-man. This is the only unqualified use of the term 'wolf' in the whole account of the ritual."

Amanda sat back in her chair, looking thoughtful.

Kyle thought they might be on to something, but didn't want to get his hopes up yet. "Does such a thing even make sense in this context?"

Amanda nodded. "Many Navajo rituals make use of a totem. They can be powerful tools. The medicine man might have used the wolf skull as some kind of spirit trap."

Kyle leaned forward, unable to hide his excitement. "That would fit the narration, wouldn't it? The medicine man drew the demon into the wolf skull and then cast it away."

Amanda pursed her lips, but the excitement in her eyes gave away her growing interest. "Let me look into this. We don't have time to create a talisman like that from scratch, but I might be able to find a substitute somewhere nearby."

Kyle tried to hold back his enthusiasm. There was no way to know if he had interpreted the passage correctly. They could be following a dead-end path. "Do you really think I might be right about this?"

Amanda looked him in the eye with a serious expression. "I really do. I should have expected the medicine man to use a totem for this ritual."

Kyle exhaled in relief. "Don't be hard on yourself. It's easy to focus on what's in front of you and never realize when something is missing."

Kyle volunteered to make lunch while Amanda started her search for a totem or some other talisman they could use for another try at the exorcism. He hoped she would find something nearby, but it was a good bet they wouldn't be able to try again that evening. That left only three more nights until First Moon.

~

Tuesday morning, Kyle and Amanda cruised south on Highway 95 in her Toyota RAV4. Kyle could hardly contain his excitement. Late Monday afternoon, Amanda had located a totem that might turn out to be exactly what they needed.

Through her connections in the Order, Amanda had found a collector of American Indian artifacts near Coeur d'Alene, about a forty-five-minute drive south of the farm. Derek Bell, the collector, welcomed Amanda's interest in his hobby and invited her to come and see it. He was willing to loan items from his collection if the borrower paid a fee and signed a contract that spelled out the terms of the loan and the penalties for loss or damage.

During the first part of their journey, Amanda didn't say much. She was still annoyed by Kyle's insistence on accompanying her. She had wanted him to stay at the farm, but he didn't trust the Pack to honor the refuge with Amanda gone and Lucille at her shop in town. He argued that he would be safer with her, and he needed to feel like he was contributing somehow.

Kyle would have lost the argument if luck hadn't intervened. When Jonathan called to check in with Amanda, he suggested that he follow them down and back; he had an errand to run that he could take care of while they visited with Mr. Bell. The last time Kyle had checked, Jonathan's green Sequoia was a couple of cars behind them.

Music from a local radio station filled the passenger compartment. As they neared the tiny community of Westmond, Kyle turned down the tunes so he could talk to Amanda and try to distract her from her mood. "I still can't believe you found a collector so close. If he has anything suitable, we could try the ritual again tonight."

Amanda shrugged. "It's not that surprising. North Idaho has several reservations. Mr. Bell is himself a descendant of the Coeur d'Alene nation, although he collects artifacts from all over the West. He said he has several Navajo items in his collection."

Kyle's voice took on a skeptical tone. "Sounds like he's got quite a racket going. A hundred bucks minimum to borrow an item for a week, and you're liable for the full value, which is however much *he* decides it's worth."

"Hey, don't knock it. We're lucky Mr. Bell is willing to loan things out to individuals at all."

Kyle couldn't argue with that. Amanda had contacted this particular collector because he was loosely affiliated with the Order. He wasn't a hunter, but he was an accomplished sorcerer who supported the aims of the Order. He recognized objects of power and understood how useful they could be for specific applications. He'd even loan them out to other practitioners—for a price.

After they cruised through Westmond and had accelerated back up to the speed limit, Amanda narrowed her eyes at her rearview mirror. Kyle turned around in his seat to see a large silver pickup truck coming up quickly behind them. Jerks in large trucks were common in North Idaho, so she was right to go on the alert.

Kyle wasn't surprised when the truck jumped into the oncoming lane of the two-lane highway to pass. No traffic came from the opposite direction, so the driver had plenty of time and room to get around them.

"Here comes an asshole in a hurry," he commented.

Amanda smirked and said, "Typical. Big truck, little brain."

Kyle laughed. "I thought that was supposed to be big truck, little *dick*."

Amanda adopted a superior air. "Yes, but a lady would never say such a thing."

As the truck came alongside them, Amanda took her foot off the gas and let her car decelerate. Kyle would have done the same because cutting back in too close was a typical maneuver for jerk drivers. The truck pulled ahead as expected, but an alarm went off in Kyle's head when the truck started to slow before its rear had cleared the front end of Amanda's car.

The truck started moving back into their lane. Amanda steered as far onto the shoulder as she could, hitting her horn at the same time. The truck's brake lights came on, but all that did was slow it down to match their speed. Amanda had just touched the brake pedal herself when the back of the truck bumped the front end of her SUV.

Although she had her speed down from sixty to about forty-five miles per hour, the truck had bumped the car over so her left tires rode on the pavement and the right tires bumped along in the dirt. Braking was no longer a good option, and she seemed to recognize that. Amanda had a tight grip on the steering wheel and carefully moved the car all the way onto the dirt, mowing down a few highway markers along the way. She was doing great and had slowed to about thirty-five when the front right tire slammed into a big rock that stuck up out of the ground, nearly tearing the steering wheel out of her hands.

"Hang on!" Amanda warned him needlessly.

Kyle had a death grip on the grab handle above the window. It was literally turning into a white-knuckle ride. Amanda struggled to keep control of the vehicle, but the rock seemed to have broken something and the car turned in a wobbling arc toward a line of trees alongside the highway. Amanda's scream was cut off by the crash that threw them forward into the airbags.

The next thing Kyle knew, he was coughing up airbag deployment dust. His face burned from the abrasion of the bag and his ears rang. He called to Amanda, but didn't hear an answer. His eyes watered and stung from the dust, but before he could rub it away, his door opened and someone pulled him from the car.

"I'm fine," he said, unable to see who was helping him. "Make sure the driver's okay."

But no one responded and he was forcefully led away from the car. His eyes cleared enough for him to see that he was being dragged toward the silver truck. He struggled to free himself, but wasn't having much luck, and then the world shifted into slow motion after something stung his neck.

He was lifted bodily into the truck. With his few remaining seconds of consciousness, he looked at the person who was fastening his seat belt, and his heart nearly stopped when he found the angry eyes of Fenris Kellen.

His last thought before passing out was, *where the hell is Jonathan?*

Chapter 16

Sedated

Kyle awoke from a deep dreamless sleep with a pounding headache. He opened his eyes but had trouble focusing them on the featureless white ceiling. Groaning, he tried to raise his head, but a cool hand pushed it back to the pillow.

He wished he were dreaming when he heard Sherry's voice say, "Hey, sleepyhead. I'm glad to see you're finally awake."

He turned his head and found her smiling down at him from a chair next to the bed he was lying on, although her smile didn't ease the pinched look of worry in her eyes. Her left hand held his while her right hand dabbed at his forehead with a cool cloth.

"Water?" Kyle croaked, trying again to sit up.

Sherry tsked at him, but she let him push himself higher on the pillow. Handing him a glass of water from the bedside table, she asked, "How do you feel?"

Kyle took a sip of the water before answering. It tasted so good that he kept drinking until it was gone. Handing the glass back to her, he said, "I feel like I've been run off the road."

Sherry squeezed his hand in sympathy. "They said there was an accident and that you were lucky they were keeping an eye on you. Your symptoms were becoming dangerous, Kyle. It's a good thing they were finally able to start treating you."

Kyle stared at her for a minute. "Is that why I've been unconscious?"

"Yes. Dr. Rutlinger said the drugs can make you drowsy, but you get a break so you can eat and drink something. He said I could talk to you as long as I make sure you eat something. There's a bathroom through that door if you need it."

Kyle levered himself off the bed and made an unsteady attempt to stand. The dark-blue pajamas he wore were a bit large on him and smelled of an unfamiliar laundry product. The idea of a werewolf in pajamas struck him as funny and he chuckled to himself. Sherry took his arm and helped him to the bathroom doorway. He disengaged his arm at the door. "I can handle the rest."

Closing the door, he turned to the mirror above the sink. He looked about as bad as he felt. His hair was sticking up everywhere and his eyelids were sagging with drowsiness. The eyes that stared back at him were the most startling sight of all. His irises were almost completely amber now. He stepped forward and leaned on the counter to catch his breath. He splashed cold water on his face, feeling better with each passing second. If they kept pumping whatever it was into his system, he would have no chance of escaping.

He used the toilet and then washed up. He gripped the door handle, bracing himself to face Sherry again. She was an ignorant pawn in this dreadful game the Pack was playing. He had to figure out a way to get both of them out of there.

Back in the room, he went around Sherry to open the blinds. His breath caught when he saw how full the moon was as it rose above the spiked tree silhouettes to the east.

"Ooh, isn't the moon pretty?" Sherry said from right behind him.

He turned to her. "What day is it? How long was I out?"

"It's Wednesday. They brought you in yesterday afternoon."

Kyle's mouth dropped open and he stumbled back several steps to sit on the bed. It was too late to escape. Thursday night was First Moon, so this was the last night he had for Amanda to do the exorcism. Even if he were able to escape immediately, would Amanda have time to perform the exorcism?

Thinking about Amanda reminded him of the violence of the crash. Had she been hurt? Even if she was okay, had she been able to get the totem? He pulled at the hair on the sides of his head. He had lost more than an entire day!

Sherry sat on the bed next to him and rubbed his back. "It will be okay, Kyle. You're getting the treatment you need."

He sighed in frustration. "Sherry, shut up."

"What? Don't be mean. I'm just trying to help you."

Kyle turned and put his finger gently over her lips. "Listen to me. Their treatment is not the cure you think it is. It has … side effects … that will change me forever. You think it will bring us together, but it won't."

Sherry shook her head and grabbed his hand. "You're in denial, Kyle. They warned me about this."

Kyle pulled his hand away from hers. "Stop and think for a second. Isn't this place a little off? Don't these people seem a little weird?"

Sherry frowned and looked down at her lap. "They're foreign," she declared with a shrug. "Well, Dr. Rutlinger is, anyway." She glanced briefly up at Kyle. "Okay, the obsession with wolves is pretty weird, but some people are into keeping wild animals. I don't agree with it, but I can't do anything about it."

Something occurred to Kyle right then. Would the Order let the Pack get away with kidnapping him while he was under the protection of sanctuary? Why hadn't they demanded his release? Or had they? He had been unconscious for a day and a half. But Sherry hadn't been.

Kyle turned on the bed to face Sherry. "Did you hear anything else about the crash? Did anyone come looking for me afterward?"

Sherry's expression changed to one of supreme disappointment. "You just want to know if *she's* okay." She flicked a glance at him, but he didn't try to deny it. "From what I hear, the dark-haired witch is fine."

Her use of the term *witch* surprised Kyle. Had the werewolves been revealing secrets? How much did Sherry understand now about what was happening?

"Did you say *witch*?"

Sherry waved a hand in apology. "Sorry. I know you like her. But that's what the lawyer calls her, and I think it fits."

"How do you know she's okay?"

"I overheard them say she ran toward the truck when they drove away from the scene. I must say it didn't sound like you to leave without making sure she was all right. I'm sure the cops would have wanted to get your statement as well." She shrugged and added, "But they said your condition is making you do strange things."

Kyle closed his eyes and buried his face in his hands. He had firsthand experience with how persuasive a werewolf could be. He didn't seem to be having much luck with it himself, so he assumed it was one of the demon's skills.

His stomach growled and Sherry got up from the bed to retrieve the food tray. She handed it to him and sat down. "Eat something. You have to be hungry after all this time."

Kyle looked down at the food and tried to figure out what he should do. His thinking was still a little fuzzy from the drugs. He'd need to keep his strength up, so food was probably a good idea. He raised a forkful of the pasta salad toward his mouth and stopped. Dropping the fork back into the bowl, he set the tray aside. He was willing to bet that the food was like Persephone's pomegranate seeds, designed to keep him at the Foundation.

Sherry gave him a quizzical look. "Try it. I had some and it's great."

"I think it might be drugged," he said.

Sherry gave him a dubious look and started to argue, but he interrupted her. "Sherry, we have to get out of here. I want to leave, but these people won't let me go. Even if you believe they have my best interest at heart, you know it's wrong of them to hold me here against my will."

"But you need treatment," she said in a pleading tone.

It was time for some selective white lies. "Their treatment is experimental. It could kill me as easily as cure me. But no matter what, it should be my choice to accept treatment or not, right?"

A slight lift in Sherry's shoulders conceded his point.

Kyle needed her on his side, and needed her to go with him. At the risk of putting her in a panic, he had to lay out some of the truth for her.

"Look, I don't know what they told you about the accident, but it was no accident. They ran Amanda's car off the road. We're lucky no one was seriously hurt. They took me out of the car while I was still disoriented and drugged me before they stuffed me into their truck. They kidnapped me, Sherry. And they nearly killed me in the process."

Sherry wasn't buying it. Her expression went from doubt to concern. "Kyle, the paranoia is part of your illness. Think about what you're saying. It doesn't even make sense. Why would they try to kill you just to bring you here so they could help you?"

"There's more going on here than a treatment facility, and there's more to their interest in me than my illness. Part of the deal, the 'contract' if you will, is that I have to stay here with them indefinitely if I accept treatment. It will change who I am, and you won't be welcome here any longer."

Sherry blinked several times, trying to process what he was telling her.

"Let me ask you this. Do they have someone out there in the hall watching the room?"

"Yes, Reggie was sitting on the bench at the end of the hall when they let me in."

Kyle wasn't familiar with the layout of the building, but after being there for four days, Sherry should be.

"Is there a staircase at that end of the hallway that leads to an exit?"

"Yes." She stood up and looked down at him with alarm. "Why are you asking me this? Are you planning to sneak out?"

"So, they are watching the room. I can go to the main building, but I can't slip out the back. Doesn't that sound like I'm a prisoner here?"

Kyle stood up. If Sherry went for the door to warn Reggie, he'd have to restrain her. He was getting nowhere. If she didn't come around, he might have to gag her and tie her up, hoping the Pack would let her go when she was no longer useful to them. So far, they hadn't killed anyone, but they were demons after all.

A light flashed on the wall through the blinds, catching Kyle's eye. He went to the window and looked out. The window was on the second floor of the building, so he could see part of the plateau near the entrance to the compound. The trees blocked his line of sight to the main gate, but a headlight shone through the trunks.

A shout out in the hallway was followed by the pounding of feet. Had Reggie left his post? While Kyle watched, another set of headlights flickered through the trees, approaching the front gate. Could it be the Order?

"What's going on?" Sherry asked.

A thrill of excitement ran through Kyle. Even if it wasn't the Order, it was a distraction. If he was going to escape, the time had arrived.

With that thought, a wave of dizziness hit him so hard he had to put his hand on the wall to maintain his balance.

Sherry put an arm around him. "Are you okay?"

He couldn't answer. The room was spinning and tipping in a way that was frighteningly familiar. The demon was trying to take over again. Kyle's vision tunneled until all that remained was the bright moon. He fought against the pressure in his mind, determined not to let the demon have its way. The moon froze in his vision while he struggled.

Slowly, he started to regain control. Images of the room flashed before his eyes and the sound of Sherry's voice stuttered in his ears like a bad phone connection.

Kyle's hand was on the doorknob, and Sherry was sitting on the bed. She sobbed into her hand as tears trickled over a red mark on her cheek.

He let go of the doorknob as if it had burned him. He slowly approached Sherry and sat next to her on the bed. Her look was wary as he gently touched her face.

"What happened?" he asked her, concern creasing his brow. "Did I do this?"

She cringed from his touch and glared at him. "What's wrong with you? I was just trying to help you back to bed. I know you don't want to be here, but that's no reason to hit me."

"I'm so sorry. You know that's not my way. This is what I've been trying to tell you. Their treatments are turning me into someone I don't want to become."

She stared into his eyes for a moment and then spoke in a hurt tone. "You've never hit me before. And you've never been so mean."

"Now you understand. I *have* to get out of here. If I stay it will only get worse. Something is going on outside, and I think this might be a good time to escape."

Sherry took a deep breath and wiped the tears from her face. After giving him a considering look, she nodded her head. "Okay. But I'm afraid to stay here now. Please let me come with you."

Kyle hugged her. "I was hoping you'd say that." She initially went rigid when he pulled her close, but she tentatively returned the hug after a few seconds.

Kyle released her and started looking around the room. "Where did they put my clothes?" He got up and checked the closet, but it was empty except for a few plastic hangers.

"I don't know," she answered. "I helped put you into those pajamas, but didn't notice what they did with the clothing you were wearing."

After a brief search, he concluded that his clothes weren't in the room. That meant the tincture Amanda had given him wasn't in the room either. Without the tincture, he had nothing to keep the demon in check. It could try to take over again at any time. Clothes or no clothes, there was no time to waste.

He evaluated the pajamas and decided they were dark enough to hide him. They'd probably rip on the first stray branch, but there was nothing he could do about that. Not having any shoes was probably going to exercise his quick-healing ability.

He glanced at Sherry. Her clothes would be adequate for an evening of slinking through the forest. Her red blouse would be practically black in the moonlight, and her jeans would keep her legs from getting scratched.

Her shoes were another story. The white-strapped sandals would do little to protect her feet, and they'd slip on damp grass or leaves. Still, they were probably better than going barefoot.

Kyle checked the window again. The headlights still glared through the trees. A vehicle had left the Foundation parking lot and was crawling up the road toward the front gate. A dark form shadowed its progress, loping through the vegetation along the road.

He turned to Sherry. "Are you ready?"

She blinked in surprise. "You can't go anywhere dressed like that!"

Kyle strode to the door. "Don't worry about me. It's now or never."

He opened the door slowly and peeked through a narrow gap into the hall. No one occupied the small couch at the end of the hallway. He stuck his head into the hall to check the other direction. The stairs to the central building were empty, but he heard a voice. Skyler was using a cell phone to stay in contact with the people who were headed to the front gate.

Kyle looked at Sherry and put his finger to his lips. She gulped and nodded, her eyes wide.

As they slipped into the hall, Kyle locked the door and closed it behind them. If someone came to check on them, the lock might buy them a few extra seconds before an alarm was sounded.

Kyle crept down the hallway toward the stairwell at the end of the wing, pleased with how quietly he could move in bare feet. Sherry did a remarkably good job of tip-toeing in her sandals, making hardly any noise herself.

When they reached the top of the stairwell, Kyle spotted a problem. The stairs went down in two flights with a landing at the middle. A big picture window at the landing would let anyone outside the building see them as they descended. They'd also be back-lit when they opened the door to exit the building.

Kyle took a calculated risk and turned off the stairwell light, hoping that no one would notice and come to investigate. He stood still and waited a minute just in case. Sherry suppressed a big yawn, but otherwise, nothing happened. *How can she be sleepy at a time like this?*

He had reached the landing with Sherry close behind when Skyler's voice got louder in the hallway. The deputy must have started up the stairs from the central building at about the same time he and Sherry started down the stairs at the opposite end of the wing.

Skyler was still talking on the phone, saying something about "going to check on them now."

Kyle and Sherry descended the second short flight of stairs as quietly as possible. Kyle turned the handle on the exterior door, hoping the latch and the hinges were well-oiled. He eased the door open, letting in the cool evening air, right about the time Skyler knocked on the door to the room they had abandoned.

"Sherry?" Skyler's voice called. "How's Kyle doing? Did you get him to eat?"

Kyle urgently waved Sherry through the door and closed it as quietly as possible. It wouldn't be long before Skyler figured out they'd left the room.

The concrete pad outside the door gave way to an expanse of grass that ended at the edge of the forest. Kyle took Sherry's hand and led her toward the trees at a run. Looking back over his shoulder, he checked their path across the grass, but he couldn't see any obvious signs of their passage. No dew had fallen yet, and the blades pressed down by Sherry's shoes were already springing back up.

They entered the trees and moved deeper into the forest. Kyle immediately lamented his lack of shoes as he stepped on dead branches and small pine cones. The moonlight filtering through the trees helped some, but it was impossible to hurry forward and simultaneously be cautious of where he stepped. Disappointingly, an improvement in night vision did not seem to be part of his wolf-upgrade package.

They were about fifty yards from the building when they encountered a narrow wildlife trail. Kyle was able to make much better progress, towing Sherry along in his wake. She stumbled several times and gasped once when a branch snagged her hair, but she was keeping up. They were about a hundred yards from the house when Kyle heard Skyler's voice calling for him. He ducked down and froze, pulling Sherry down with him. Light from a flashlight flickered through the tree trunks far behind them, but the trees were too dense for the beam to reach their position. Kyle rose and continued forward, but Sherry pulled back on his hand.

"Kyle, wait," she whispered. "I can't see where I'm going and I'm getting dizzy. I need to rest."

"Rest? We can't rest. We have to get to the fence line and find a weak spot. We need to flag down one of those cars at the gate before they leave."

Sherry sat down and leaned against a trunk with a sigh. She waved him on and yawned. "You go ahead. It's you they're after anyway. I'll go home tomorrow."

Kyle had his answer about the possibility of drugs in the food.

He took her hand and made her stand. She wavered on her feet. "Nope. I'm not leaving you here." He leaned forward and picked her up in a fireman's carry across his shoulders. She feebly protested and kicked her legs, but he ignored her and continued down the game trail as fast as he dared. Within a minute, her protests trailed off and she went completely limp.

Because of his enhanced strength, her weight was an insignificant burden. He smiled wryly to himself, thinking about how he was using the gifts of his *lupusdaemon* against itself.

Kyle followed the trail until it started curving toward the right, away from the main gate. He left it then and had to move more carefully to keep from damaging himself or Sherry. More than once, something punched into the bottom of his foot, but he ignored the pain and kept moving. He marveled at the way the pain receded almost as soon as it began, the wounds healing within a dozen steps.

He looked down the trail behind them, but could no longer see the beam of Skyler's flashlight. He doubted Skyler would have given up on him, and with a chill, he realized that she may have shifted. If she tracked him in wolf form, she would probably catch up any second.

Kyle increased his pace, accepting more scrapes and bruises for both Sherry and himself. He figured he was about halfway to the gate when he reached an obstacle. A short, rocky cliff separated the upper plateau where the main gate was located from the lower elevation of the Foundation building. It wasn't much more than ten feet high, but Kyle didn't see a way to climb up while carrying Sherry.

He could go left until he reached the road or go right and hope he could find a way up the cliff. He was guaranteed to get up onto the plateau if he took the road, but he was also more likely to encounter Pack members. He went to the right.

The going was easier along the cliff bottom, although the loose rock bruised his feet. He had traveled only about thirty yards when he found the game trail again and also discovered what he had been looking for. The trail had veered to the right earlier because it went directly to a tumble of eroded stone that created a natural staircase up the cliff. Cursing to himself for leaving the trail and wasting precious time, he clambered up the rocky steps.

Kyle topped the cliff to find himself standing in a small grassy area bordered by boulders and aspen. An angry exchange of voices carried from the gate. He was tempted to run toward the voices, but he was still on the wrong side of the fence. Rocky ridges and tall trees prevented him from seeing anything but a bright glow in the direction of the gate. The game trail continued at a tangent to the gate, so he decided to stay with it. If the forest critters had found a way through the perimeter, he could use it as well.

In spite of his superior strength, Sherry's weight was starting to slow him down. He was sure he could carry her off the property, but he hoped he wouldn't have to face any more steep inclines.

A rustling from below the cliff gave him the impetus he needed to get moving again. With the moon almost directly above, he could clearly see where the path entered the slender silvery aspen trunks. Sherry groaned in discomfort as he shifted her higher onto his shoulder and moved forward. He reached up with his free hand and patted her butt in apology, smiling when he thought about how little she would appreciate the sentiment.

The aspen gave way to pines after a few dozen yards, and the trail started to climb through a fold between two rocky hillsides.

Kyle froze when he heard the snap of a twig from the trail ahead. Had the werewolves already flanked him? He had no idea how many trails led off the property, so he didn't know what the odds were that they would look for him on the path he'd chosen. He had turned halfway around when a growl came from the trail behind him. He was trapped.

With nowhere to go but up the side of the ravine, he lunged and scrabbled as far as he could up the loose rocky soil. He reached out to grab a low branch from one of the trees at the top of the incline, but a strong grip on his ankle pulled him back down to the trail. He slid down on his hip to keep Sherry up off the rocks. The instant he stopped sliding, he twisted and laid her down as gently as possible. Springing to his feet, he turned to face his attackers and was momentarily blinded by a flashlight.

"Kyle?"

The voice behind the flashlight was Amanda's. She pointed the light toward the ground, but all he could make out was two silhouettes blocking the trail. The larger one came toward him, and he dropped into a defensive crouch.

"Kyle, it's okay. It's Amanda and Jonathan. We came to get you out of here."

His vision recovered enough to see that she was telling the truth. He straightened and started to say, "Boy, am I glad …."

Before he could finish his sentence, something large and snarling hurtled past him so close that it brushed his arm. Jonathan went down under the assault, rolling aside to separate himself from the large wolf. He was on his feet with the next roll in a remarkable display of agility.

The animal stood between Kyle and the others, growling fiercely with its hackles raised. This wolf was not Reggie. It was lighter in color and smaller. Kyle guessed that Skyler had shifted form to track him. She apparently could not speak while in wolf form, but her message to Jonathan and Amanda was clear. *He's ours. Get out.*

Amanda pointed a wand of some sort toward the animal as it gathered itself for a leap. "Sleep," Amanda commanded. A blue glow enveloped the wolf right as its rear legs began to uncoil. Its growl changed to a weak canine whine and it collapsed to the ground at Amanda's feet.

"We need to get out of here," Jonathan said. He raised his shirt to reveal a long bloody scratch along his ribs. "Damned wolf."

Amanda shined her flashlight on Sherry as Jonathan kneeled by her side. "What's wrong with her?" Amanda asked. "Did they do this to her?"

"Indirectly," Kyle answered. "She ate some drugged food that was intended for me. She's not hurt, just asleep."

Amanda met his gaze. "That's convenient, actually." She glanced at the wolf. "Less to explain."

"Ignorance is bliss," Jonathan mumbled.

Kyle briefly wished *he* were still ignorant regarding werewolves and witches. He'd love to go back to work tomorrow and forget about everything that happened over the past four weeks.

Jonathan offered to carry Sherry, but Kyle didn't know when she would start to wake up. She'd probably panic if she regained consciousness while being carried by a stranger. Besides, after the brief respite during the wolf encounter, Kyle felt somewhat restored.

Jonathan stood over the wolf, which was twitching in its forced slumber. "Can you shield us, Amanda? I don't want to run into more of them."

Amanda frowned up at the moon. It had progressed across the sky past meridian. She glanced at Kyle and then exchanged a significant look with Jonathan.

He shrugged. "I know it will cost you some energy, but do we have a choice? That sleep spell was a one-shot, right? What if we run into more of them?"

Amanda sighed. "We'll have to fall back on other defenses, and things could get ugly." She leveled an assessing gaze on Sherry's somnolent form, and then she nodded. "Okay, we'll do it your way."

Amanda wore a lightweight vest over a dark long-sleeved t-shirt. The vest was the kind that fishermen wear, with dozens of pockets. She tucked her wand into one of the pockets and extracted a metallic disk from another. The disk had symbols etched into its circumference and a reddish-orange gem of some kind set in the center. Holding the disk in her left hand, she went through a quick ritual, appealing to the spirits for help. She kneeled down and picked up a pinch of soil, which she sprinkled over the disk. A tube of water came from yet another pocket. She levered the stopper off the top with her thumb and slowly washed the dirt away. Finally, she blew gently across the top of the disk, and the gem in the center glowed faintly.

The air was still that evening, but when Amanda blew on the disk, her breath seemed to evoke a stiff breeze. The breeze circled them all, ruffling their clothes as it passed, and then raced off toward the Foundation. Moments later, a deep howl split the night air. Another wolf was hunting them.

"That's our cue," Jonathan remarked.

Kyle picked up Sherry and matched Amanda's swift stride down the trail while Jonathan took rear guard. "What did you do?" Kyle asked Amanda.

"Shh," she admonished. In a whisper, she added, "I obscured our trail. No more talking or the effort will be wasted."

Kyle followed Amanda to the property boundary. When they reached the Foundation's block perimeter wall, he discovered that it merged into a rocky hillside, leaving the wildlife pathway to cross over a steep tumble of boulders. Kyle's bare feet gripped well on the smooth rock, but he had to use his free hand to pull himself and Sherry up and over the peak.

Once they had crossed the boundary, Amanda altered her course and went straight toward the gateway. When the sound of arguing voices became clearer, Amanda crouched and sneaked forward through the trees. Kyle followed as cautiously as he could. Two vehicles were stopped at the floodlit gate entrance.

When Amanda came to a stop, Kyle took advantage of the opportunity to set Sherry down. She moaned, and he worried that she might be waking up, but the voices at the gateway distracted him.

"We aren't leaving until we speak with Mr. Nelson," a woman's voice insisted. It was Noreen. She stood next to the passenger door of the lead car. Her right hand gripped a gnarled staff that was nearly as tall as she was. Lucille stood next to the passenger door of the second vehicle. Both driver seats were occupied, but Kyle had no idea who the drivers might be.

Noreen's demand was met with the smooth and amused voice of Dr. Rutlinger on the opposite side of the closed gate. "Then you will be waiting a long time. As I said, Kyle is resting right now, and I imagine it would be quite difficult to wake him."

"You drugged him," Noreen guessed with sharp disapproval. After a moment's silence, she said, "Then let us speak to his girlfriend. We know she's still here."

Dr. Rutlinger spread his hands. "She refuses to leave his side. It's quite touching."

Noreen angled her staff toward the gate. "You know that there are consequences to kidnapping normals. Turn them over now, or we will be forced to retrieve them."

"Mr. Nelson is *not* a normal, as you well know, and Ms. Baxter is free to leave whenever she wishes. I'm sure she will be more than happy to be on her way Friday after Kyle is feeling better." His voice took on a warning tone. "You have no justification for trespassing on Foundation property."

Amanda crept backward to Kyle and motioned Jonathan to get closer. "We should go out there before Noreen escalates the confrontation."

Jonathan nodded. "I agree. She didn't like being part of the distraction and may try to take a more active role."

Amanda grimaced. "That would be her style." She looked at Kyle. "Follow me out to the second car. I want you and Sherry in the back seat." She then turned to Jonathan. "I'll send Lucille to ride with you in the first car. Stay alert. I don't know how the Pack will react when they see that we have Kyle with us. I'm going to tell Franz to start rolling as soon as we get in."

Jonathan nodded. "Let's do it."

Amanda waited until Kyle had Sherry in his arms and was ready to move. This time, he cradled her with her head resting on his chest so he could quickly slip her into the car.

The need for stealth was behind them, so they boldly walked out of the trees. Jonathan headed toward the first car, waving Lucille to come forward with him. Amanda went straight to the back door of the second car and opened it for Kyle. Leaning in, she said, "We've got them, Franz. Start the engine."

Kyle put Sherry on the seat and closed the door. He ran around to the other side of the car right behind Amanda and slid in next to Sherry. He fastened a seat belt around Sherry while Amanda got in the front and told Franz to leave immediately. The car had already backed around and was driving away by the time he had his own belt buckled.

He looked back toward the gateway through the dust raised by his ride. The last thing he saw was Noreen's intense gaze and an expression of smug satisfaction. Noreen seemed to delight in annoying people. Her parting conversation with Dr. Rutlinger would undoubtedly make her night.

"Thanks for the rescue," Kyle said to Amanda. "I'm glad you weren't seriously hurt in the car accident."

She turned around in her seat and smiled at him. "Hey, you practically rescued yourself. I think everyone was surprised at how quickly we returned from our rescue mission. We thought we were going to have to sneak into the Foundation and liberate you."

"Just the two of you? That was bold."

"Oh, we have a few tricks up our sleeves. Jonathan and I got out before the cars reached the gate. Noreen's job was to keep them distracted while we went to get you."

"Speaking of Jonathan, where was he when we were pushed off the road?"

Amanda raised an eyebrow. "Getting pulled over by a certain deputy sheriff. By the time he arrived at the scene, you were long gone. I was still yelling obscenities at myself for letting you ride with me and at you for talking me into it.

The Pack has been monitoring our movements and waiting for us to make a mistake like that."

Kyle sighed and looked over at Sherry. She had slid into the corner of the seat near the door and was gently snoring through her open mouth. She was going to be fine, but *he* wasn't much better off than he had been in his drug-induced coma. "I'm glad we got Sherry out, but this is probably all a waste as far as I'm concerned. I'll either be dead or going back there on my own by Friday."

Amanda gave him a puzzled expression. "What makes you say that? The protection ward drained me too much to attempt another exorcism tonight, but we still have tomorrow."

Kyle was genuinely confused. "But tomorrow is First Moon, and you need moonlight to do your thing. When the moon rises, it will be too late."

"I don't *need* moonlight to perform magic, but I'm at my strongest in the moonlight. Moonrise is ten minutes after sunset tomorrow. I can get started just before sunset and have the exorcism in progress as the moon rises. As the demon grows stronger, so will I."

Kyle shook his head. "But what about the totem? We never made it to Coeur d'Alene to pick it up."

Amanda gave him a secret smile and winked. "*You* didn't make it to Coeur d'Alene, but *I* did."

Kyle leaned forward, his eyes wide. "You got it?"

"Yep."

A tiny glimmer of hope sparked in his chest. What she was proposing sounded terribly risky, but he had nothing to lose. If she was willing to fight the demon as it emerged on First Moon, he would do everything he could to protect her while she did so.

Chapter 17

Standoff

Kyle lay in the dark, unable to sleep. In truth, he was afraid to sleep. He could feel the demon pushing insistently against his consciousness. When his mind started to wander, the slow chuckle of the demon echoing in the recesses of his mind made him sit up in bed and return to full alertness.

Staying awake wasn't that difficult. He had a lot on his mind, and much of it was frightening. Earlier in the evening, he had partially raised the window of the room he was using at Hayworth Farm, but he jumped at every noise that came in from the outside. Would the werewolves violate sanctuary and kidnap him again? What was that scrabbling sound? Finally, he closed the window and locked it, hoping to calm his nerves.

His room was equipped with two twin beds. Sherry was sleeping in the second one, although her sleep was far from restful. She tossed and turned and made little noises of distress occasionally.

At about three o'clock in the morning, she gasped and sat up. "Kyle?"

"I'm here," he answered. He went over to her bed and sat next to her. The moment she felt his weight settle on the mattress, she reached out and hugged him close.

She looked around at the dimly moonlit room. "Where are we?" she asked in a groggy voice.

"We're at a friend's house. We'll be safe here for now. Go on back to sleep."

Sherry released him from her embrace and scrunched up her forehead. "What friend?"

Kyle didn't think it would be a good idea to tell her they were staying with Amanda. "We're at Hayworth Farm. It belongs to Lucille, the nice lady who runs Butterflies and Rainbows in town."

Sherry was quiet for a moment. She wobbled a little while she tried to process his answer. "That New Age store? How do you know her?"

"It's a long story. Go back to sleep, and I'll tell you about it in the morning."

Sherry grabbed his hand with hers and lay back down. "Okay, but don't leave me here alone."

Kyle patted her arm with his free hand and tilted his head toward his own bed. "I'll be right over there if you need me." He stood up and disengaged her hand from his.

She reluctantly let go. As he walked back to his bed, she turned onto her side so she was facing him. She watched him get back into his own bed and then she finally closed her eyes. Within a minute, her breathing had returned to a slow and steady rhythm.

Kyle spent the remainder of the night leaning against propped-up pillows and imagining all the things that might go wrong with Amanda's exorcism. If it worked, he would be able to walk away from all this insanity. If it didn't, he'd become a permanent prisoner of the sensory abyss.

With nothing to do except think and be terrified by the possibilities, Kyle began to put together a contingency plan.

~

Kyle poured himself a second cup of coffee, draining the last of it from the carafe. He held the pot up and waggled it toward Lucille. "That was it. Should I make more?"

Lucille was chopping onion for the scrambled eggs she was making for breakfast. She glanced over and shook her head. "I'm good. But feel free to make more if you want it."

"How about you, Amanda?" Kyle asked.

"I'm fine," she answered.

Kyle carried his cup over to where Amanda was sitting at the kitchen table. Sitting down with a sigh, he said, "I'll make a fresh pot when Sherry gets up."

Amanda gave him an appraising look. "I think it's going to take more than caffeine to erase those dark circles under your eyes. Did you sleep at all last night?"

"No. I was afraid the demon would take advantage. It's getting stronger."

Amanda swallowed the last of her coffee. "I doubt it will make you feel any better, but I didn't sleep well last night either."

Kyle adopted a thoughtful expression, then shook his head. "Nope. That doesn't make me feel better. You'll need to be at full capacity tonight."

A thump upstairs interrupted Amanda's response and drew both of their eyes toward the ceiling. Kyle said, "Sounds like she's finally awake."

"Hey, give her a break. She was drugged."

Kyle scoffed. "Even without drugs, that woman has an infinite capacity for sleep, believe me."

Amanda grew serious. "We're going to have to watch what we say around her. Have you thought about how you're going to explain what we'll be doing tonight?"

Kyle had indeed thought about that. It was one of the many plans he'd made during his sleepless night. "There's no way to explain it. I have to get her out of here, but is it safe for her to leave?"

"I'm sure she's in no danger from the Pack. Using her to get to you didn't work before, and now there's no time left."

"Don't remind me," Kyle said under his breath. He took a sip of his coffee, but the flavor no longer appealed. "You want some of this?" he asked, poising his cup over Amanda's.

"Sure, I'll take a little more."

Kyle poured some of the steaming brown liquid from his cup into hers.

"Thanks," she said, taking a sip.

"Aw, that's so sweet," came a mocking voice from the doorway. Sherry stepped into the room with her arms folded across her chest and a glare on her face. "You told me this house belonged to someone else."

Kyle got up and motioned for Sherry to take his seat. Amanda leaned away from the table, looking displeased as Sherry hesitantly sat down.

"This is Lucille's house," Kyle said, stepping aside so Sherry could see the woman standing at the stove. Lucille waved a spatula in greeting and went back to her cooking.

Kyle backed away from the table and said, "I'll put on some fresh coffee." He gave Amanda an apologetic look for leaving her with Sherry. The narrow-eyed look Amanda returned told him she thought he was being a coward.

When Kyle went into the kitchen, Lucille raised an eyebrow at him. He tried to ignore her and went about starting a new pot of coffee while keeping an eye on the uncomfortable pair at the kitchen table.

Sherry crossed her legs and arms, and she started bouncing the suspended foot. Kyle held his breath, recognizing her shift into belligerent mode. "What brings you here?" she asked Amanda.

"I live here," Amanda answered in a flat voice.

The foot paused and Sherry cut her eyes to Kyle. "Bastard," she said, just loud enough for him to hear.

She returned her poisonous gaze to Amanda. "So *this* is where he's been hiding? With *you*? I knew it."

Kyle pushed the button to start the coffee and stood watching the glowing red light, postponing the inevitable for as long as possible. Lucille nudged him and tilted her head toward the table. Kyle sighed and walked back to face the two women.

Sherry looked up at him. She was mad, but she also looked hurt. "I understand now why you didn't want to stay with those weirdos at the Foundation, but why did you dump me at the hotel with no explanation? Is this fling with Miranda your way of getting back at me?"

Amanda blinked in shock and her face turned red. Kyle didn't know if she was capable of turning Sherry into a toad, but he was willing to bet that Sherry was one croak away from finding out.

"No, it's nothing like that," Kyle said quickly. "And her name is Amanda. We aren't … involved."

"You two seem pretty cozy to me," Sherry said with a pout in her voice.

Amanda interrupted. "We're just friends. That's all."

Even though her statements were true, they hurt him a little. Kyle knew for certain right then that he would like to become more than friends with her.

Sherry pressed her lips together and looked from Amanda to Kyle. "Fine. Let's say I believe you. When do we leave? We should see if the house is ready yet. We may not have to go back to the hotel."

Kyle wet his lips. This was the part of the conversation he'd been avoiding. "There's no *we*. *You* need to go, but I'm staying here for now."

Sherry stared up at him. Her lower lip trembled and her eyes filled with tears. "After all we've been through, you're giving up now?"

Kyle reminded himself that she didn't understand what was truly at stake. To Sherry, it was all about rebuilding their relationship and helping him get over some mysterious illness. But he had no time left to be gentle with her. So far, being supportive had done nothing but encourage her to think they would get together again.

He hardened his voice. "I gave up when you handed me your engagement ring and walked out the door. I was stupid enough to try to help when you came back broke and lonely. We aren't getting back together, Sherry. Ever."

Tears spilling down her cheeks, Sherry looked at him like he was some kind of monster. "But ... but we had sex."

Kyle threw up his hands and rolled his eyes. "You got naked," was all he said by way of explanation.

Sherry's horror turned instantly to anger. She stood up and slapped him so hard that his ears rang. She ran from the room sobbing. Her feet pounded up the stairs and the door to their room slammed closed.

Lucille set two plates on the table. While she removed her apron, she said, "I'll go talk to her and take her into town with me when I go to the shop. Amanda, please get a couple of tortillas out of the refrigerator and make two breakfast burritos out of the eggs that are still in the pan. We'll eat them on the road."

Amanda seemed stunned by the turn of events. She stammered her response to Lucille. "Sure ... okay ... no problem."

Kyle sat down and started eating, attacking his eggs with his fork and popping them into his mouth forcefully. He was embarrassed and angry, but he was also starving. When he realized Amanda wasn't eating, he glanced up at her and did a double-take. She was staring at him, and although she was keeping a straight face, her eyes crinkled with mirth.

"What?" he demanded.

"*You got naked?*"

He blushed and swallowed. "Well, she did. What was I supposed to do? Tell her, 'No thanks' ?"

Amanda picked up her fork and sighed. "Men," she said before taking a bite of her breakfast.

~

Kyle helped Amanda clean up the kitchen and was careful to stay out of sight when Sherry left with Lucille a half-hour later. Sherry made no attempt to find him or to say goodbye.

When they were gone, Amanda brought Kyle up to the moon shrine to show him the totem she had borrowed from the collector in Coeur d'Alene. She had a proud smile as she lifted it from the altar with both hands.

Kyle shuddered when Amanda held up the wolf skull. With its long fearsome canine teeth and hollow eye sockets, he found it to be repellent in a primal way. Upon closer inspection, he found a small symbol above each of the long upper canine teeth and each eye socket. Those symbols were not the only evidence that the wolf skull was special. It had a faint glow to it, as if a tiny LED had been placed inside. From the shadows of his mind, the demon urged him to slap the artifact from Amanda's hands. Kyle pushed the demon back and reconsidered the skull, liking it better because of the demon's reaction.

"It's smaller than I expected," Kyle observed.

Amanda nodded enthusiastically. "I noticed that too. I asked Mr. Bell about it, but he didn't know the reason. He speculated that it might have come from a young wolf, or perhaps a female. It's also possible that the skull came from one of the smaller wolf species."

Amanda seemed exceptionally excited about the wolf skull, and Kyle started to wonder why. She kept giving him sidelong glances, as if she were expecting him to notice something.

"What's up with you?" he asked her.

She turned the skull in her hands, giving him a view from all angles. "Did you notice anything else about it, other than the fact that it's small?"

Kyle looked carefully to see what she was getting at, but didn't see anything else unusual. "Just the symbols and the weird glow. Is that what you're hinting about?"

Amanda seemed taken aback. She held the skull away from her and tilted her head. "What glow?"

Kyle thought he might have been mistaken, but as Amanda angled the skull to face him, a faint white light flickered around the empty eye sockets and the symbols. "It has a white glow to it, especially here and here," he said, pointing to the areas that glimmered.

Amanda stared at him with a nonplussed expression. She inspected the skull again and then glanced over at her altar. "Does anything on the altar glow?"

Kyle looked carefully at the items sitting on the altar, but the crucible, knife, and other items looked pretty much the same as always. "Nope. Only the skull."

"Interesting," she said, barely above a whisper. Putting the skull down on the altar, she seemed lost in thought. "Have you seen anything else glow with light that didn't seem natural?"

Kyle thought back over some of the crazy things he'd witnessed in the past several days. "Well, your crucible glowed briefly when you consecrated it. And the light from your spell-casting seemed pretty unnatural. The first time I saw the green shimmer while you were refreshing the wards was kind of weird, but the force pushing me against the fence freaked me out a lot more."

Amanda's mouth dropped open and she blinked a couple of times before recovering her composure. "You see a green shimmer when I cast spells?"

"Don't you?"

"No!" Amanda put her hand to her head and furrowed her brow in concentration. "That sounds like the effects of a magic aura spell. I've used it to check objects for enchantments. If someone happens to use magic while the spell is operating, I can see auras related to their casting, similar to what you just described." She looked up at him. "But it's a short-term spell. It lasts maybe five minutes at the most."

Kyle shook his head. "I don't know what to tell you. Could it be another thing I'm getting through the demon?"

Amanda's eyes went wide. "It has to be. I'm glad you mentioned it. That ability has ... ramifications. I need to tell Noreen about this."

Kyle grimaced. The last thing he needed was for Noreen to associate more *ramifications* with him. "Should we get back to the skull? Was there something special about the symbols?"

Amanda nodded absently. "Yeah ... I wanted to make sure you saw them." With a quick shake of her head, she started for the door, waving for him to follow her. "Come on. I've got something else to show you."

She descended the stairs quickly and entered her office. Kyle followed, his curiosity aroused.

She went to the table with the notes about the exorcism ritual. She had spread them out again, and sitting on top were photocopies of the original diary that contained the trader's account of the ritual. Kyle had never bothered to look at the handwritten text. He had worked from the typed version that was much easier to read.

At the bottom of the last page, the trader had drawn four symbols. They drew Kyle's eye before Amanda's index finger pointed them out.

"Look familiar?" she asked with a triumphant smile.

Kyle's mind refused to put it together immediately. The odds were too impossible.

"Are you saying that you think the skull upstairs is the same one the medicine man used in his ritual a hundred and fifty years ago? How can that be?"

"I don't know, but those symbols match the ones on the skull *exactly*. I've looked through every word of this part of the diary, but the trader never says why he drew those symbols or where they came from. He might have copied them from the skull, or maybe from some other artifact the medicine man was using. Either way, the symbols are somehow related to the exorcism ritual, and that skull has those symbols. I believe we've stumbled upon a powerful totem that was specifically designed to be used in an exorcism. It's *possible* it's the same one this medicine man used."

Kyle stared at the symbols in speechless shock. "Holy crap," he finally managed to say.

She laughed and gave him a hug. "Vulgar, but possibly accurate."

Amanda took a moment to check her e-mail while Kyle looked through the diary. She asked him to verify that she hadn't missed something that might explain the reason for the symbols, but he had no luck finding anything either. He was about to ask her what they were going to do next when the phone rang.

Amanda answered the phone. As she listened, her expression grew intent. She got up and pulled back the lace curtain from the window next to her desk, peering outside. "I see them," she said. "What should we do? Okay … thanks."

She hung up, and when she turned around, she had a wild look in her eyes. "The Pack has surrounded the farm. Lucille saw them on her way out and called to warn us. She is contacting the Order to see if we can get additional protection."

Kyle's heart pounded as he followed Amanda around the house. In every direction, they could see someone standing or sitting next to the fence. A van and an SUV were outside the front gate, parked in the grass on either side of the driveway. So far, they weren't blocking access to the property.

Amanda ran downstairs and locked all the doors.

"Are they coming onto the property?" Kyle asked, panic in his voice. It would figure that right when things were starting to look good for the exorcism, the Pack was going to interfere again.

"Not yet," Amanda answered. "I would feel it if any of them penetrated the ward."

After rushing to lock the doors and windows, they had ended up in the kitchen by unspoken agreement.

Kyle eyed the knife block, but he hoped they wouldn't get close enough for him to need a knife. "Do you have a gun somewhere?" he asked. "And maybe some silver bullets?" he added jokingly.

Amanda nodded absently. "There's a shotgun. We're fresh out of silver bullets, but double-ought buckshot should slow them down." She was silent for a moment, and then shook her head. "I can't figure out why they're here."

"Well, the Order sent you onto Foundation property to retrieve Sherry and me. Maybe this is their idea of payback."

"I don't think so. The Pack has never been particularly vindictive in the past. Something else is going on. The car crash, kidnapping you, and now this all add up to something important. Something that makes them willing to take big risks."

Kyle shrugged. "Maybe they're afraid you'll succeed tonight."

Amanda stared at him. "They haven't been worried about that up to now."

"That's true. But everything changed when—"

"When we went to get the skull," she finished for him.

"You now have what it takes," Kyle concluded.

They both jumped at the sound of car engines roaring up the driveway. Was the Pack making its move? Amanda leaped for the broom closet and withdrew a shotgun that was hidden at the back. She pumped it once to chamber a shell and ran for the front door. Kyle grabbed a big knife from the block and followed her.

Some of the people pouring from the three vehicles in the driveway were familiar. Noreen and Jonathan exited the lead car and strode toward the screen door while others took up positions around the house. The cars were parked in a semi-circle centered on the front door, much like circled wagons in the Old West.

Amanda set the safety on the shotgun and leaned it next to the door. Kyle took the hint and put the kitchen knife down on an end table. Turning the doorknob, Amanda barely had time to open the door and step out of the way before Noreen breezed in with Jonathan on her heels.

"Lucille warned us of the siege," Noreen said. "What is your current status?"

"Status? We have nothing to report yet. We just found out about the Pack being here. How did you manage to assemble a team and get here so quickly?"

Noreen frowned at Kyle. He got the impression that she wanted him to leave so she could talk privately with Amanda, but there was no way he was missing this. Pressing her lips together, she turned back to Amanda.

"Your little project has attracted a lot of attention over the past week. The director has taken notice." She mentioned the director's interest as if it were not necessarily a good thing. Judging by the way Amanda's face went pale, Kyle guessed she was concerned as well. "The teams were already assigned and on alert when our observers warned us the Pack was mobilizing."

"What's the plan?" Amanda asked.

Noreen folded her arms. "The plan is to help you complete the exorcism. If you are unsuccessful, our job is to contain the danger and see that the demon is returned to its kind." The finality of her tone showed that she anticipated no other result.

Amanda's face tensed in annoyance. She leaned forward. "And if I succeed?"

Noreen's shrug, clearly discounting the possibility of a successful conclusion, infuriated Kyle. "We will make sure that the Pack does not attempt some kind of retribution on you or the victim."

Kyle was starting to feel like some kind of lab rat. To Noreen, he wasn't a person with real feelings and a real name who was standing right in front of her; she had demoted him to "the victim."

Amanda narrowed her eyes at her coven leader. "You said the plan was to help me complete the exorcism. What kind of help are you talking about? Are you summoning the entire coven?"

Jonathan interrupted by throwing up his hands in exasperation. "That's exactly what I suggested."

Noreen waved a hand in dismissal at Jonathan and continued to address Amanda. "Absolutely not. I will not put the entire coven at risk. I can protect myself well enough, and you have chosen to ignore the danger."

Seething, Kyle couldn't keep quiet any longer. "How can you stand this?" he asked Amanda. "Can't you join a different coven with a more reasonable leader?"

Noreen folded her arms and raised her eyebrows, watching Amanda with a bemused expression and waiting for her answer.

Amanda took a deep breath and blew it out. "Kyle, please stay out of this. I don't have time to explain. Just be glad we'll have Noreen's help."

Chastised, Kyle frowned and tried to temper his dislike for the arrogant older witch. Amanda was right. Any help was probably better than no help.

Jonathan started toward the kitchen. "You got anything to eat in this place?"

With the brittle moment behind them, Noreen pushed between Kyle and Amanda on her way toward the stairs. "We've wasted enough time. If I'm going to help, I need to understand what we'll be doing tonight. Show me your research and the exorcism you've crafted. I'm sure I can find ways to improve it."

Kyle turned an incredulous expression toward Amanda. How could she work with this woman?

Amanda shrugged apologetically. "I know she's a pain in the ass, but believe it or not, she's worth it."

"I heard that," Noreen called in a singsong voice as she ascended the stairs.

Kyle rolled his eyes and Amanda put a placating hand on his shoulder. "Trust me," she said, her hazel eyes staring into his.

He nodded his head and sighed. "I do. You know I do."

Chapter 18

Bad Moon Rising

Kyle spent most of the afternoon downstairs with Jonathan, who was responsible for coordinating the hunters on the farm grounds. The older man brought in a radio unit and set it up on the big table in the dining room. All of the hunters wore ear pieces and checked in regularly. It was like being surrounded by the Secret Service.

Nothing much happened for most of the day. Pack members moved around the perimeter, appearing and disappearing at various points along the fence, sometimes in human form, sometimes as wolves. It kept the hunters on their toes, but the Pack seemed content to watch the farm from the outside.

Kyle had the disturbing feeling that the Pack was waiting for night to fall or for some other signal to attack. He moved Amanda's shotgun from the front door to the dining room so it would be closer at hand. Jonathan seemed amused by his caution.

Noticing Jonathan's smile, Kyle asked, "What? You don't think it will do any good?"

"Sure it will. You probably won't kill any of them unless you put the barrel right up against their head, but it will definitely keep them back. It's just that I doubt you'll need it with all the support we have outside."

Kyle had remained quiet for most of the day, lost in his own thoughts and trying not to interfere with Jonathan. The man initiated a few friendly conversations about their shared passion for sailing, but the distraction was only partly successful.

Kyle's anxiety increased as the afternoon wore on. Amanda and Noreen thumped around up in the moon shrine preparing for the evening's activity. All of the werewolves disappeared for a short while and then returned, putting Kyle and Jonathan's entire team on edge. Since then, things had calmed down, but Kyle continually had to remind himself to breathe and unclench his hands. He decided to try distracting himself with conversation again.

"May I ask a few questions about the Order?" he ventured.

Jonathan turned away from the radio set and leaned back in his seat. "Go ahead."

"I'm confused about how it all fits together. Amanda is part of a coven, but she's also a hunter. There's a director somewhere, but most of the action seems to be coordinated by team leaders like you. Is the Order some kind of military organization?"

"Not exactly. Most of us have normal private lives, but we've pledged to protect humanity from rogue paranormals."

"Like the werewolves?"

"Truthfully, the werewolves rarely cause trouble. They contribute to the community and keep a low profile." He motioned toward the window. "What we've been seeing lately is unusual. If they hadn't alarmed the director by kidnapping you, we wouldn't have been prepared to respond today."

Kyle estimated that the Order had at least eight hunters on the farm. It was hard to imagine all of those people having lives that they could drop whenever the Order called. "So the director gives the orders and all of the hunters report to him or her?"

Jonathan chuckled and shook his head. "Not quite. Few of us meet with the director. He works through master hunters. The master hunters manage the crisis teams, each of which is led by a journeyman hunter. The team members are mostly apprentice hunters and a few journeymen mentors."

"That makes you a journeyman hunter," Kyle surmised, and Jonathan nodded. "Where does Noreen's coven fit into the order?"

"It doesn't, at least not directly. Noreen and Amanda are the only hunters in their coven. The other three witches know about the Order but haven't chosen to take the hunter pledge. That's partly why Noreen doesn't want them involved here tonight."

"As the leader of the team, couldn't you force the issue?"

Jonathan laughed. "Setting aside the difficulty of getting Noreen to do anything she doesn't want to do, there's the problem of her outranking me. Noreen is a master hunter. My authority extends only to the tactical team outside. She leads the transcendental team, which is only her and Amanda at the moment."

It reminded Kyle of how the project teams were sometimes organized at his former employer. Programmers reported to their managers in the information technology group, but they were occasionally teamed up with business analysts from other departments for the duration of a specific project. A project manager usually led these intra-departmental teams. Kyle explained what he was thinking to Jonathan.

The blond sailor pursed his lips and nodded. "That's fairly accurate. Our crisis teams combine members from all three disciplines and we select a primary leader based on who has the most relevant experience. Noreen is in charge of this conflict because it falls under her area of expertise."

Jonathan turned back to the radio to ask for an update from the hunters posted outside. The consensus was that nothing had changed.

The dining-room window gave Kyle a view of the front gate. The meadow between the gate and the house was turning golden from the sun sinking lower in the sky.

Only one vehicle was parked outside the gate now. A man stood leaning against the front of the car with his arms and legs crossed. He wore a cowboy hat and a long-sleeved shirt. To passers-by, he probably looked like a rancher kicking back for a rest before going back to work on his fence. "How many of them are out there?" he asked Jonathan.

"They keep moving and shifting, so we can't tell for sure. We know that eight live in this area, and I'm betting every one of them is here."

Kyle almost asked him if the eight included him, since Clarissa's demon had become his demon, but he didn't want to have that conversation.

Footsteps thumping down the creaky stairs announced Amanda's arrival. She was dressed in her dark-blue kimono again and looked breathtaking. "We're ready for you, Kyle. We went over the timing of the spell, and decided that we'd better get started soon."

Kyle's heart seemed to stop for a moment, and then it pounded in his chest. When he stood, his knees nearly gave out and Jonathan grabbed Kyle's arm to steady him. Amanda came forward and took his other arm, nodding to Jonathan that he could let go.

As Amanda led Kyle to the stairs, they exchanged a long glance. Although she spoke no words, her eyes and face said plenty. Her wide eyes spoke of excitement mixed with fear. Her tight smile was meant to be reassuring, but it also admitted to the danger of what they were about to do. She would do her best, but there was no guarantee that she would succeed.

The moon shrine might as well have been called a sun shrine, Kyle thought when he entered. The setting sun bathed the space in warm color, making everything in the room seem mundane and rustic. Sunlight emphasized every speck of dust and overwhelmed the sparkle of the various gems and glass objects around the room. The dark and mysterious atmosphere imparted by the stars and moon was washed away in a haze of golden light.

Shocked by the change in ambiance, Kyle stopped just inside the doorway.

Amanda twisted her lip up in a half-smile. "The room feels pretty ordinary in daylight, doesn't it?"

"Yeah. How strange."

"Amanda, come here for a minute," Noreen called to her. Amanda joined her at the concrete pad, where Noreen pointed and talked in a hushed voice about where they would place the tools needed for the exorcism.

A glint on the altar caught his eye. It was the bone-handled knife Amanda used to cut up herbs and other ingredients for her magical workings. He had intended to grab a knife from the kitchen in preparation for his backup plan, but in all the excitement, he'd forgotten. Lifting his feet carefully, he sidled over to the altar. Two small piles of leaves sat on the cutting board next to the wickedly curved, six-inch blade. Kyle guessed that she was done with it since the blade had been wiped clean and Amanda had said they were ready for him.

He reached out and plucked the knife from the altar, cupping his fingers around the end of the hilt so the blade was held against the back of his forearm. Hoping that Amanda wouldn't notice it was missing, he took a step away from the altar a moment before the two women turned to face him.

Amanda smiled and motioned for him to come over to the circle. "Have a seat, Kyle. We're ready to start the purification ceremony."

Kyle took a roundabout course to the chair so he could keep the knife hidden. Both witches apparently thought he'd chosen his path to avoid going near Noreen. Amanda rolled her eyes and Noreen huffed impatiently.

Once seated in the chair, it was easy for him to conceal the knife between his arm and his leg. He had a moment of panic when Amanda went to the altar to sweep the chopped herbs into a small bowl, but she didn't seem to notice his theft.

A moment later Amanda was in the circle with him, putting the bowl down next to his chair. "You know the drill," she said. "We won't be able to talk once I get started. Is there anything you want to say or ask right now?"

Kyle gave her a wry grin. "Are you asking me for last words? You make this sound like an execution." The disturbed look that came over her face made him regret that he'd teased her. "Sorry. Bad joke. Thank you for doing all this."

Amanda leaned forward and surprised him by kissing him on the lips. "Good luck to both of us," she said as she pulled away.

Kyle hadn't been prepared for the brief kiss. His lips tingled and his heart swelled in a way that made him want to stand and take her into his arms for another try. But Noreen's disapproving frown and narrow-eyed glare kept him pinned to his chair.

Amanda prepared for the exorcism using the same purification ritual he'd seen her perform before. She banished the dark spirits using her new crucible, purified the circle with holy water, and raised a protective column of air around them with her feather fan.

While she worked, Kyle felt the demon stirring in the recesses of his mind. Amanda's ritual was putting pressure on him as it had before, and the demon was reacting.

To make matters worse, Noreen was positioned outside the circle directly in front of him. She watched his every move and change of expression, looking ready to strike him dead should she decide it was the right course of action.

When Amanda called upon the earth spirits, the chest-constricting boom that followed made Kyle sway in his chair and nearly pass out. He shook his head to break out of the swoon and took deep breaths while he tried to focus his eyes. He knew instinctively that it would be fatal to lose consciousness with the demon clawing at his mind for control over his body.

And this was just the purification ceremony! He began to wonder how he could possibly keep the demon at bay through the exorcism.

For the final step of the purification, Amanda stood in front of him with her back to him. It was a much better view than staring into Noreen's angry eyes. Kyle tried not to stare at the way Amanda's silky outfit draped over her shapely bottom, but then decided that he didn't care. Hers might be the last he would ever see.

Noreen took over for Amanda when it was time to call the fire spirits. It was the first time Kyle had heard Noreen put a respectful tone into her strong voice. When the spirits responded, all four of the candles around the circle flared up like gas-powered jets for several seconds. Amanda stepped back from the candle in front of her, nearly stumbling on Kyle's feet. He quickly moved the knife to the side of his leg in case she accidentally fell into his lap. He was mildly disappointed when she regained her balance.

Noreen's contribution seemed to do much more than make the candles go wild. The protective column of air had become so strong that its shimmering obscured the details of the room. For the first time, Kyle felt something other than confidence and hunger from the demon. It became silent and watchful, even as it continued its assault on his will.

Amanda glanced up at the cupola with an expression of nervous excitement as the light of the room shifted to dusky tones. The sun was setting, and the ceremony was progressing right on schedule. She kneeled next to Kyle's chair.

Having reviewed the exorcism ritual Amanda had put together, Kyle knew more or less what to expect. Noreen might have altered it, but he doubted she would risk messing with the original ritual too much.

Amanda lit a piece of charcoal inside the crucible and added the herbs she'd prepared. Thin, pungent smoke rose from the herbs and floated around the circle. Kyle hadn't noticed it before, but the shimmering air column had a distinct swirling flow to it. The smoke was drawn toward the edges of the circle, where it rippled against the air column and spread up its inner surface.

Amanda stood and positioned herself directly in front of Kyle. She held the wolf skull at chest height with the jaw facing her. The ruddy colors of sunset eclipsed the glow of the skull, even though the sun's light was fading from the room. Amanda called on the spirits to help her drive the demon from Kyle, as she had during the first exorcism.

Kyle's vision narrowed and he could feel the demon coming forth, but this time he wasn't going to let it take over. He was never going to the abyss again. He gripped the knife in his fist and placed the point under his chin. The demon halted its assault on his mind for a moment, but then it continued. Kyle pressed the blade into his flesh until it drew blood. The demon paused again.

That's right, you bastard. If you try to take over, we both die.

Amanda gasped and glanced over her shoulder toward the altar when she saw Kyle raise the knife. Noreen leaned to see around Amanda and cursed when she saw what was happening.

Amanda's voice took on a desperate edge as she continued to call upon the spirits for help. The column of air became more turbulent, creating a breeze within the circle that fluttered against Amanda's clothing.

Kyle was aware of the instant the sun dropped completely below the horizon. A chorus of muted howls leaked into the room through the cupola windows as the werewolves called to their companion.

The demon changed tactics. Rather than clawing for control over Kyle's body, it tried a direct assault on his consciousness. The effect was like being repeatedly hit on the back of the head with a baseball bat. If the demon succeeded in knocking him out, it would be sitting an arm's length away from Amanda with a knife in its hand.

He couldn't let that happen. The ritual wasn't working, and he couldn't hold the demon back much longer. He closed his eyes and tilted his head back, bracing himself to plunge the knife up and into his brain. The demon cringed and growled across his mind. It was so close to winning.

A cold hand gripped his forearm. "Kyle, wait. Give me the knife."

Amanda didn't understand what he was doing and he couldn't let her stop him. He opened his eyes to look into hers one last time, immune to the desperate plea they held. He tightened his grip and shook his head once, painfully deepening the puncture in his neck.

"You have to let the demon manifest," she insisted. "I can't trap it until you let it come forth."

Shit.

The demon's presence was like a looming shadow. It waited to see what Kyle would decide.

What if Amanda was wrong? Kyle would be forever locked in the abyss. He was far better off dead.

But what if she succeeded? Kyle would get his life back, and this whole nightmare of werewolves, magic, and demons would be over.

It all came down to one question. Did he believe in Amanda enough to give her control over whether he survived or spent the rest of his existence in the abyss?

Kyle lowered the knife and held it out in his open palm. Amanda grabbed it from him and kneeled, slipping it under his chair.

The wolf skull was in her hands again when she straightened. She raised it, positioning the skull over Kyle's head, and started calling to the spirits again.

Sensing Kyle's surrender, the demon wasted no time. Its presence slipped over his mind like ink spreading from a tipped bottle. His awareness was unceremoniously shoved into the abyss.

But this time was different. Rather than plummeting endlessly in dark silence, he was buoyed just beyond the edge of sensation. Amanda's voice was an echo of sound from far away. The pain from the wound on his neck was a disconnected throb that belonged to someone else.

He wasn't alone. Warm sensations buffeted him, calming him and giving him patience.

Then came the scream. It was unlike anything Kyle had heard before. It tore through the abyss like the blaring horn of a freight train, shocking Kyle into numbness. The demon's departure created a forceful vacuum that sucked Kyle's awareness back into his body with a slamming jolt of confusing sensations.

His vision slowly cleared. Amanda still held the wolf skull over his head and called to the spirits to banish the demon. Her braid whipped over her shoulder and her clothes rippled in a tornado of wind that scoured the inside of the circle.

Amanda took a deep breath. In an authoritative bellow, she demanded, "Spirits of light, banish this dark spirit and let it plague the living no more!" Green filaments of light appeared in a lacy eggshell around Amanda. The shell expanded until the whirling wall around the circle absorbed it.

The wolves outside howled in unison again, and they were joined by a howl that came from the skull. Kyle cringed from the totem as a thin, silver bolt of lightning flashed from the swirling column of air and struck the skull with a thunderous crash. The howl from the skull stopped instantly, and the werewolf chorus outside slowly faded away.

Amanda lowered her arms and blew out her breath in relief. She swayed for a second and Kyle reached forward to steady her. She stopped him with a look that told him they weren't done yet. Kyle sat back, recognizing the danger of the unseen forces that still swirled around them and had yet to be released.

Kyle had difficulty remaining seated while Amanda completed the ritual and released the spirits. He itched to stand up and whoop while waving his arms in the air. He wanted to hug Amanda and twirl her around in a circle. He was alive! The demon was gone from his mind like a black stain bleached from a white cloth. He would not be turning into a werewolf tonight or any other night.

By the time Amanda finished, Kyle's initial euphoria had passed. For the first time in many days, he dared to think about what he was going to do after First Moon. Would the werewolves leave him alone now, or would he have to leave the area? Would they follow him if he did leave? Could he get his job back? Did he want it back?

Amanda reached out a hand to help him up from the chair. He ignored her hand and got up to envelop her in a tight hug. He closed his eyes over her shoulder so he wouldn't have to look at Noreen's disapproving face. "Thank you, Amanda. I owe you my life."

She hugged him back just as tightly. "I'm so glad it worked. I was afraid I'd lose you."

As much as he wanted to, Kyle tried not to read too much into her remark. A friendship had grown between them over the past few weeks, and they had flirted with each other a little, but he didn't expect a romantic relationship to suddenly blossom. He smiled to himself. All in good time.

Hunter

Kyle hurried down the walkway, dodging the few pedestrians who strolled through town on the blustery day. Gunmetal gray clouds hid the midday sun, making it feel much later in the day than it really was.

When he reached McWort's, Kyle pulled open the heavy wooden door and stepped into the warm interior. Other patrons enjoying their lunch filled the space with the noisy clink of glasses and scattered conversation.

Amanda waved to him from her seat at the table where they'd first met. Tiny streams of bubbles rose in her half-empty glass of golden beer.

"Sorry I'm late," Kyle said, pulling out the chair opposite her and sitting down. "I hope you haven't been waiting long."

"Only about ten minutes," she said with a smile. "Long enough for the waitress to ask about my order a half-dozen times and for me to fend off a few guys who wanted to join me."

Kyle looked around the restaurant with narrowed eyes. "Which guys?"

Amanda reached out and touched his hand. He almost missed the tingle he used to get from her touch, but didn't care to repeat the conditions that had made it possible. Amanda had explained that the mild shock they had experienced was because of her magical alignment with the light forces, which had reacted to the dark spirit within him.

"I'm kidding," she said. "But it's cute that you care."

Kyle squeezed her hand with his and waved with the other to get the waitress's attention. "Of course I care. If this seat is in demand, I want top dollar for it."

Amanda let go and pinched him. "Very funny. If anyone gets the money, I think it should be me."

Kyle mocked a thoughtful look and then shook his head. "Nope. They have a name for girls who do that sort of thing."

"I would have a name for you too," she said, and they laughed together.

The waitress came by and took their lunch order, returning only moments later with the dark beer Kyle had requested.

He lifted his glass toward Amanda and said, "Happy Equinox." She raised her glass and clinked it against his, repeating the toast.

When Kyle found out that Amanda celebrated the equinoxes and solstices rather than the typical religious holidays, he invited her to lunch at the brewpub as his treat.

He was glad to see that she seemed happy and relaxed. She was dressed in blue jeans with a green and teal flannel shirt, and her hair hung to either side of her face in dark waves. His breath caught as it often did when he looked deeply into her intelligent hazel eyes. She was leaning back in her chair, smiling slightly at him, while her hand turned her beer glass.

He leaned forward to explain his tardiness. "I got a call as I was headed out the door to meet you. I should have let it go to voicemail, but I had a feeling I should answer it. I'm glad I did."

Amanda caught the emphasis he placed on his last sentence. She wrinkled her forehead and asked, "Is everything okay?"

"Yes, actually. It was Garrin Brisbane."

The name caught Amanda's attention. She sat forward with excitement in her eyes. "As in the master hunter from the Order's technology discipline?"

Kyle smiled and nodded. "The very same."

"What did he want?"

Kyle watched Amanda's reaction closely. After the exorcism, they had seen each other only a couple of times over the subsequent weeks. They had decided to "just be friends" while Kyle got his life back in order and figured out what he wanted to do. He had done that and wanted to ask her if she would still be willing to pursue something more with him.

He took a deep breath and answered her question. "Garrin wants to interview me. I've been talking with Jonathan about joining the Order, and he agreed to sponsor my request."

Kyle had been working with Jonathan off and on at the marina doing guided kayak tours. The money wasn't good, but it was a lot of fun.

The two of them had spent a lot of time talking about the possibility of Kyle joining the Order. Many of the physical alterations the demon had wrought on his body remained. He was still supernaturally strong and fast. He wore colored contacts to hide the fact that his irises were still amber. Unfortunately, the quick healing was magical in origin, so it had left with the demon. Everyone had expected that he would lose his ability to see magical auras as well, but he hadn't. That one still baffled everyone at the Ternion Order.

Regardless, the abilities he retained made him a paranormal by Order definitions, and he suspected they would want to keep an eye on him, one way or another.

Amanda's gaze was steady and unreadable. "When did you decide to join the Order?"

Kyle chose his next words carefully. This wasn't all about her, and he didn't want her to worry that it was. "When I decided that I didn't want to leave the area."

She drained the last of her beer and looked down at the empty glass, still with a blank expression. "I thought you had things to work out before you made that decision."

"I did. And I worked them out. Sherry has moved on. She won't even talk to me. Last I heard, she was planning to leave town again. I haven't heard anything from the Pack since the ceremony, either. In fact, I was offered my old job back, so it seems they've stopped trying to sabotage my life. However, I'm looking into freelance programming, in case I'm accepted by the Order. The income wouldn't be as steady, but I could work from home and my schedule would be flexible. I could even continue to work with Jonathan once in a while."

Their food arrived, and they waited until the waitress had left before continuing their conversation.

Amanda stared at her food for a moment. She didn't seem interested in eating it. When she looked up at him, he thought he saw disappointment. Had he said something wrong?

"That's great, Kyle," she finally said. "Congratulations."

Kyle couldn't stand not knowing what she was thinking. "Is something wrong, Amanda?"

"No, I'm good." She started eating. Between bites, she said, "I've just been really busy. Lots of work to do. Great money, but no time."

She didn't have to tell him about that. Over the previous weeks he'd had to beg her to leave the farm. He'd been able to pry her away from her work on only two occasions—once to go hiking and once to meet him for lunch. Maybe she'd decided he wasn't a good match for her after all.

He dug into his own lunch while he tried to figure out what was up with her. After a few minutes of uncomfortable silence, he tried again.

"Hey, maybe we'll end up working together some time," he said.

The idea seemed to surprise her. "Maybe we will. That would be interesting."

Interesting was one of those words that could be taken at face value or interpreted as something sarcastic or even ominous. Once again, her tone gave him no clues to go on.

He tried the direct approach. "Maybe we could see each other again before that. Like soon. Repeatedly, even."

She put down her sandwich and wiped her hands. There was something at the corner of her eyes, a telltale wrinkle hinting at amusement. "You mean like a date?"

"Yeah."

"Sorry, I don't date co-workers."

Kyle swallowed hard and stared at her in disbelief.

Amanda laughed and leaned forward. "I'm kidding! You should have seen your face. Of course I'd like to go out with you. I was starting to think you preferred being just friends."

Thinking back on it, Kyle could see how she might have misinterpreted his behavior over the past month. He had been trying to respect their mutual agreement to keep their relationship on a friendship level. Had he become a little too distant?

"I'd prefer to be more than friends," Kyle said.

Amanda looked into his eyes for a long time. When she spoke, her voice was husky. "I'd like that too."

THANK YOU FOR READING

Thank you for dedicating some of your reading time to *First Moon*. I hope you enjoyed the adventures of Kyle and Amanda and that you look forward to more tales of the Ternion Order.

If you would like to be notified by email when I release a new book, please subscribe to the New Releases list at my blog: www.DanielRMarvello.com/releases. I only use the list for release announcements, and you may unsubscribe at any time.

I know that not everyone likes to write book reviews, but if you are willing to spare the time to write a sentence or two about what you thought of *First Moon*, I encourage you to post a review at your favorite book vendor site or recommend the story to your social networking friends.

I love hearing from fans. If you would like to share your thoughts with me privately, you can reach me through the contact page on my blog: DanielRMarvello.com/contact. I look forward to meeting you.

Happy reading,
Daniel R. Marvello

Acknowledgements

M y thanks go out to my readers and my family for supporting my writing career. I couldn't have done it without you.

Thanks also to my beta readers, who helped me make *First Moon* a better book than it would have been without their feedback. I sincerely appreciate their time and effort:

- Susan Daffron (author of the Alpine Grove Romantic Comedy series)
- Becca Mills (author of the Emanations series)
- Nancy Brashear (contributing author of the *Grimm & Grimmer Volume Two* anthology)
- Paul Sheriff (author of the PDSA programming series).
- Ken Rahmoeller
- Cynthia Daffron
- Melanie Griffin

Finally, I'd like to thank the 70's rock band Klaatu for giving me decades of listening entertainment, and especially for their song, "Howl at the Moon," which inspired me to write my first werewolf story.

ABOUT THE AUTHOR

Daniel R. Marvello writes fantasy adventure stories from his log home on forty acres of forest and meadow in the North Idaho panhandle. The setting for his Vaetra Chronicles book series was inspired by the scenic beauty of his surroundings. Daniel shares his home with his loving wife of 20 years and several wonderful animals.

Books by Daniel R. Marvello

The Vaetra Chronicles

- *Vaetra Unveiled*
- *Vaetra Untrained*
- *Vaetra Unleashed*

Find out more at www.vaetra.com

The Ternion Order

First Moon

Visit Daniel's blog at:
www.DanielRMarvello.com